His Vampire Harem
Book Two
By Lily Harlem

Gay Romance Books By Lily Harlem
Caught on Camera
His Vampire Harem
His Vampire Harem 2
Dark Warrior
High-Sticked
The Chase
Who Dares Wins
Bad Idea
Mile High Kink Club
Kangorilla

His Vampire Harem Book Two: text copyright © Lily Harlem 2019
All Rights Reserved

With the exception of quotes used in reviews, this book may not be reproduced or used in whole or in part by any means existing without written permission from Lily Harlem.

Warning: The unauthorized reproduction or distribution of this copyrighted work is illegal. No part of this book may be scanned, uploaded or distributed via the Internet or any other means, electronic or print, without the author's written permission.

This book is a work of fiction and any resemblance to persons, living or dead is purely coincidental. The characters are productions of the author's imagination and used fictitiously.

Please note this book is intended for mature readers.

Artwork by Studioenp.

Edited by Studioenp.

Chapter One

Darius

The full moon hovering over Stonehenge shone on my newest vampire. Patrick was devilishly handsome, his eyes were bright red, and his short hair messy after his ordeal of being turned.

He was still breathing hard, his brilliant-white fangs visible, and he was staring at me as if I were the only thing in his world.

But I wasn't. Oscar and Rhys very much existed and were holding him tight. They each had a grip on his arms, spreading them outward, sacrificial almost. Which in a way he had been—sacrificed, that was. My demon father had possessed his body in an attempt to get close to me then possess mine. He'd had evil deeds on his mind that he needed a human body for. Wicked intentions, and while he performed his vile plans, I would have been burning in Hell.

Which hardly seemed fair when my cambion blood had saved my vampires from an eternity of damnation, flames, and agony.

"Vampire harem?" Patrick repeated, his voice a snarl, his throat sounding tight and dry, which I guessed it would be after being burned alive.

"Yes." I gestured to George and Lloyd at my side. "These four men are vampires. They're all in love with me, the same way I am them."

I took a step closer.

George rested his hand on my shoulder. "That'll do."

"Yeah," Lloyd said. "Don't be fooled by his stillness. He can move like the wind."

I nodded and flexed and unflexed my fingers. My hands and arms were still hot despite having discharged my sparks. I had no doubt Patrick was fast and strong. My vampires were, and apparently newly turned vampires were even more so.

"And the thing is, Patrick," I went on.

He drew back his lips, as if tasting the air with his gums, his tongue, and the insides of his cheeks.

"You're one of us now," I said, "and you'll have to accept that, no matter how hard it is."

"I want blood." He was unblinking, just staring.

"And you'll get some," Oscar said sternly. "In good time."

Patrick suddenly jerked his entire body, his arms seeming to fly backward and his chest forward. It was a surge of energy so violent, Rhys dropped his hold on Patrick.

It happened so fast. Patrick lunged at Oscar, sent him reeling, then was pushing me with unyielding force.

I hit the hard ground. The wind whooshed from my lungs.

Patrick was above me, the moon directly behind his head giving him a weird diamond-white halo.

Except he was no angel

His fangs were out and angling toward my neck.

I shoved at him. It was no good. He was too damn heavy and too damn strong.

Then he was gone. As fast as it had happened, his weight was off me.

I pushed up, hands behind myself, elbows locked, and watched as George, Lloyd, Oscar, and Rhys all piled on top of him.

Patrick was writhing and shouting, a long bellow of curse words, and his Scottish accent lay thickly within the sounds. He arched his back, kicked, twisted his head this way and that.

"For the love of Benedict, calm down," George said. He'd lost his cap, and his hair hung forward. "You won't win this."

"Blood!" Patrick yelled. "Give me blood."

"Typical I get a tough-guy soldier for my first turn," Rhys said. "He's wild."

"Yeah, I'll give him that." Oscar was scowling as he pinned one of Patrick's legs to the ground.

"You okay?" Lloyd threw over his shoulder in my direction.

"Yeah, fine." I touched the cross on my necklace. "But will *he* be?"

I thought we'd done the right thing by saving Patrick, even though being turned into a vampire wasn't going to be life as he knew it. But right now, Patrick seemed to be in agony because of his craving for blood. He was shouting and screaming for it as though he'd die all over again without it.

"He'll be okay." George shifted position, still holding Patrick's left arm.

"And what the bloody hell are we going to do until then?" Lloyd asked.

I was keen to hear the answer to that. Until we'd come to Stonehenge to perform the ceremony, to use my key to unlock the destiny of my vampires, we'd been a close unit. I'd felt safe and secure with these four otherworldly men. I knew they'd do anything in their considerable power to protect me.

But now?

Now we had a stranger in our midst—an out-of-control, feral, bloodthirsty creature.

"We need to get to the cabin," George said.

Lloyd shook his head. "I don't think so."

"You got a better idea?" Oscar asked gruffly.

Lloyd clamped his lips together.

"What cabin?" I asked, pushing myself to standing and swiping my palms together.

Oscar and George shared a look.

"What?" I asked again. "What are you planning?"

Patrick lunged forward with a roar.

All four vampires grunted and shoved him down again.

"I do believe," George said, "that we have to get Patrick to Siberia. To our cabin there."

"Siberia!" I was a well-traveled guy. My modeling career had taken me all over the word. But Siberia—that had never been on my to-go list.

"Yeah," Rhys said, slightly breathless as he battled to hold Patrick's arms. "I'm happy with that. We need him isolated, away from humans."

"Including Darius. We need them separated," George said. "You'll have to stay here, Darius."

"No." The thought horrified me. We all needed to be together. Siberia or not, we were family now. Lovers. I didn't want one of my vampires in Russia with Patrick, so far away from me.

"Yes." George lowered his eyebrows. "I don't want you around him, Darius."

"I'm only *half* human, remember." I folded my arms and held his gaze. "Half human. Half demon."

"And does it seem like being a cambion makes a difference to how much a new vampire wants your blood?" Oscar asked.

I pressed my lips together and scowled. This wasn't a great solution. How could I not be with one of my vampires while he babysat Patrick?

"Would you keep still!" Lloyd shouted at Patrick, his voice echoing around the huge stones and out onto the moor.

Patrick took no notice, bucking and bowing within the hold. He was snarling, too, his fangs gleaming.

"We need a silver collar and cuffs," Oscar said. "It's the only way we'll be able to transport him."

"But where?" Rhys looked around. "I don't see any here."

"No, but there's some at The Order."

"In London?" I asked. "That's a long way to go."

"Not for us," Oscar said. He glanced up at the moon. "It's a bit bright tonight, might get spotted, but we have no choice."

"It won't be a problem." George gestured to Lloyd. "You go, you're fast."

Lloyd nodded.

"But surely the bike," I said, "would be the fastest—"

"I'll run." Lloyd shifted Patrick's leg so Oscar could sit over both of them and hold his hips at the same time. He stood and adjusted his hoody so his face was partially covered by the material.

For a moment I took in the sight of him—big, tough, dark, and dangerous.

So damn sexy.

And he'd fucked me so good and hard only minutes before my demon father had arrived at Stonehenge. It was a pity there'd been no post-coital cuddle, but this was the situation we'd found ourselves in.

Lloyd stepped up to me and cupped my jaw. "Darius," he said softly. "Please don't be so worried."

"What do you expect? We have another man's soul on our conscience. He's our responsibility and he's violent and crazed. Plus, there's the thought of one of you going to Siberia with him and being so far away from me." I tapped my chest. "That's not sitting well here, in my heart."

Lloyd glanced at George who frowned and tugged down the corners of his mouth.

"Don't worry about that." Lloyd turned back to me. "Right now, we need to subdue Patrick for your safety and his." He leaned forward and breezed his lips over mine. "I won't be long."

And then he was gone. Where he'd stood was an empty space. I looked to the left, thinking he'd headed that way, though I wasn't completely sure. Perhaps I could make out a streak of darkness in the distance, but it was only there for a split-second, and I wouldn't have bet money on it.

"Get yourself under control," Rhys snarled at Patrick.

Patrick glared up at him, his dazzling red eyes creepy as fuck glowing in the moonlight. For a moment he was still, then he resumed his battle.

"He can't," George said. "The impulse is too strong."

"How long will this last?" I asked, seeming to remember from a previous conversation that it might take years.

"It depends," George said. "If we can give him animal blood—big mammal blood—then he might calm down enough for us to rationalize with him."

"Big mammal? Like what?" I asked.

"Bear, wolf, elk…"

"Wolf." Oscar grimaced. "I could do without coming into contact with them in Siberia."

"Me, too." Rhys pulled a face.

"You don't like wolves?" I asked. "I didn't think any creature would scare a vampire."

"Wolves are devious," George said, "and a common shifter."

"Ah, yes." I nodded. I'd been told about wolf shifters that lived in Canada. Oscar had lost his first love, Jack, to them. They'd chained him in silver then murdered him. Oscar's heart still had a crack in it, one that would never truly heal.

I looked at Oscar. His face was dark, his mouth a tight line.

George glanced at him, too. "It's okay," he said. "You're not coming to Siberia."

"What?" Oscar glared at him. "Of course I am."

"No." George nodded at me. "You can stay here with Darius."

"I don't understand," I said. "Does that mean you're going to take Patrick alone to the lodge, George?"

"No, I can't handle him on my own. Not while he's freshly turned and manic. Three of us will go. Oscar can stay here with you, Darius. Your father is dead, we hope, so it seems the sensible solution is to keep you completely out of harm's way."

"Sensible!" I rammed my hands onto my hips. "I don't want to be thousands of miles away from you, Rhys and Lloyd." I paused, emotion welling. "I've only just found you all."

"I understand that, and I feel the same," George said. "But it's what must happen, and it's not like we have a shortage of time to be together."

"Here, this should do it." Lloyd appeared before me.

I glanced to my left and right. Where the hell had he come from so fast?

He grinned and held up a small black sack that appeared heavy at the base. He was wearing black rubber gloves—at least they appeared to be rubber, not the sort you'd do the washing up in, more like biker gloves but thicker.

"How did you... I mean...you've been...?"

"To The Order, in London, yes." He dropped the bag on the grass next to Patrick. "Doesn't take long, and there's always a few bags of silver in reception in case it's needed for newly turned vampires."

"Oh." His speed, his super-human ability had my head spinning, despite the fact I knew he wasn't human.

"Did Samree see you?" George asked.

"Yes, of course. She doesn't miss a thing." Lloyd huffed.

I thought of The Order's glamorous vampire receptionist. She'd seemed sharp and nosey, in my opinion.

"What did you tell her?" Rhys asked.

"That you'd made your first turn and we're going to Siberia for a while with the newbie." Lloyd directed his attention to George, as if daring him to question his judgment about the information he'd delivered to Samree.

"Good," George said. "Master Concorde will hear of it from her, without a doubt."

"Which will suit us," Lloyd said. He pulled open the bag and reached inside. From it he withdrew a silver collar with a chain hanging from it.

"Let's get it on him," Oscar said. "The sooner he's restrained and calm the better."

"I agree." Rhys was still battling with Patrick's right arm which was jerking and twisting.

Lloyd bent between George and Rhys, holding the collar in his gloved hands. He slipped it around Patrick's neck.

The moment the silver touched Patrick's neck, he stilled, opened his mouth, and released an agonized scream.

I slapped my hands over my ears. The sound was horrendous. Almost worse than when he'd been burned alive.

"It's for your own good, Corporal," George said, watching as Lloyd fastened the collar securely.

Patrick continued to wail, one long sound that took all the air from his lungs. When they were empty, he lay silent with his eyes wide and staring up at the moon.

"Cuffs?" Oscar said.

"Yeah, hang on." Lloyd reached into the bag again. He produced silver handcuffs with a thick link in the center chain.

Patrick didn't put up any resistance to his arms being drawn together and his wrists fastened. Once the cuffs were secure, Lloyd connected the chain on the collar to the middle of the cuffs.

"All okay?" Oscar said, rising from Patrick's now still legs.

"Yes, he's stable." George stood, then retrieved his flat cap and put it on.

"Thank goodness." Rhys unfolded to his full height and shoved his hand through his now messy hair. "That was intense."

"You did well," Oscar said. "For a first time."

"Thanks." Rhys glanced at me. A frown marred his usually perfectly smooth brow.

"Hey." I stepped up to him and curled my arm around his waist. "There's a first time for everything, remember." I kissed his cheek.

It was clear the experience had shaken Rhys.

He smiled at me, though there was still worry in his eyes. "I just hope we can keep him contained while we teach him control, because if he ever does anything to harm you, Darius, I'll never forgive myself."

"And I'd never have forgiven myself if we'd let a human, a *good* human, a soldier who serves his country, die at the hands of my father. You did the only thing we could all live with, and I'm including Patrick in that statement." I squeezed Rhys closer.

"Yeah, you did well, kid," Oscar said. "And don't worry about Darius. Nothing will happen to him, not while I'm on watch."

Chapter Two

Darius

George pulled out his pocket watch. "And now, it's time for the next stage of this plan. Which I'm afraid is going to mean a spell apart."

"It is?" Lloyd said. "How come?"

"We'll take Patrick to Siberia," George said, "and work on him, me, you and Rhys, while Oscar stays here with Darius."

"And who decided that?" Lloyd glanced at Oscar and then me. "I could stay here with Darius."

George hesitated for a moment. "I'm proposing it as the most sensible plan. It means Patrick is well away from Darius and—"

"As are we all." Lloyd crossed his arms and frowned. "Hardly ideal."

George jabbed his chest. "I don't want to be away from him either." He looked at me. "And he knows that, don't you?"

I nodded.

"But it's too dangerous." George went on, "When the time comes, we can't test Patrick out on Darius to see if he's got control of his thirst. That would be crazy."

"It would be damn stupid," Oscar added.

"So who will you test Patrick out on?" I asked.

George shot a look at Lloyd.

Lloyd studied the floor.

Oscar cleared his throat and shifted from one foot to the other.

"Rhys?" I asked, studying his face. "Who will you test him out on?"

"I don't know," he said. "I haven't done this before."

"We'll use big mammals," George said. "Don't you concern yourself with it, Darius."

I wasn't sure I believed him.

"Let's get him up." Lloyd stooped and grabbed Patrick under his arm. It was clear he wasn't happy about going to Siberia, but it seemed he'd accepted the decision. "Give me a hand, Oscar."

Oscar was quick to help.

Between them they dragged the new vampire to standing. His body had been weakened by the silver; his legs barely held him up. In fact, he would have fallen had my two men not been supporting him.

"Hey." George ran his hand into Patrick's hair and tugged so he wasn't facing the ground. "It'll be okay," he said, his voice gentle. "Once you get through this first bit."

Patrick gritted his teeth and hissed. His eyes were closed, as if he'd folded in on himself. As though the pain of the silver was all he could think of and he'd retreated from everyone and everything around him.

"So when will you go?" I asked.

"Now." George released Patrick's hair, stepped up to me, and took my hand. "No time like the present, and he's at his most dangerous in this initial period."

"Yeah," Rhys said, "I agree."

"Me, too." Oscar studied the cuffs through narrowed eyes. "Get him out of here."

"You would say that." Lloyd snorted.

"What?" Oscar said.

"You're staying, here with Darius." A muscle flexed in Lloyd's jaw. "You've got the best deal by far."

So he hasn't totally accepted the decision.

"That might be the case," Oscar said. "But it's also one hell of a responsibility."

"Hey." I rested my palm on Lloyd's shoulder. "We'll all be together again before we know it. And the sooner you start working on Patrick's control, the sooner that will happen."

I couldn't see there was any other option than what George had proposed. Not at this point at least.

Lloyd sighed. "Yeah, I guess you're right."

"I am." I brushed my lips over his. "And if you need to see me, or I need to see you, you can just do that fast thing, like you just did to London and back."

"You mean run?"

"I don't think it can be described as a run, certainly not the way a human would use the word at any rate."

Lloyd smiled.

It was what I'd wanted him to do, before we parted. I needed my memory of him to be with his lips turned up and not down. "I'll see you soon." I kissed him.

"Mmm..." With his free arm, he dragged me close and deepened the kiss.

I sagged against him, wanting to get as near to him as possible. Our tongues tangled, and the embrace tightened.

After a few minutes, Rhys cleared his throat.

"Come on now," George said. "While we still have the cover of night."

Lloyd pulled back. "I'll miss you."

"I'll miss you, too."

"We all will." Rhys was before me, taking me from Lloyd. He set his mouth over mine, kissing me with the same passion Lloyd had.

And then it was George, sliding his arms around my torso and taking my mouth the moment my lips left Rhys's.

I clung to him. These men were part of my soul. Saying goodbye hurt. Already there was a real physical ache in my chest. Siberia was so far away. To me it sounded alien, dangerous, and inaccessible.

"Don't worry," Oscar said as Rhys took Patrick from him. "If you need to get anywhere, I'll take you."

George stepped away.

I hugged my arms around myself. "Thank you."

"No thanks required." Oscar straightened his leather jacket then shoved his thumbs into the front pockets of his tight biker pants. "Making sure you're happy and safe is my job."

"All of our jobs," Rhys added.

"And you can add satisfied to that list." Lloyd raised one eyebrow at me.

My heart was clattering against my ribs, and my fingers tingled. Emotion was building up heat again.

"It's okay." George looped an arm through Patrick's. "Try not to let your heart run away with itself, Darius."

"What do you mean?"

"I can hear it." He smiled.

I pressed my hand over my chest and dragged in a deep breath. George's incredible hearing could be a little disconcerting at times.

"Come on then, if we're doing it, let's do it." Lloyd tilted his chin as if bracing himself for the distance that was going to be between us.

"Yeah," Rhys said. "Let's go."

And then they were gone. This time I did see the first second of them breaking into a run, Patrick between them, before they became a blur then a flash fading into the distant dark hills.

All was silent. Still.

I blinked rapidly a few times and hoped the cool night air would dampen down the heat inside me.

"It's okay," Oscar said, nodding at my hands. "If you need to—"

"I don't. I can control it." I'd released enough sparks for one night. More than ever before, in fact. I had a grip on the burn that usually wouldn't subside until fire had left the tips of my fingers.

"Sorry, I just..." Oscar looked concerned.

"No. It's me." I pressed the heels of my hands to my eyes. "I just wasn't expecting to say goodbye so soon."

"It's temporary."

"I know but…"

I was in his arms, his leather jacket creaking as he trapped me in a tight embrace. I always felt small against Oscar; he was huge and muscled and super-strong.

But that suited me, and I allowed him to hold me, knowing he wouldn't think less of me for being vulnerable in my moment of sadness, or weak because I missed the men he considered brothers with every beat of my still galloping heart.

"It's okay," he said, stroking my hair. "It will go in a flash, and we're all much happier having distance between you and Patrick."

"But not forever?"

"No, not forever. I'm sure one day you and him will have a very special bond."

I pulled back. "What do you mean?"

"As you said, he's one of your harem, babe." The right side of his mouth tilted into a smile.

"Yes, but…special, as in…?" I wasn't quite sure what he was getting at.

"As in whatever you want it to be. Rhys turned him, so they'll always be close, and Rhys loves you, so it's inevitable Patrick will also be close to you."

I thought about the handsome young soldier Patrick had been, and the devastatingly gorgeous vampire he'd just become. There was no knowing if he was attracted to men or women or even if he'd be the kind of soul who could control his thirst.

"They'll teach him," Oscar said. "Techniques for managing his new desires and urges."

"Blood?"

"Yes." Oscar touched his lips to mine. "But let's get away from Stonehenge now. It's been quite a night, what with killing demons and creating vampires."

A sudden shiver went up my spine. A dead-of-the-night chill had seeped into the air. Laced with damp, it had created small dewy stars in the grass which sparkled in the moonlight.

Oscar kept one arm wrapped around me, and after a last glance at the ancient stones, we headed in the direction of his bike.

"You want me to carry you and run?" he asked.

"No." I pressed closer to him. "I'm happy to have the walk. Clear my head a bit."

"And then we'll go find that hotel George booked. You need to eat, drink tea, and sleep."

"I won't deny that sounds like a very good plan."

* * * *

The Foxhill Hotel was a quaint affair with Tudor beams and a thatched roof. A covered porch with lollipop-shaped bay trees led the way to a polished black door with a large brass fox-head knocker.

"They won't let us in now," I said, removing my helmet. "It's so late."

"Sure they will." Oscar waited for me to climb off the bike then did the same.

The car park was half empty, and a single light shone from one of the upstairs bedrooms.

"Well, I guess we can try." I shrugged.

"We have a room booked," Oscar said. "Come on, don't worry. I'll get you what you need, I promise."

It was nice to be so cared for, but I wasn't sure he was going to deliver on this occasion. I had every expectation of having to drive back to London in my weary state.

Oscar led me to the door, then pushed it open.

To my surprise, it wasn't locked.

The reception area was overwhelmingly red, with carpet, walls, and soft furnishings all a rich scarlet. A mahogany counter was set in the wall, behind which a suited man sat. I'd have put him in his late sixties, early seventies. He was resting back, eyes closed, mouth open, and snoring softly.

Oscar and I looked at each other. I suppressed a giggle.

Then Oscar cleared his throat.

"Oh…oh…good evening. Foxhill Hotel and Spa, how can I help you?" The man bolted forward, his eyes pinging open but not quite focusing.

"Good evening," Oscar said, stepping up to the desk. "We have a room booked."

The man was scrabbling for glasses. When he'd opened the arms and slipped them on, he gestured to the cuckoo clock on the wall behind him. "I see, sir…it's…it's two a.m. You're a little later than planned."

"I don't recall giving a time."

"We've been out for dinner with friends," I said. "The night ran away with us."

"Of course. Of course." He swung his attention to me, and then to Oscar. For a moment he froze, as if taking in Oscar's size and frame. That alone was impressive, but dressed head to toe in black leather and with a dark expression, Oscar was nothing short of menacing.

"Can we have the key to our room?" Oscar said.

"Certainly, sir… What's the name?"

"George Bartlett."

"One moment, please." He clicked the mouse on his computer then turned to a rack of long brass keys. "Here you go, room twelve. The room has already been charged and paid for. Breakfast is included in your rate and will be served in the orangery."

"Good, my companion needs to eat." Oscar took the key. "In fact, can we get room service now?"

"I'm sorry." He shook his head. "The chef went home hours ago." He paused and eyed Oscar as though he didn't want to do anything to displease him. Which was probably wise. "I could rustle you up some sandwiches, though? Beef, chicken?"

"Yeah, you do that." Oscar took out a wallet and flipped it open. He placed a fifty-pound note on the desk. "I appreciate it."

We headed to room twelve. The winding corridors were a little uneven underfoot, and old pictures of the village and Stonehenge adorned the walls.

"I hope this is nice," Oscar said. "I only want you to have the best."

"If it's got a shower and a bed, it will be the best."

As it turned out, the room was stunning. With a large four-poster bed dressed in gold and blue swags and drapes. A massive fireplace with ornate tiles featuring foxes, pheasants, badgers, and hunting hounds. The window was lead-paned and was directed over the hills rather than the car park.

"Yeah, this will do." Oscar slung his biker's helmet onto a low plush couch then took mine from me.

"It certainly will." Despite my tiredness, the sight of the bed thrilled me. To be sleeping in there with Oscar would be a treat. We'd yet to have full sex. He'd insisted I wasn't his first because of his big cock.

And what a cock. I'd had it in my mouth, tasted it, felt him come, and I wanted more.

Much more.

"Go shower," he said. "I'll wait for that food to arrive."

I peeled off my clothes in front of Oscar.

He stood by the door, arms folded, and didn't hide his study of me. Once naked, I raised my arms above my head, linked my fingers, and did a full body stretch, groaning as I did so. My back ached from the long journey on the bike earlier that day, and my arms were still aching from producing sparks.

"For the love of Benedict," Oscar muttered. "You want me to come over there, tip you facedown on the bed, and fuck you so hard you'll be orgasming for a month?"

"That sounds like a promise." I dropped my arms to my sides and gripped my cock. It was rapidly going from soft to semi.

"Get in the damn shower," he said, his voice a growl. "You've had enough for one day. I'm not going to push it."

I pouted.

"Unless you pull that face, then I might not be held responsible for all the wicked things I do to your sexy body." He shoved one hand down the front of his pants and adjusted himself.

I chuckled, enjoying seeing big, macho Oscar battling with his willpower. If he did decide to release his passion, I'd handle it.

Wouldn't I?

Chapter Three

Lloyd

Siberia had its useful aspects, sure, but basically the place was a cold, white version of Hell. I'd been here on several occasions, once only for a month, the longest instance for eight years. That had been kind of a sabbatical. I'd needed time alone, to think, to come to terms with my destiny. The solitariness of the icy wilderness had done me both good and bad. Yeah, I'd accepted my lot, but equally the sense of aloneness had been suffocating. Even with the chill wind blowing it had been hard to breathe, to get a sense of purpose.

But all that had changed now I'd met Darius. With him in my life I was complete. Not just because he'd secured my fate as a better one than burning in Hell for all eternity, but also because I loved him. I no longer felt alone. A human mate was what I'd needed. Someone warm of body as well as heart. For my vampire brothers were all well and good and we'd go to the ends of the earth to help each other, Darius was something different. Our souls had connected in the most beautiful of ways, and I knew I would love him always.

"This snowdrift has frozen solid." George dragged the door of the cabin open, moving a huge, heavy drift as he did so. Humans would have spent dangerous outdoor time in the brutal cold shifting it with shovels, but George moved it easily, and it created a small mountain beneath the window which looked out from a never-used kitchen.

Unless Darius joins us here, then it will be stocked and filled with the scents and sounds of cooking.

That thought gave me hope. I didn't know when it could or would happen, or even if it was wise, but I had to have hope, even if it was just undiscovered disappointment.

"Come on." Rhys pulled Patrick through the doorway by the arm.

I followed, gripping Patrick's other arm.

"We should smarten this place up." George stepped in, stamping snow from his boots.

"Yeah." Rhys wrinkled his nose. "It's damp."

"Basically, it's a bit shit." I sighed.

"Well, it's home for a while." George nodded at Patrick. "Put him in the back bedroom for now. I expect he'll sleep for a few weeks."

Rhys and I maneuvered the new vampire down a wooden-paneled corridor into one of the rear bedrooms. The double bed was covered with a duvet patterned with tiny Russian flags and images of the Kremlin. It was strangely patriotic considering we were over three thousand miles from Moscow. Beside it, a table held a lamp with a wonky pink shade. A cupboard stood in the corner, one of the doors slightly ajar, and the window faced the huge expanse of white tundra stretching north for miles before hitting the semi-frozen sea. The curtains were thin pink cotton.

"Rest here." Rhys helped Patrick lie on the bed.

He groaned; his eyes were still closed, and his cuffed hands shook violently.

I hoisted his legs up, and he curled into a foetal position.

"Perhaps we should have let him die." Rhys wore a concerned expression.

"If he was dead, there would be nothing we could do for him." I held out my hands, palms up.

"But at least he wouldn't be in silver agony."

"He won't be forever, it's just until we have him under control." I hesitated. "Besides, Darius might have never forgiven us if we'd let him die. Patrick, the man before he was possessed, did nothing wrong. He didn't deserve to be murdered because we were killing the demon inside him."

Rhys rubbed his chin and pressed his lips together, then, "Did you see the fire coming from Darius's hands?"

"Yeah, I did." I blew out a breath. "I've seen him release sparks before, but that was something else. That was full-on flame throwing. His emotions must have been wildly intense."

"He was fighting, for himself and us. For our lives."

"And he did a damn good job."

Rhys nodded and stroked Patrick's hair. "And now it's time for us to do a good job, with this one."

"We will." I paused, watching Rhys's softer side as he touched the first vampire he'd created. "And you mustn't feel alone, Rhys. You might have turned him, but we all take responsibility for the situation."

"Thanks, Lloyd, I appreciate that."

I smiled. "Come on, let's leave him to rest."

We shut the door, confident that Patrick wouldn't do any harm to himself or others, and walked into the living room. Like all the rooms in the cabin, it had walls made of logs lying horizontal. Several mismatched chairs and a sofa sat around, and on the wall were several framed photographs of prior Russian leaders—Stalin, Lenin, Khruschev, and Brezhnev.

"What you doing?" Rhys placed his hands on his hips and frowned at George.

"What does it look like?" George was kneeling by the fireplace stacking kindling and logs.

"Okay, I'll rephrase: Why are you lighting a fire?"

"Well, it's not for heat, I couldn't care less about the cold." He turned and shriveled his nose. "It's the damp smell."

"Yeah, I agree." I walked to the picture of Stalin and straightened it. "I'd rather smell a fire."

"It will dry the cabin out, too." George struck a spark from a piece of flint. It landed on the kindling.

Rhys flopped onto the sofa nearest the fire. "I've only been here once. It doesn't change, though, does it."

"No, might as well be fossilized up here, with only one true summer month and the rest of the year temperatures hitting as low as minus eighty. People still live in that village to the west?" I asked.

"Oymyakon, yeah," George said, "and they will while there's diamonds to be mined. There's about five hundred humans permanently there."

"Humans." Rhys licked his lips. "Warm, blood-filled humans."

"Hey." I frowned at him.

"Can't blame a guy for thinking about it," he said. "We're gonna get pretty damn bored here over the coming months."

"You have your own willing human now, with exquisite blood. No need to take from others."

"And that would risk our cover immensely out here. No crowds to lose ourselves in." George shook his head.

"Okay, okay, chill out." Rhys frowned and crossed one leg over the other. "I was only saying."

After a moment, George spoke. "Is Patrick okay?" He stoked the fire which had burst into flames.

"As well as can be expected with silver around his neck and wrists," I said.

"We'll give him a couple of days and then take the collar off. The cuffs should be enough to subdue his new instincts while we talk some sense into him."

I nodded. "And there's no human smell around here to set him off."

"Which is why, like I said, it's perfect for our needs." George stood, the fire going well now, and walked to a large window. "I heard musk deer in the forest over there."

"You did?"

"Yes, when we arrived."

I stood next to him. The tree line was half a mile away, the evergreens heavy with snow, the ground thick with it. In the half-light the forest appeared shrouded in an eerie mist, and shadows stretched onto the virginal snowfield before it.

"Are you going to feed from the deer?" I asked.

"Yeah, I might." He licked his teeth, as if feeling for his fangs. "Been a hell of a few hours. And I've grown rather fond of musk deer blood over the years."

"Suit yourself." I had no need of blood. I was still satisfied after drinking from Darius at midnight.

"I will." He turned to Rhys. "Keep a watch on your charge."

"I'm not going anywhere." Rhys shrugged and chose a book from the shelf at his side.

George didn't reply. Instead, he let himself out of the door into the arctic wind. As he shut it, several wisps of snow entered the lodge and skittered about my feet.

"This place is a tip." Rhys gestured around. "There's nothing nice about it."

"I know."

"Can't we tidy it up a bit? If we're going to be hunkering down for a while."

"I guess it would give us something to do."

"We need that. I've got cabin fever already."

I went to the kitchen area and wiped my fingers along the counter. It was filthy with dust, though beneath it was good solid wood. Again I thought about Darius joining us here. How he'd need the kitchen, because unlike us, he'd have to eat. From memory, I knew all the bedrooms were just as crap as the one we'd put Patrick in. And although it was fine for a vampire, I didn't want the love of my life having to put up with such dire surroundings.

"In fact, I think it's a great idea." I nodded at Rhys. "To smarten it up a bit."

"You do?" He grinned and slotted the book away.

"Yeah."

"Excellent." He stood and rubbed his hands together. "Where shall we start?"

"How about you clean the kitchen, and I'll get to work on the main bedroom?"

"The main bedroom." He narrowed his eyes. "Are you thinking what I'm thinking?"

"That Darius might join us here—yeah, I am. Exactly that." I held up my dusty finger. "And this is nowhere near to the standards he's used to in swanky hotels."

"And his apartment. That's pretty nice, too, remember."

I had a feeling, knowing Darius the way I did now, that he wouldn't complain. But equally I wanted him to be happy, to enjoy being where he was in the world. Okay, the middle of Siberia was as remote as the moon, but we could make the best of it. It wasn't as if money and labor was an issue for us.

"And if he doesn't ever come here," Rhys said, "at least it'll be a bit nicer for us to sit around in."

I nodded. "Okay, we'll clean, and then when George is back, one of us can go and get some stuff to…" I flicked my hand toward the sofa and the walls.

"Brighten it up."

"Yeah, I guess." I pushed my hood down. "And get things Darius needs. We'll have them in, you know, just in case."

"I know what he needs." Rhys grinned and cupped his groin.

I turned away. Sometimes it was hard sharing a lover, but it was the only way. And Darius had enough room in his heart for all of us, and he certainly seemed physically capable.

I wonder how he's managing with Oscar?

I pushed that thought from my mind. It would be easy to worry. Oscar was a big guy, but I knew he'd be considerate and gentle. Or at least I hoped he would be, otherwise he'd have me to deal with. Oscar didn't scare me.

I went into the largest bedroom and shut the door. For a moment the absolute silence was deafening—the air was still, the outside landscape was still. There wasn't even my heartbeat to hear.

I blew out a breath and walked to the bed. Sitting on the dark-blue blanket, I stared out of the window. Like the others, the view was little other than snow and a white-gray sky.

Did I feel any different now I had the key to salvation? I'd drunk from the cambion—Darius—at midnight, at the place we were sure Master Benedict had sent us to. In all honesty, no, I didn't feel any different. More in love with Darius than ever, and ready to face the challenge that was Patrick. But as for not going to Hell one day—that, I had no idea.

I thought back to the stroke of midnight, and my cock hardened. It had been so hot, all of us taking a drink from Darius, the drink that would save our souls. Except it had been so much more than that. Our saliva, combined, had sent Darius near crazed with lust.

Oh, I knew we had that effect on humans when we bit them, but this was off the scale. He hadn't known what to do with himself. Need had swamped him, he'd cried out, demanded, and then bent over right in front of me.

I groaned at the memory and flicked the top button on my jeans. My erection was growing by the second. It was becoming damn uncomfortable.

Shoving at my pants, I released my cock and took the shaft in my hand. I stroked and leaned back, supporting myself on one arm.

The vision of Darius bent before me hovered in my mind. His perfect ass, his long, lean back, and the shiver that had traveled up his spine.

"Fuck yeah," I muttered. The image was seriously hot. Definitely wank fodder.

I worked my cock, root to tip, and my balls tingled. I knew I'd come soon. Thoughts of Darius could do that. We'd arrived in

Siberia, and George wanted a feed, Rhys needed to clean, but I wanted to replay the incredible first time I'd entered Darius.

I sped up, my cock thickening with each stroke. Darius's little hole had been there, quivering, waiting for me. I'd started off being careful, but his demands had been raw and impossible not to obey.

Within seconds, we'd been fucking hard, Rhys working Darius's cock with his hand and Oscar sinking his big dick into Darius's mouth.

I gritted my teeth. My slit was peeking from my fist and sparkling with the first drip of cum.

Darius had been so tight, so warm inside, and I'd taken him so high and hard. He'd been so trusting and giving.

I held my breath and closed my eyes. My orgasm was threatening, the pressure building. I allowed every sense to remember Darius in his wonderful moment of climax. He'd shot sparks from his fingers as his body had writhed in ecstasy, crying out around Oscar's cock.

"Oh yeah." I allowed my own release to happen. In three blissful spurts, I coated my hand and the base of my hoody in cum. It was almost like being there again, with him. Coming hard and fast.

I slowed, then stilled and opened my eyes. "Damn it." I tutted and looked at the mess on the black material. I'd have to clean it. But I wasn't too bothered. The memoires and the solo time had been worth it.

Chapter Four

Darius

"Sleep now," Oscar said when the plate was clear.

I'd wolfed down all the sandwiches, enough for two people, and a cake.

"Sleep?" I rested back on the pillow and crossed my ankles. I wore only tight black boxers and knew he was admiring the bulge of my cock.

"Yeah." Oscar chuckled, tugged the blanket, and covered me. "And stop testing my self-control."

"Maybe I like testing your self-control." I reached for his big hand. The back of it was hair-coated and his knuckles wide. "Maybe I want to see you lose control."

"Trust me." He shook his head, and his eyebrows pulled low. "You don't, babe."

"Why can't I have it the way you and Jack used to?"

"Because that was different. *Very* different."

"How?" I looked up at his handsome face.

His stubble was thick, and he still had on his biker jacket and leathers, as though he didn't trust himself to take them off.

"You know why. He was a vampire. I wouldn't break him or hurt him. We were as tough as each other, but you…"

"Do not say I'm delicate. That really is an affront to my manhood."

"I'm not questioning your manhood, Darius, far from it. More my reluctance to accidently break your bones."

Break my bones.

I sighed, rested deeper into the pillow, and let my eyelids droop. "In that case, if I must sleep at your insistence, that's what I'll do."

His lips brushed mine, his chin abrading my skin. "Yes, sleep. We had some fun earlier. Thinking about that blow job you gave me could keep me going for decades."

I popped my eyes wide open. "If you don't get down and dirty with me for decades, Oscar Yale, you and I are going to have a problem."

He smiled, his lips moving against mine. "You're cute when you're angry, you know that."

"I am *not* cute."

His smile widened. "Sleep before I go and keep watch over you from the other side of the hotel room door, the way I did in Paris."

"No, don't do that." I squeezed his hand. "I like you being in here with me."

"I like it, too." He rested back.

I closed my eyes, allowing the weariness that had been creeping up on me to take hold. My body ached in a good way, and my arms were still warm from the incredible release of fire from my fingertips.

The room was quiet and warm, and Oscar's breaths were slow and steady.

It didn't take long for sleep to steal me away.

I found myself in the usual place. London. Tower Bridge.

The Thames stretched before me, a dark-chocolate color rippling with the tide. To the right The Tower of London rose into the night sky, and behind me an old-fashioned car went past, its exhaust wheezing and spluttering.

A scruffy urchin came up to me, hands outstretched, begging, and a breeze lifted my hair, taking with it the stink of the city.

I turned back to the river, running my hands over my body. To my surprise, I was male. No breasts and my hips slim. This was very different to how this dream had been in the past. Then I'd been a voluptuous female, drawing attention from males in the dream—one in particular.

I scanned the river, looking for the lone rowing boat with its three occupants. That was always what I saw next in my recurring dream.

But that had changed, too. There was nothing there. The small archway leading to Traitor's Gate was, but no one was making their way toward it.

Usually I'd feel a desperate sense of urgency to get to the prisoner, but that wasn't growing in me. Instead, I took in the sight of the towers, the stars, and a crescent moon.

And then it all went dark, faded away. My sleep deepened into a dreamless abyss that healed my soul.

When I woke, I was lying on my side, Oscar spooning me from behind.

I stared at the curtains and the sun peeking in around them. I couldn't remember when I'd last slept so well. It was bliss to just lose myself in nothingness. No scary demons trying to win my attention and affection. No threats or mysterious riddles.

"Morning." Oscar kissed my ear.

"Hey." I spun within his arms. The leather on his jacket creaked and was cool on my skin.

"You slept well." He kissed the tip of my nose.

"Yes." I smiled.

"Dreams?" He raised his eyebrows and studied my face.

"No...well, yes, to start with."

"Was he there? Your father?"

"No." I thought back. "And neither was Master Benedict."

"Neither of them?" He seemed surprised.

"No, neither of them. It was a nice change. There was no lurking menace, you know what I mean?"

"I do. Dreams were the way they'd been communicating with you. On your father's part, that was devious and underhand."

"What do you expect from someone who sides with the Devil?"

"True." He ran his hand over my hair. "I hope everyone stays away from your dreams; it can only be a good sign."

"I agree. And it's certainly good to sleep so well." I yawned and flipped over onto my back, stretched my arms over my head, and pointed my toes, knees locked. It was a full body stretch that rid me of all the overnight kinks and knots, and it felt great.

"Darius." Oscar was close again, his body in alignment with mine. "It's driving me crazy being this close to you when you have so little clothing on."

He slipped his hand beneath the blanket, running it over my chest and down to my belly.

I trembled under his touch. His palm was a little rough.

"So do something about it," I said.

He opened his mouth, but I quickly pressed my finger over his lips.

"And don't say you're worried you'll hurt me. I want you. I want everything you can give me, Oscar. I have since the first moment I saw you."

"You have?"

"Yes, you're super fucking hot in a macho, brooding biker way."

He chuckled and kissed me, sending his hand lower and cupping my cock over my boxers.

I was at a semi anyway, but his caress quickly brought me to full hardness.

"You're hot, literally," he said.

I smiled and ran my hand into his thick, dark hair. I had no idea how far he wanted to take this; up until now he'd been holding back. But I was happy to go all the way, if Oscar felt it was time.

"Let me play," he said, slipping under the waistband of my boxers and taking a hold of my shaft, flesh on flesh.

I sighed and fluttered my eyelids closed. The stimulation was exactly what I needed. "Play as much as you want."

He shoved at my boxers some more so they were at my thighs, and then settled in to stroke my growing erection.

His movements were slow and indulgent. Occasionally, he twisted his hand a little just beneath my glans, sending a shudder of longing through my balls to my asshole.

"Relax," he whispered.

"I am."

I wondered if and when he was going to get naked but resisted asking. I didn't want to break the spell of him touching me, enjoying me.

Outside, a bird squawked, and there was a scrabble above. It was on the roof. There was a voice in the corridor outside our room; it quickly passed.

On and on, Oscar masturbated me. Not with enough friction or pressure to make me come, just enough to have me hovering on the edge of need and want.

"Lift your knees up," he whispered.

I did as he'd asked, dragging my heels on the sheet and the blanket tenting.

He released me and pulled a tube from his pocket. Lube. After coating his fingers, he was touching me again.

I groaned at the new coolness, and again my asshole quivered.

"Keep still," he said onto my lips. "Very still." He stroked over my balls, the thin strip of skin behind them, then circled my hole.

"Oscar." I was breathing light and shallow, desperate for his touch there now. "Please."

"Shh, don't speak either."

I pressed my lips together. He had such a look of concentration on his face.

He kept on stroking my hole, orbiting it. My cock twitched, blood pumping through my shaft.

"You have no idea what you do to me," he said. "Your taste, your smell, the feel of you here."

I clenched as he slipped the tip of his finger into my ass.

"Damn it," he muttered. "You're too tight."

"I'm not, give me more... Oscar." I gripped his shoulder.

He stared into my eyes and gave it, riding knuckle deep.

I groaned and tried to release the tension. But it was so nice having him there. I wanted to clench and relish the moment.

"I'll never be able to fuck you," he said.

"No, no, don't say that." I cupped his face. "I've seen your cock. Hell, I've sucked it. I can take it. Just prepare me for it." I paused. "The way you're doing now."

He shook his head.

"Oscar!"

"I'll hate myself if I hurt you."

"You won't. What hurts me more is you not even being willing to give it a try."

"Babe." He kissed me, his tongue stroking over mine as he retreated and then sank his finger deep into my ass.

"Give me two fingers," I said. "Please."

He hesitated, then found my lips again.

My asshole stretched wider. I concentrated on relaxing while he filled me, but it wasn't difficult. I was so turned on. I wanted him there. And thanks to George, I was no longer a virgin.

"You feel amazing," he murmured onto my mouth.

"So do you."

He fucked me with his fingers, the lube easing his way.

I took hold of my cock and held it gently. We were nowhere near climax yet, and when I came, I wanted Oscar to as well.

After a few minutes, he lifted from our kiss, closed his eyes, and grimaced.

"What's up?" I asked.

"My cock. It's getting damn painful in these leathers."

"So take them off."

"If I do we'll..."

"Fuck, yes, I get that." I smiled. "Do it."

"You're a demanding cambion, you know that?"

"Have you ever had a man who's half demon, half human before?"

"You know I haven't."

"So maybe all cambions are demanding." I twitched my eyebrows. "Or maybe you just got lucky."

"Oh, I got seven fucking shades of lucky."

He slipped from my ass, stood at the side of the bed, and stripped. He did it in super-human time, then, completely naked, he crawled back next to me.

I ran my hand down his hair-coated chest. "Where were we?"

"I was getting you ready to fuck."

"Oh yeah." A tremble of anticipation seized me.

"But we're going to do it like this, so you have the control." He rested onto his back. "Sit up and over me."

I stared at his huge cock pointing directly upward. It was thicker than I ever thought a cock could be, longer, too. On his belly and down his thighs, the hair was thick and curled, and his balls sat heavy.

"Like this." He gripped my waist, and in one swift movement, had me sitting straddling his hips.

I rested my hands on his chest and stared down at his face.

A crease had etched onto his usually smooth forehead.

"I don't want this to be anything but a good experience." He handed me the lube. "So you can sit on me."

"What...just sit...on your cock?"

He brushed my hair back from my face. "That's the general idea."

"Jesus," I muttered, the cross at my neck swinging forward.

"*He* doesn't need to watch." Oscar grinned, a sexy-as-sin smile that did strange things to my heartbeat.

I sat upright and wriggled back, my cock tapping against my belly, then took hold of Oscar's dick.

I squirted lube onto the tip then began to work it down his length.

He hissed in a breath and pressed his head onto the pillow, eyes closed.

I knew I'd have to be careful, otherwise I'd be flipped over and this huge cock would be ramming into my ass at lightning speed—taking it at my pace would be out of the window.

The lubrication was cool on my hot fingers. I hoped I'd be able to contain the sparks and not ruin this nice bedding with scorch marks. But when I came, control seemed to slip out of the window. And orgasming around this big cock, that I couldn't even begin to imagine.

"Damn, I'm so hard," he muttered.

"Yes, you are." I ran my thumb over his slit, then around the ridge of his glans.

"Darius," he murmured, the words quiet but desperation lacing his tone.

"It's okay, I'm here. No rush."

I released his cock and sat forward again so the end stroked the gap between my buttocks.

He shot his hands out and gripped my waist. "I've got you."

"I know." And he did; his firm support allowed me to concentrate on nothing but what I was about to do.

Gripping his muscle-roped forearms, I sank lower, finding purchase with my ass on his cock.

He stared at my face, his jaw tense, the tendons on his neck standing flush. The effort of not ramming upward, entering me hard and fast, was clearly a strain.

I closed my eyes and sat lower, my hole opening around his tip. Pausing, I blew out a breath, then took him some more.

"Yeah..." He hissed. "Yeah, that's it..."

I bore down, allowing my hole to open as I impaled myself on his cock. I was stretching so wide, wider still. A nip of pain joined the filling sensation.

"Darius, you're...doing it."

I didn't answer. I was concentrating.

I continued to take him until the rim of his glans popped inside me.

He groaned and squeezed my waist.

I released his right forearm and took hold of my cock. It was throbbing with need.

And then I went on a slow journey down his cock, filling myself with him.

He held his breath. So did I.

The denseness of him was amazing. I'd taken his width and now was accommodating his length.

"Benedict give me strength." His fingers were pincers on my skin.

I didn't care. I tugged my cock and sat until my ass cheeks were on his thighs.

"Oscar," I moaned, not knowing where he ended and I began. It was out-of-this-world incredible. He was so deep inside me. I was stretched to the max, owned by him, taken by him.

"You did it." He was breathing hard.

"Yes."

"Now fuck me." He gritted his teeth. "Fuck me until we both come."

I didn't need telling twice and began to work myself on him, grinding my hips, pulling almost off and sitting back down. Each drag of his cock on my ass had me groaning and losing myself in the ecstasy of being skewered on him.

"I need to come. Darius… I need…to come."

The old four-poster bed was squeaking with each of my bounces over him.

I upped the pace on my cock, the cum dragging at my balls. They'd retracted, and I could hold off no longer.

Releasing a long wail of satisfaction, I spurted, my ass clamping around him.

He yelled out, too, the deep sound echoing around the old room.

My climax extended, another rope of cum coating my hand as I wanked harder, faster.

He filled me with a cool release, each pulse of his cock thudding on my internal walls.

And then it was over, the ecstasy faded, and I hauled in air. I released my cock and tipped my head back, stared at the drapes over the bed.

Oscar kept a tight hold of me while I sat on his cock, unmoving.

"That was… I can't believe…"

"That I can handle you?" I said, setting my attention on him. "Don't underestimate me."

He chuckled. "I won't, and it's also good you didn't burn this bed down. It's likely an antique."

I glanced around. There was no evidence of scorch marks in the bedding. And I certainly couldn't smell burning.

"That's good." I checked my fingertips. They were hot and tingling, sure, but it was under control. I didn't have the need to fire off sparks.

"I shouldn't think there's any left," Oscar said, "after the flame throwing at Stonehenge."

"Yeah, that was extreme." I squeezed my asshole around the base of his cock.

"Oh fuck," he moaned, his eyes rolling back. "Would you stop teasing."

"Why?"

"Or we'll never get out of this place."

"But where do we have to be?" I grinned. "I thought we were just passing time anyway."

He raised his eyebrows. "You've got a point there. Tease all you want. We're staying at Foxhill Hotel for a while."

Chapter Five

Patrick

Agony.

That was all I could think of.

The screaming, burning agony in my neck and hands. It radiated around my entire body. It was exhausting, this blistering pain; it had drained everything from me—my energy, my thoughts, the very essence of my soul. I didn't even have the strength to groan or ask for help.

"How are you doing, Corporal?"

Someone stroked my hair. I couldn't respond. It was as if my teeth were glued together in a weird jaw cramp.

My spine shook, a constant tremble that had knotted all the tendons, muscles, and nerves around it.

"It's been a week," someone else said. "Time to take one piece of silver off."

I heard the words, but they made no sense.

"Yes, it's time. Go get his feed, Rhys."

"I'm on the case."

And I craved something. A taste, a nourishment that was raw and primal, tangy and warm.

Blood.

I remembered it at the exact moment the delicious scent of it came to my nose. It was in the room now—beautiful, metallic, rich blood.

A gurgle rumbled up from my chest, my vain attempt at begging for what I needed most barely a sound even though I needed the blood I could smell.

My mouth watered, and a strange, sharp tingling burned in my upper gums—it had done that a lot while I'd laid there in torment, just to add insult to injury.

"Take the collar off, Lloyd," someone said, the one with the posh English accent.

"Was just about to." A gruff, murmur of a voice.

"There was a fiddling at the back of my neck. Pain shot up the base of my skull and down my spine, spreading over my shoulders and making my internal organs shake all the harder.

And then it was lifting away, the searing torture that had been there for as long as I could remember, my skin now cool and smarting, my neck stiff.

I dared to move my head, just a little. The bones didn't hurt anymore, my ears stopped ringing, and I managed to unclench my teeth and peel my tongue from the roof of my mouth.

"See, you're okay." A gentle, soothing tone from the guy at my side. "How is that, Patrick?"

I was moved—by strong hands—onto my back then tugged upward to a sitting position on soft pillows.

My hands were still in ice-hot suffering. Whatever was around my wrists keeping them shackled was inducing some kind of painful, energy-sapping force.

"You should open your eyes now."

A shoulder squeeze.

I snarled and twitched away. Where was that blood?

"It's okay, Corporal. We'll look after you."

I'm not a corporal.

I grunted and twitched my head from side to side to sniff out the red stuff.

"He's not ready for this."

"He is. And if he's not, it doesn't matter. We'll collar him again for a few weeks. Let's face it, we're in no rush. This could go on for decades if necessary.

Decades?

I pinged my eyes open, then immediately blinked in the stark lighting.

Where the hell am I?

"Ah, see, he is with us."

Another shoulder squeeze.

I wished I had the energy to shake the guy off and rid my shackles. But I didn't, I was exhausted the way I had been after my Special Forces selection week—a dark, dense fatigue that ate a hole in the very heart of me. My skills and my physical fitness were rendered useless by whatever drug these men had used on me.

Are they terrorists? Extremists? Am I to be held to ransom?

"Close the curtains."

"Doing it."

The room dimmed; the blinding white light flooding through the window disappeared.

I cleared my throat. It was dry and tight.

"You're safe, Corporal."

"Officer," I managed, staring at my cuffed wrists that were sitting over my camo combats. "I'm a goddamn officer." I coughed.

"My apologies."

I looked at the man who'd spoken. He was white, wore a flat cap, stiff starched shirt, and tweed waistcoat. Clean-shaven and with sharp intelligent eyes. His attention was as fixed on me as mine was on him. He certainly wasn't a typical insurgent, at least not going by my last deployment experience.

"Get these...off me." I managed to raise my hands a little. Without whatever had been fastened around my neck, some of my strength was returning.

"I'm afraid not. They're on for your own safety at this stage." He shook his head. "I'm George Bartlett." He held up one hand. "We'll shake later. I don't want to get too near those cuffs."

The strange tingling was back in my upper gums, sharp and greedy. Like a hard-on, it was growing to the point I couldn't ignore it.

I studied the other two men standing beside the bed. Again, both white, and going by their accents, also English born.

The older one was tall, wearing a black hoody which framed his handsome face. His skin was pale, his shoulders broad. I reckoned he could handle himself.

The other was nibbling on his bottom lip, his hair brushed into a quiff, and he had on a retro Beatles t-shirt. He was cute, just my type had I not been so fucking furious with him, and the others, for holding me hostage.

It was then I saw what he was holding. Need surged within me, overtaking my confusing thoughts and the pains in my hands, wrists, and arms.

"Give." I nodded at the tankard.

"Yeah, do it," Hoody Guy said. "We might be able to speak to him then."

Beatles t-shirt bloke came closer, clutching a pewter tankard.

A strange excitement, despite my predicament, swirled within me. I needed that tankard. I needed what it was in it with a desperation I'd never known before. I'd run miles for it...kill for it.

"Here."

The tankard was at my mouth, the beautiful red liquid within sparkling up at me. I inhaled, then, as it touched my lips, I began to swallow.

Its warmth slid over my tongue, filled my cheeks, and passed down my throat.

I closed my eyes and gulped, taking it fast, as much as I could. Each swallow eased an ache in me, a longing. It was dampening a fire that was raging in my soul.

He kept on tipping the tankard, until I'd had every last drop. Then he stepped away.

I was breathing fast as I licked my lips, gathering up the last drips. There were two strange, hard protrusions on my top gum where the tingling had been. I didn't know what they were, but they didn't worry me; they felt like a part of me despite being sharp on their points.

"Better?" the cap guy, George, asked.

I nodded and breathed deep, in and out, my nostrils flaring. I had to get out of this place.

"I'm sorry it's only deer blood," he went on. "Best we could get for now. The bears are still hibernating, and the wolves, I'm pleased to say, haven't been around here for a while from what we can tell."

"Deer blood," I repeated.

"Quite fresh," Cute Guy said. "I drained it myself, this morning...for you."

I glared at him, trying to make some kind of sense of his words.

He smiled, dimples appearing in his smooth cheeks. "I'm Rhys, by the way. I'm glad you're awake. We wanted to talk to you."

I didn't reply. If they were going to interrogate me, torture me, they'd have a tough task on their hands. I'd been trained to handle this kind of situation.

"And I'm Lloyd." Hoody Guy shoved his hands into the pocket of his hoody. There was a small box shape in there, so I guessed he was a smoker.

"Where am I?" I glanced at the window. It had to be midday, the light was so vivid. Somewhere hot, though I didn't feel hot, not even warm really. It was quiet, too. Perhaps we were near a lake or the desert. No traffic, no other noises, not even the low rumble of a jet in the sky.

"Siberia," Lloyd said. "Or as I like to call it, the middle of bloody nowhere."

Rhys huffed. "You can say that again."

Siberia?

Who were these guys? Why the hell would they bring me to Russia? They clearly had a plan they didn't want anyone to know about. I racked my muddled mind for intelligence on insurgents in this part of the world—Russians who were on the radar or offshoot groups who might be operating here.

"Can I please...get these off?" I tried to raise my hands. They lifted about an inch, then the cuffs shifted, and new shots of pain went up my arms. I grimaced.

"No." Rhys set his hand on my shoulder. "Not yet, not until you understand a few things."

"Like what?" I gritted my teeth.

Rhys looked at George.

I guessed he was the ringleader. The one I'd have to watch. This Rhys, perhaps I could get him on side, use him. He seemed a softer touch and the youngest of the group.

"Go on, you tell him." George nodded.

Rhys pulled in a deep breath. Whatever he was going to say, he'd been building up to it.

"Well?" I asked, trying to project some kind of control into the room.

"The thing is..." Rhys wound his hands together. He glanced at Lloyd.

Lloyd bobbed his head, as if giving encouragement.

"The thing is..." Rhys said again. "You're a vampire."

"What?" I'd heard the word, the sound, the syllables, but it made no sense.

"You're a vampire. I turned you. I had no choice. I'm sorry." Rhys stretched his hands wide. "You were dead. A demon had possessed you, and we had to...well...kill you to kill him. But then Darius wanted to save you. Darius that's our cambion, he's a good soul, and we try to be, you know, no harm in that. So I drained you dry, took every last drop of your blood, and in doing so, you became a vampire."

Vampire.

"It was the best and only thing we could think to do," Rhys went on. "It was that or death, permanent death, for you. We figured being a vampire was better than it being the end. At least you'll still have something, even if you are a different species."

These guys were off their rockers. I knew that now. It was why I hadn't been able to place them with any groups on the Military of Defence's watchlists. They were simply a bunch of nutters living up here in the snowy wilderness and pretending to be vampires. Likely they'd played too many video games or read too many fucking comics.

"Do you remember it happening?" George asked.

"Remember what?" I asked.

"Being drained, at Stonehenge?" Rhys tapped his neck. "When you woke and it all clicked back into place."

"I've never been to Stonehenge." I eyed the tankard again, wondering if I'd get more blood.

Blood!

Shit. I'd just drunk blood...like a vampire. I'd more than just drunk it, I'd craved it, smelled it, and it had satisfied a need deep inside. A hunger I'd never experienced before.

Vampires drink blood.

I swallowed, my breaths becoming a little shallow. What the heck kind of drug had they used on me? Some kind of mind-altering shit, it had to be.

"Of course he won't remember," Lloyd said. "The demon had possessed his body when he went there. Then afterward, when he was freshly turned, he was manic, wild. All he could see was Darius."

"Who...who is Darius?" It was the second time I'd heard the name.

"He's our lover."

"Your lover?"

"*Our* lover." George gestured to the other two men. "We share him."

"Fuck." I closed my eyes. This wasn't making sense. These guys were all gay and thought I was a vampire. I hoped to hell they weren't thinking of doing any weird crap to me. I'd rather have my toenails pulled or be waterboarded than be the star of gay movies for YouTube that featured me getting off while covered in blood.

I'd die of shame if anyone knew I was gay. My squadron would never let me live it down. It would be the end of my career, everything I've worked for.

"It's okay." Rhys stroked his hand over my hair. It was as though he liked touching me or something. "We've all been where you are right now. It passes, this confusion, this urge to kill and drink, I promise."

"What do you mean you've all been here?" I studied his eyes. They were full of compassion and patience. He didn't want to hurt me, not with the usual torture techniques.

"When we were turned." Lloyd tugged the box of cigarettes from his pocket. He had a lighter, too, with a picture of the Eiffel Tower on it. "We all went through exactly the same thing."

"And it was George who turned me." Rhys nodded at George. "And he's looked after me, helped me ever since, the same way I will you."

"We're all here for you, Officer," George said, his expression serious and his back rod-straight, shoulders set down.

"Yeah, we're a team, and you're in it." Lloyd lit a cigarette. "You just need to let the information sink in."

"Do you have to smoke?" George said, frowning at Lloyd. "In here?"

"What? You worried about getting lung cancer and kicking the bucket?" Lloyd blew out a stream of smoke.

"I don't like the smell." George wrinkled his nose.

Lloyd rolled his eyes. "I'm going out anyway. I'll do a routine sweep for human and wolf tracks, just in case, you know."

"Good idea." George sighed.

Lloyd wandered from the room, his swagger confident, as though he didn't think anything or anyone on this earth could hurt him.

Is he really a vampire?

I shook my head, trying to get my brain into gear. Was Rhys trying to tell me that he, George, and Lloyd were vampires and they'd made me one?

Yes, that's exactly what they're saying.

It had to be a pile of crap. Some kind of warped trick they were playing. It was fucked up. Some game show host would likely jump out of the wardrobe in a minute with a microphone, and I'd have won a shed load of money for being such a good sport on television.

"It's hard to take in, I know that. But you'll get used to it." George smiled—one heck of a smile, a model smile with straight white teeth, and eyes that held depth and wisdom. The guy was dressed old-fashioned, but his perfect skin was young, and he was gorgeous.

"Get used to being a vampire and being around vampires, yeah right." I'd tried to sound disparaging, but doubts were niggling at me. Some of the things they'd said did make sense.

"Vampires are real." Rhys turned and walked to the window. His jeans were tight, his ass small, the perfect handful. "We just like to keep a low profile; it's better for our species."

I didn't say anything. I needed all the information I could get on these guys so I could outwit them and escape. And then I'd go to the top. I'd get the whole damn weight of the British military coming down on them, Siberia or not. They didn't know who the fuck they'd messed with by kidnapping me.

"Remember drinking that?" George nodded at the tankard Rhys had left beside the bed. "Can you explain why you needed it so badly? Why you craved it? How the blood satisfied a part of you you'd never even known existed?"

I shook my head, narrowing my eyes at him.

"Because before you were turned, that part of you *didn't* exist. Now it does, now you're vampire, complete with fangs, urges, a perfect body, and immortality."

I stared at him and ran my tongue over those new protrusions on my top gums. No, they weren't protrusions...they were fangs.

Fangs!

Fuck. How the hell had they managed that? They'd inserted them, some kind of freaky dentistry while I'd been under the influence of drugs.

"Don't be so alarmed, Officer," George said. "If you concentrate, you can retract them."

Rhys turned from where he'd been looking through a gap in the thin curtains. "Yeah, try. Try it now."

"All you have to do is think about it." George peeled back his top lip.

I watched in amazement, my breathing shallow, as he slid two long pointed fangs from his top gum. They stayed for a few seconds, then slipped upward and disappeared.

"See, easy."

"Shit a brick," I muttered. "How'd you do that?"

"Same way you can. Concentrate."

Rhys was by the bed again. His smile was broad, showcasing those damn cute dimples.

I ran my tongue over the extra teeth in my mouth then imagined them retracting, disappearing. To my amazement, a tickling sensation grew, then the teeth slid away.

"What the fuck?" I went to lift my hands, wanting to feel my mouth. Pains shot up my arms.

I moaned and dropped my head back onto the pillow. A wave of exhaustion came over me. Pain could do that. It was draining when there was no end to it.

"See, you did it." Rhys sounded so proud of me it was weird.

"He needs to rest," George said. "The silver is still very effective on him, as you can see."

I blew out a breath. I knew I wouldn't sleep. I hadn't slept since I'd arrived. Every second of pain had been experienced. But I had to give my brain a break from thinking. I needed to just be, with the torment, and let the rest of this fucked-up world slip away.

Chapter Six

Darius

Oscar and I had been guests at Foxhill Hotel and Spa for over a month in the bridal suite. We'd barely left the room, just ordered room service that he'd watched me eat, and fucked—a lot.

We'd fucked in every position, over every bit of furniture—in the shower, in the tub, and once against the window in the middle of the night as bats had swooped over the fields.

The cost didn't matter. The vampires had plenty of money, an endless supply they told me, so it all got charged to the account George had booked the room on, and we thought no more of it.

But now I was starting to crave the outside world again—and three men, or rather three vampires, in particular.

"What's up, babe?" Oscar asked. "You just spoke with your mother, she's well and understands that you're taking a well-earned holiday."

"I know." I poked at a blueberry on the pancakes I was eating for breakfast. My mother wasn't the problem. She'd sounded happy on the phone, busy too with her voluntary job and her friends at the church. "I'm missing the others." I paused. "Aren't you?"

He tipped his head and studied me. He'd not long since showered and had a towel wrapped around his waist. His chest was bare, the hairs a little damp. "A bit." He shrugged. "We may be a team, best mates, but we're not joined at the hip. We've gone years without seeing each other in the past."

"They're more than mates to me, though." I smiled and popped the blueberry into my mouth. "As you well know."

"I do." He set his hand on my knee, over my jeans. "But I can't deny I'm enjoying having you to myself."

"Ditto. It's nice for it to just be us after waiting."

"Do you think we've made up for it yet?"

"Mmm, not quite." I waggled my eyebrows. "But I've proved I can handle you, don't you think?"

"Yeah, I do. You're one in a million, Darius. No, make that one in a billion or so." He leaned forward and kissed me.

I sighed happily. Every time we touched or kissed, our connection grew. The love I felt for Oscar was so intense it was like a flame living inside me. In fact, on several occasions when we'd fucked since that first time, I'd created sparks that had damaged the bedding. We'd had to have the cost of replacing it added to our bill.

"Maybe it's time to head to Siberia," I said when he pulled back so I could carry on with my breakfast. He was quite particular about making sure I ate and had my special tea.

"It's too soon." He shook his head. "Trust me on that one."

"But if Patrick is subdued by the silver, I'll be safe." I shrugged. "How can I not be safe when I have you three there?"

"Of course we'll always keep you safe," he said. "You must never doubt that, but..."

"But what?"

"They've taken Patrick there so he's far from you, far from everyone. It's the best way while he's acclimatizing to what he is and controlling his thirst. And don't you see?" He leaned forward and cupped my face. "You have the blood he craves the most, the way we all do."

"I can't stand it if it's years before I see the others, before we're all together again. It's hurting a piece of my heart." I swallowed, hating that a lump had formed in my throat. I wasn't a crier, never had been. But to have found the men I loved and then so quickly parted from them hurt, even if Oscar was here.

"Ah shit," he muttered. "Don't."

"I'm not." I blinked and shook my head. "I just wish there was another way."

His phone vibrated on the table.

He frowned and looked at the screen. "It's George. I didn't think he'd have signal."

"Answer it." My heart leaped. Just when I'd been thinking of him, and Rhys and Lloyd, there he was, making a call.

"Hey, boss."

He was quiet, then, "So you want us there?"

"Siberia?" I stood, the cutlery rattling. "Are we're going?"

Oscar shook his head. "Yes, we can do that. It's closer, I guess." Another pause. "He misses you, all of you."

"Can I speak to him?" I knotted my hands together.

"He wants you." Oscar handed me the phone.

"Hey, George," I said, my heart ballooning in anticipation of hearing his voice.

"I'm missing you."

"I'm missing you, too. How's it going in Siberia?"

"According to plan."

"Patrick okay?" I hoped desperately that he was.

"As well as can be expected. He's still shackled at the wrists which is keeping him subdued so we can talk to him."

"And how's he taking the whole being a vampire thing?"

"I think he's going from believing it to thinking we're all off our heads and part of some weird cult."

"Oh dear."

"It'll work out, and it's to be expected. He's a tough bloke, though."

"He is a soldier."

"I'd guess Special Forces. He's got the mental toughness as well as physical from what I can tell."

"How long will it be until I can join you there?"

There was a pause, then, "I really can't say."

That wasn't the answer I'd wanted. "How are Rhys and Lloyd?"

"They're well. They made it their mission to clean up the cabin, make it more cozy for when you come."

"They did?" I smiled. That was much more positive. "I can't wait to see it."

There was a crackle down the line, then silence.

"George. George. Are you still there?"

A moment of quiet. "Yes, I'm here. I'm surprised I've got any reception, but I've come to the local town today."

"You have? Why?"

"Lloyd wanted cigarettes. I offered to get them, fancied the trip out."

"In the snow? Or has it melted? It is spring."

"Spring. Siberia hasn't even thought about spring yet. The snow is thick; it's well below zero and will stay that way for a while yet."

"Brr, you keep warm."

"I don't need to worry about that, as you well know."

The phone clicked and went quiet. I was losing him. "I should say goodbye, Darius... Oscar will...fill you in."

"Okay, and I love you. Goodbye."

He was gone. I stared at the phone for a moment before handing it back to Oscar. "He said you'd fill me in."

"Yeah, babe, we're going to Krakow."

* * * *

Twenty-four hours later, we were on a flight from Bristol to Krakow.

"Shall I get you a drink?" Oscar asked as the air steward moved along the aisle.

"No, I'm fine." I looked at him squashed into the seat.

With no first class on this short hop to Poland, he'd had no choice but to squeeze into a standard chair. His knees were bunched up and his back stooped. He overspilled into the aisle and into my space. Not that I minded, but the woman sitting to my right, by the window, kept giving him wary glances. She likely felt completely trapped.

"Perhaps you should listen to music, or read or something, to pass the time?" I suggested.

"No." He took my hand. "I'll just sit still. Safest thing."

I nodded, enjoying holding his hand in public. No one would dare make a snide remark to Oscar, and if they did…they'd regret it before they could even realize their mistake.

George had informed Oscar that we needed to speak to Concorde, the Master of the Worshipful Company of The Ancient Order. He knew about Patrick, thanks to Samree's predictable gossip, but was committed to jury service in the Central European Order in Krakow.

"And we're going to the Krakow Order first?" I asked.

"Yeah, we'll head straight there."

"Will it be your first time visiting?"

"No." He shook his head. "I've been there lots of times over the years. It's nice, you'll like it."

"I will?"

"Yeah, it'll appeal to your cultural side."

I raised my eyebrows. "You think I have a cultural side?"

"Sure, you appreciate the world around you." He leaned closer. "It's one of the many things I love about you."

I smiled. I'd never get tired of hearing Oscar say he loved me and seeing the truth glistening in his eyes.

The plane touched down in Krakow on time, and we took a taxi to the city center.

When we alighted onto the cobbled streets surrounding the town square, I stopped and stared. The buildings were grand and old; history seemed to pour from their bricks. A huge clock tower stretched a shadow over market stalls selling flowers, cakes, and amber jewelry. Tourists swarmed, and fancy horses pulled white carriages, their occupants beaming and taking photographs.

It was a sunny spring day, and as Oscar directed us past restaurants whose tables had leaked onto the square to serve hungry customers, I enjoyed the sounds and scents of somewhere new.

"George spent some time here during the Russian Revolution," Oscar said. "It was a different place then."

"I'm sure it was. But this is beautiful now."

"*Peace* is a beautiful thing."

"You're quite deep for a rough-and-tough biker dude, you know that?"

He laughed, a gruff sound I'd come to adore. "I can be whatever you want me to be."

"I just want you to be you."

"That's what you've got." He winked then nodded ahead. "That's where we're going."

Before us stood a majestic castle perched atop a hillock. It rose from the city into the perfect blue sky, its ancient turrets and ornaments catching the light.

"Wow, impressive."

"Wawel Castle. Its history is as impressive as its old stones. It dates back to medieval times."

"And that's where The Order has a base? In the castle?"

"It's a long-standing arrangement that I hope will continue for many more centuries."

"How long-standing?"

"Many years ago." Oscar paused and pointed to a pointy-roofed turret with lead-paned windows looking down on the city. "A young prince was shot at from the street, about here actually. The arrow went into his bedroom situated in that turret and narrowly missed him. His father, King Sigismund the First, was keen to catch the culprit who'd vanished as soon as the shot was fired into the warren of alleys that is Krakow."

"So he was never caught?"

"He was...by a vampire."

"And killed?" We were walking up a steep path now, toward a huge archway.

"No, the vampire, Elridge the Dane, captured him and brought him to the king, along with his bow and identical arrows. The king was so pleased to have found the would-be murderer he allowed Elridge to choose his reward. Elridge asked for a room in Wawel castle."

"Which he gave?"

"Absolutely. And then, as was Eldridge's plan, over the next few years he and the king became firm friends. Several years later, a servant attempted to poison Sigismund, but Elridge discovered it and brought the man to the king. Again the king was grateful and asked Elridge what he could do to repay him this time. Elridge replied that he wanted the man's blood, he wanted to drain him almost dry, not enough to turn him, but enough to kill him."

"And the king allowed that?"

"Yes, he was fascinated by his friend's request and ordered him to do it there and then on the spot."

"In this castle?"

"Of course, in the Royal Chambers, while the king sat on his throne."

"And what did he say when he realized the truth about his friend?" The vampires were usually so secretive. This story fascinated me.

"He said he couldn't be happier to have such a powerful ally and that other vampires were welcome to join him at Wawel Castle so long as they swore allegiance to Sigismund and his heirs."

"And others came?"

"Yes, others came. It's a fortress, this place, a safe haven. If we wanted, we could completely take it over."

"And the vampires want that?"

"No, here they work peacefully. It's a base for upholding vampire law and punishing those who break it."

"Which is why the Master is here on jury service."

"Exactly." We walked past a huge cathedral with a throng of visitors waiting to go in. "We're not going in there. This way."

We carried on, dodging people of all nationalities who were carrying tourist guides and cameras.

"It's busy here," I said.

"Always a good place to hide, in a crowd."

"I suppose."

We left the stream of people and arrived in a huge courtyard with an overhanging roof supported by beams angled from the uppermost sections of the walls. Murals depicting dragons, fish, flowers, and arrows were painted on the whitewash, and dark windows reflected the sky.

"Stick with me." Oscar steered me to the right.

Within a minute we were indoors, the only sound our footsteps accompanying us as we headed down a long corridor.

I glanced out of a window. We were high now, Krakow stretched out before us, the orange-peaked roofs giving way to forest and hills.

Oscar stopped at a dark-wooden door. Its hinges were shaped like dragon's heads, and the handle was a heavy iron affair. He rapped, twice.

"Is this the Master's room?" I asked.

"No, this is the entrance to the Worshipful Company of the Ancient Order, Krakow."

A bubble of excitement went through me. I'd been overwhelmed when we'd visiting the vampires' London headquarters. Then it had all been so new, this world, plus I was coping with a demon father trying to possess me so he could spread his evil around the world.

"Don't look so worried." Oscar pulled his eyebrows low and studied me.

"I'm not. I'm excited to see it. Does it have a..."

"What?"

"You know...a sex dungeon?"

"There is a room, yes."

"Will we go?"

"You haven't been fucked by me enough?"

"Never."

"Good." He swept his lips over mine.

The door opened.

We both turned.

"Oscar. Darius."

Master Concorde stood before us. Like before, he wore a heavy cape fastened with ropes over his chest. The rest of his clothing was dark, and he held a cane, the top of which was a severed wolf's head with black holes for eyes.

"Master." Oscar dipped his head. "Thank you for seeing us."

"It is a good day to be here. The jury has been given some time off." He gestured behind himself. "This way. We'll go to my office. There is much to discuss."

Chapter Seven

Oscar

"How is the trial going?" I said, "if I'm allowed to ask, Master?"

We were following behind him. He walked slowly, though I knew damn well he could go fast if he wanted to.

"You may ask," he said without turning.

Darius squeezed my hand and looked at me.

"It's going as I'd expected," Master Concorde went on. "Three of our own, preying without consideration on a family of Bombays in Romania. The evidence is damning, and I don't use that word lightly."

"Did The Order know there were humans with Bombay blood in Romania?" Darius asked. "I thought it was a rare blood type, almost extinct."

"Exactly, almost extinct, which is why if a vampire discovers a Bombay they must report it to the elders of The Order so the blood line can be documented and protected. Keeping that knowledge a secret is a sin in our world."

He pushed open another heavy door that led to a room shrouded in shadows. Its window faced a river with mountains in the distance, and a huge fireplace dominated one wall. It was lit.

"I was concerned you might get cold in here, Darius." The Master nodded at the fire. "We don't notice such things, but I try to be considerate to human guests." He set his cane aside, sat, and rubbed his chin. "Though you're not entirely human, are you."

It wasn't a question, so Darius didn't answer.

"You spoke to George," I said, sitting when the Master indicated two chairs on the opposite side of his desk.

"Yes, I did. And I was glad to hear from my son. When I last saw him, and indeed you all, you were in a very precarious position."

"We still are. Darius is still a cambion, much sought-after, the way Bombays are. Though luckily, keeping him a secret is not a punishable offence under vampire law."

"This is true, even though his key is very precious." The Master sat forward and linked his hands on the desk. "The key has performed its duty of unlocking the future, though, for the four of you?"

"Yes. Didn't George tell you?" I was sure he would have. He and George—his son because he'd turned him—were very close.

"He did. But I'd like you to tell me also, Oscar."

"Yes, sir." I nodded. "We drank from him." I paused and took Darius's hand again. "We drank from Darius at midnight on the spring equinox at Stonehenge. We believe that will save us from eternal damnation."

"I believe that, too, and I welcome you into the same position I am, thanks to my cambion many years ago."

"Who I trust is well," Darius said. "In his monastery."

The Master set his attention on Darius, and a smile tugged his lips. "Thank you for asking, and yes, from what I know, he is." He pushed up his sleeve. He wore a thin red bracelet made of fabric that was knotted several times. "He sent me a gift recently, a rare event. This, he tells me, is to invoke compassion in what is left of my soul. We could all do with more of that, don't you agree?"

"The world can never have enough kindness and compassion," Darius said. "It's a noble truth."

The Master smiled at that; I wasn't sure why.

"So back to this demon father of yours," he said. "George tells me you killed him."

"Yes, we believe him to be dead." I nodded.

"But we can't prove it," Darius said with a disheartened shrug. "We never actually saw him."

"Mmm..." Master Concorde tapped his fingers together. "Last time I saw you, Darius, you told me about your dreams. Dreams in which our great and much revered Master Benedict visited you along with your demon father."

"Yes." Darius dipped his head. "That's right."

"Tell him," I said.

"Tell me what?" The Master raised his eyebrows.

"They've changed." Darius let out a sigh, as if pleased to be able to say the words. "The dreams."

"How?" The Master asked.

"Neither my father or Benedict are in my dreams anymore. They've gone."

"Gone? Completely?"

"Yes, now it's a peaceful dream, no angst, no threat. I'm no longer afraid to go to sleep."

"This is very good news." The Master stood, reached for his cane, and banged it on the wooden floor. "Excellent, in fact."

"It is?" Darius said then bit on his bottom lip.

I smiled at him, pleased with the Master's reaction.

"Yes, I believe you were successful in killing the demon. You all did a marvelous job."

"So if he was still a presence, he'd be in Darius's dreams?" I asked.

"Absolutely." The Master stepped up to the window and stared out. "I believe that with all my heart."

Darius sagged in the chair, seeming to finally relax.

"You did so well," I said quietly to him.

He nodded. "Thank you."

"Which leads me to ask: How exactly did you kill this demon?"

"How?" I said.

"Yes." The Master turned and faced us. "How?"

"It was a combination of things," I said. There was no point telling him anything other than the truth if he'd spoken to George. "The demon had possessed Patrick, a young solider. Then when he tried to get close to Darius, Darius produced sparks—"

"I'm quite fascinated by these sparks." The Master nodded. "It wasn't something my cambion could do. His special skill was water."

"Water?" Darius asked.

"Yes, he could move it around, part it, produce it from nowhere. Came in quite useful on several occasions."

"Just like Darius's sparks were that night," I said. "We'd fed to fulfil the prophesy of the key, and then..." I paused as I remembered the wild fucking that had followed. It had been intense, so hot, Darius had come so hard; so had I.

"Go on." The Master frowned.

"We'd fed," I said, a rise of heat making my back itch and my balls tighten. "And then this guy appeared, a soldier, and he was overly interested in Darius. He made a beeline for him while pretending to take photographs of the stones in the moonlight."

"He sucked my thoughts from my mind," Darius added. "As if he was getting into it, into me."

"Damn demons," the Master muttered.

"But we realized this," Oscar said. "Just in time, perhaps, but we saw what was going on."

"I hear he had a staked crossbow with a silver-tipped arrow."

"Yes, Master. He did."

"It was wooden." Darius stood, as though reciting events was releasing energy inside him. He flexed and unflexed his fingers. "Old-fashioned-looking but lethal, you know." He walked up to the window and stared out. "A functioning wooden crossbow."

"Yes, Darius, I know." The Master studied him.

"Which was fortunate," Darius went on, "because it meant it was flammable." He held up his hands. "And one thing I have is fire."

"You burnt it. Clever."

"Yes, and the soldier, which doesn't make me proud, because he was in innocent in all of this, taken by my father for his body and nothing more."

"You saved yourself and your vampires." Master Concorde stepped close and set his hand on Darius's shoulder. "You *should* be proud."

"Your words give me strength." Darius touched his cross; it was beneath his clothing, but he knew where it was. "Thank you."

"And the soldier was turned, by Rhys, I hear."

"Yes, Master," I said, also standing. "And is currently in Siberia with George, Lloyd, and Rhys."

"I have no doubt they'll be successful in calming him and teaching him control. George and Lloyd are experienced with this."

"As am I," I said, "though my job is to protect Darius while Patrick, that's the soldier, goes through his transition."

"A job made easier now the demon is gone." The Master reached for Darius's right hand. "I have to admit, I *really* am quite fascinated. The sparks come from your fingertips? The ends? All of them?"

"Yes, sir." Darius watched the Master examine his hands.

"And does it hurt? Burn you?"

"It hurts if I don't release them. It's like a volcano trying to erupt but the lid is too tight. My hands, my arms, my whole body is on fire. The sparks have to come out."

"And you have full control?"

"Not quite, do you, Darius?" I stood, then moved to Darius and set my hand on his shoulder.

"No, but I'm working on it," Darius said.

"Would you release some now, so I can see?" The Master used his cane to gesture to the fire. "Wouldn't be any harm done if they landed in there."

Darius set his attention on me, his lips parted as though not knowing what to say.

"It's up to you, babe," I said.

"I'd like to. I mean, it's not a problem, but..." His cheeks went that adorable shade of red they did on occasion, the blood rushing to the surface. My mouth watered to taste him. "It's just..."

I knew what Darius's problem was. Releasing sparks was a very personal and private thing for him; he also had to have his emotions running high.

"Do you want me to help?" I asked.

He nodded.

I took his hand. "If you stand there," I said to Master Concorde and gestured to the right, "it might be possible to show you."

He did as I'd asked and gripped the top of his cane with both hands, covering the wolf's head completely.

I led Darius to the fire, then stood behind him. Wrapping my arms around his warm, neat waist, I tipped my head so my mouth was by his ear. "Close your eyes. I've got you, I'll always have you."

He leaned back onto me, his hands on my forearms.

The sensation of his body, full of life and blood, against mine had my cock swelling. His scent, too, added to the discomfort in my groin.

"Do you remember," I started, "when we were in the Foxhill?"

He nodded.

"There was one day," I said, "when we'd had some toys delivered." I paused, though I knew he wouldn't answer. There was no way Darius would have forgotten about that day. "We opened our purchases, the sight of each one making us harder. Damn, your cock was so hard, so fucking hard, Darius, by the time I took it in my mouth."

He groaned softly and tightened his hold on my arms.

"And I sucked you, licked you, took you down my throat, so low, and then you came. I remember how you cried out, pulling on my hair, your knees trembling, your cum so sweet for me to taste."

"Oscar." He pressed his butt back, making firmer contact with my groin.

I bit on my bottom lip, holding in a moan. The last thing I wanted was to get aroused in front of Master Concorde, despite that fact it was exactly what I was doing to Darius.

"And then it was my turn, and you wanted to do something to me no one had ever done before, not even Jack."

"I remember." His fingers stretched wide, splaying outward, then he curled them over my forearms, his fingers digging into my cold flesh. "It was so hot."

Darius was getting hot right now. I recognized the signs. He was twitching, his breaths coming short and shallow, and it was clear his fingers were tingling.

"Remember the plug?" I murmured, my lips moving on the shell of his ear. "How you lubed it up, then worked it into me. I thought I was going to hit the damn ceiling. It was amazing to have you touching me there, putting something in me, invading me."

"Fuck," he muttered, his shoulders tensing.

"Yes, then we fucked, hard, and all the time, the plug, it worked me from the inside the way I was working you. Up against the shower wall. Do you remember? Can you see it now? We were wild, like animals. The sounds, the wails, the cries when we came together."

"Jesus, Oscar, I'm..."

"You shot sparks from your fingers then, didn't you. They hissed on the shower floor, spitting and steaming. On and on we fucked, like we'd never stop."

He released my arm and held his arms forward, hands aimed at the fire.

Anticipation shot through me; he was getting ready. Master Concorde would see what we had. How special Darius was—so unique and worthy of every effort of protection from the highest authorities at The Order.

"Can you feel it now? My cock pulsing in your ass? I can feel the plug in mine? The memory of it is so real. The plug you slid into me, taking a part of me no one else has. When I came with you, it was so intense, so damn amazing."

"Oh God," he groaned, his fingers flexed, and then sparks shot from the tip of each one, including his thumbs. They rained toward the fire, some landing in the flames, some splashing onto the hearth.

I sensed Master Concorde moving a little closer.

"And you came so hard, too, my big cock slamming in and out of your cute little ass." I hoped Master Concorde couldn't hear what I was whispering. He wasn't gay, wasn't even into sex, so he'd once said. I couldn't imagine ever being like that.

Darius moaned and dropped his head back. I was holding him tight. The sparks were draining his energy.

More came, bursting like fireworks from his hands.

"Incredible," Master Concorde said, staring at the hearth then Darius's hands. "Truly an incredible sight, and coming from someone who is centuries old, that is really saying something."

The sparks trickled to a stop, and Darius let his arms hang at his sides. I was supporting him entirely now; he was exhausted.

"I've got you," I whispered

I helped him to the chair, and he sank into it, his eyelids heavy.

I stood behind him, my hands on his shoulders, ready to support him should he need me.

"And that's how you burned the crossbow?" Master Concorde asked.

"It was more of a flame thrower on that occasion," I said. "There must have been something in Darius that knew we were all in mortal danger, if I can use that expression."

Master Concorde chuckled. "A flame thrower I would also like to see."

I squeezed Darius's shoulders.

He set his hands over mine. "I'm okay."

"Thank you, Darius, for showing me that." Master Concorde sat. "And if I may, what are your plans now? Siberia?"

"No, it's too soon." I said. "We will stay here, in Krakow, until we hear from George again. I don't know how long that will be."

"I would agree with your plan at this stage, and there are spare chambers in the west wing of our block. You're welcome to use them."

"That would be most kind." I smiled. It had really come to something special when Master Concorde was inviting me, a lowly ex-miner vampire and of no station within The Order, to stay at headquarters.

"I think it would be prudent to stay in separate rooms, though." The Master raised his eyebrows.

"You do?" I frowned.

"Yes. Don't you recall, when you were in London with Darius, you all made it very clear that he was with Rhys, not with you, George, or Lloyd. If you are seen as a couple here, without Rhys, suspicions will be raised about your loyalty to a fellow vampire, and following that will be the question of what Darius's lure is to you all."

Damn it. With everything going on, and then our self-imposed confinement in Foxhill, I'd forgotten that we'd used the ruse of Rhys and Darius being an item to keep him safe. Hell, they'd even gone to the dungeon together in London, been seeing entering and leaving a private sex room.

I nodded.

The Master made sense, even if I didn't like it, and I had to agree.

Chapter Eight

Darius

Releasing sparks zapped my energy, it always had done, and this was no exception.

But I'd managed to show Master Concorde my ability. Once upon a time, I'd have hated to let someone I hardly know see it. In my old life, only my mother was witness to it. But now, with my vampires, that had changed.

We're all different.

Maybe this was where I belonged. It certainly felt that way. Ethereal men who roamed Earth for centuries were my destiny. Now being able to create fire wasn't so strange. Neither, it seemed, was a power over water, draining people of blood, and protecting rare blood groups.

"Perhaps you should take Darius to his chamber," Master Concorde had spoken to Oscar. "I'll spread word that Rhys's human mate has become unwell while you were accompanying him to Siberia to be with Rhys. I'll say that you are resting up here for a while."

"Won't questions about Siberia be asked?" Oscar said.

"It is perfectly acceptable for Rhys to have turned his first human and taken the new vampire to Siberia—that cabin is perfect for the job."

"And no one would expect Rhys to want his human around in the initial phase," Oscar added.

"Exactly, so who better to entrust him to than one of his best friends."

"Thank you, Master Concorde, for all of your help."

"Mmm, thank you." I managed a smile at him, even though my head felt heavy and my legs dense.

"Come on, babe." Oscar scooped me into his arms.

I clung to him as he held me close.

"And calling him *babe* will definitely not help your situation," Master Concorde said sternly.

"Yes, Master. Sorry."

I closed my eyes and was aware of Oscar carrying me down another corridor, up a set of stairs, and through a few doorways. I'd be okay soon. A few minutes rest, and I'd be back to normal.

He set me on a bed, the mattress harder than I was used to and the material covering the pillow a little scratchy. The door clicked shut, and I guessed I was alone with Oscar. I could sense his presence.

After a few minutes he stroked my hair. "I'm going to get you tea, to give you strength."

I licked my lips. That would help.

He, too, left, and I allowed myself to drift into a doze in the silent room. I visualized a turret, the ceiling above me a Heaven-angled point and the city sprawling beneath the window. Up here it was calm and safe, my breaths came easy, and the tension that had been in my body dissipated.

I was aware of my thoughts scattering. Images coming and going like clouds drifting past, there for a moment, then gone. I saw faces, heard voices. Some I recognized, some I didn't.

And then he was there.

Standing before me, vital and handsome, his clothes hugging his fit body.

Patrick.

He had his hands outstretched, as if trying to pull me to him. His eyes were unblinking, staring straight at me.

It was a dream, yes, I was aware of that. But he was so real. I could see every hair, eyelash, dot of stubble over his top lip. The swirling patterns of his tattooed arms.

He didn't speak, but a wave of anguish came from him. He was aching, aching so badly.

I touched my dream-self. I was male, myself. Thank goodness.

"Patrick," I said. "I'm here."

"But you're not." He shook his head. "Are you."

A stab of pain went through my heart. I hated to see him this way—a young man with so much to give to life and to his country, yet taken possession of by my father. Then I'd done what I'd had to do, burned him. Guilt racked me. I let out a sob of regret for the whole situation.

"No," he said, stepping closer, his face filling my vision. "It was not your fault."

I couldn't speak, couldn't answer. I had a longing to go to him, to hold him, take him in my arms. But that wouldn't happen. It couldn't. My arms were locked at my sides.

There was pain in his eyes, as if he didn't understand why I wasn't comforting him or taking away his agony.

"I'm so confused," he said. "Why aren't you here?"

"I'm sorry…I'm sorry…I'm sorry."

"Hey, babe, wake up."

My hair was being stroked by a cool hand.

"Darius, wake up."

I flicked open my eyes.

Oscar was sitting on the bed, a concerned crease over his brow. "What is it?"

I cleared my throat then rubbed my hand over my face. My strength was returning, but the dream had disturbed me. It still felt real. "Patrick."

"What about him?"

"He was in my dream?"

"Doing what?"

"He's in pain. He's confused."

"Yes, that's most likely what's happening to him this very moment."

"I hate that." I pushed to sitting. "That he's going through this."

"It's the only way."

"But I feel…" I tapped my chest. "Responsible and connected to him. Does that sound strange?"

"You have no need to feel responsible, that's on Rhys's shoulders."

"But Rhys turned Patrick for me, for my conscience. He knew I couldn't live with myself if we let him die."

"That is true." Oscar nodded.

"And I feel connected to him because he's one of mine." I paused. "The way you and George, Lloyd, and Rhys are mine, Patrick is, too."

"Are you saying you're in love with him?" Oscar's voice was low and quiet.

"I don't know." I shook my head. "I'll be honest, that was one powerful dream, and I'm used to my dreams meaning something."

"I'll give you that."

"And as for love." I held out my hands. "I hardly know him; in fact, I don't know him at all. None of us do, so how could I love him?"

He swallowed, his Adam's apple moving within his thick, stubbled throat. "I can share you with one more, if that's how it's got to be."

I quickly took his hands in mine. "That's not what I'm saying. What I'm trying to explain, and not very well, is that I need to go there, to Siberia. To see him. He needs me."

"That's impossible."

"It's perfectly possible."

"He's too dangerous."

"But I don't think he is. Not now. Not to me."

"You saw how he was at Stonehenge. He was ready to kill for a taste of you."

"That was weeks ago now. I'm sure he's settled."

"Weeks are a blink of time in a matter like this."

Frustration built inside me. I knew what I'd seen in the dream. Patrick, my fifth vampire, needed me. I didn't know if he needed me as a friend, a protector, a confidant, or a lover, but he needed me. The draw to be with him was growing more powerful by the second. "What will they be doing with him? Right now?"

"Likely he'll still be handcuffed in silver to keep him calm and subdued."

"But that hurts him, right?"

"Yeah." Oscar stood and went to a tray holding a china teapot decorated with small pink flowers. His hands looked ridiculously big and macho as he removed the lid and stirred the contents.

"I don't like thinking of him in pain."

"Neither do I. I don't like thinking of any of our own in pain." His voice was a little sharp. "But what choice do we have?"

"You can take me there, to talk to him."

"George will stake my heart himself if I do that."

"Not if we ask him first."

"He'll say no." He turned, holding a cup and saucer. "He, like me, is keeping you away from Patrick because he loves you."

"But we can't stay here for long." I stood and took the tea from him, grateful that my body felt like my own again. "Pretending that we're not an item, Oscar, living a lie."

"We can while we have to."

"I don't want to *have* to do anything." I clenched my jaw, knowing I was sounding petulant but unable to stop myself.

He sat on a straight-backed chair. He crossed one ankle over the opposite knee, his leather trousers stretching over his wide legs.

I sighed, a sharp puff of frustration, and walked to the window.

I'd been right. Krakow was far below and stretched into the distance. People were ants, the horses and carriage small toys. "What else will they be doing?"

"To Patrick?"

"Yes, to Patrick."

"They'll be talking to him, explaining what happened and what he is now."

"And how do you think he'll take it?"

"I have no idea."

"You must have. How did you take it?"

He was quiet for a moment, then, "It was different for me."

"How?" I turned to him and took a sip of tea.

"We were trapped, Jack and I. Down a mine. He told me beforehand, when I was dying and he wasn't, what he was and what he was going to do. When he sank his fangs into my neck, I knew I was going to wake up a vampire."

"So you were calm."

"Calm about that, yeah. Horny as fuck, too." He smiled, as if recalling the moment.

"Will Patrick be horny?"

"He'll be everything: confused, horny, thirsty, angry. Imagine every emotion you've ever had at its maximum and existing in the same instant."

"I don't think I should imagine that." I managed a small smile. "I might burst into flames."

"True." He held up his hand, a smile tugging his lips, too. "Forget I said it."

I sat in the chair next to him and studied a tapestry on the wall. It depicted what looked like a Russian tsar on horseback and going to battle.

"The problem is," Oscar went on, "it's getting the message through to him. The silver dulls his considerable strength, but also his mind."

"So they have to repeat themselves."

"Yes, that and it takes a while for it to sink in."

"How do you think Rhys is managing? With his first turn?"

"George and Lloyd are there for him."

"That's not what I asked.

Oscar sighed. "Rhys is..."

"What?"

"He's so young."

"He isn't really, he's older than any human I've ever known."

"But just a kid in vampire terms."

"So you think he won't be coping?"

"I didn't say that. He's got a good head on his shoulders."

"I'm worried about him."

"Don't be."

I sighed and rested back. The room was strange, as if within its walls time stood still. "I can't help it—worry, that is." My heart skipped a beat, and heat spread over my shoulders.

No, not again. Not more sparks.

"I'm here for you, babe."

"I know, and don't think it's because you're not enough, you are. It's just..."

He waited for me to go on.

"I've got to go there, Oscar." I set the cup and saucer to one side and leaned forward, dangling my hands between my legs. I needed Oscar to understand how badly I had to be with the others, with Patrick. "You have to take me to Siberia. Please." I twisted to look at him.

He studied me with his eyebrows pulled low and his lips in a tight line.

"Please," I said again and took his hand.

He shook his head.

"Oscar." An image of Patrick flashed in my mind, his voice contorted with agony. "If you don't take me, I'll find my own way there."

"Damn it!" He snapped his hand away, stood, and raked his fingers through his hair. He turned so his back was to me.

I gulped, never having been on the receiving end of his frustration before.

He was so damn big and broad. Strength oozed from him.

"We could wait here for a week," I said. "And then go."

He turned. "A month."

"Two weeks."

"Deal."

He didn't seem happy, but I was. Two weeks, and I'd be in deepest, darkest Siberia with my vampires—all of them.

Chapter Nine

Rhys

Patrick had been trapped on the bed for weeks with his wrists cuffed in silver. He wasn't sleeping, despite his eyes being closed. He was simply lost in his own world of pain.

I hated seeing him like this. He was a strong, vibrant, intelligent guy. Clearly highly trained and highly skilled, he'd been reduced to a mass of torment, both mental and physical.

I'd rarely left his side. A strange possessive instinct had come over me. It hadn't been something I'd been expecting with my first turn, but just the same, it was there.

Patrick found himself in this situation—a new vampire—because of me. Although it had been a joint decision to turn him, I'd been the one to drain his last drip of blood.

Me.

So he was mine.

Kind of.

That was certainly how it felt. And with that emotion my sense of responsibility to him was almost overwhelming. I wanted to make sure he was okay. That this stage, the first weeks and months of becoming a new species were as smooth as possible for him. And then I wanted to help him learn to control his urges to drink human blood. In doing that, he'd be able to live amongst the vampire community, maybe even be happy.

I stroked his short hair. It was soft on my fingertips.

He was trembling, something he did often.

"You'll like Darius," I said softly, "when he eventually joins us here."

No response. I didn't expect any, but talking to him was better than the endless silence, and Darius was one of my favorite subjects.

"Darius is so fucking handsome. He's a model, you know; yeah, you do, I told you that." I paused to smile. "He's worked all over the world, been on the cover of magazines, billboards. Everyone wants to either be him or be with him. Yet, he's ours." My heart swelled with love. "He loves us, and we love him. He's our soul mate, the one we searched for over many centuries. And then we found him, a rarity, a needle in a haystack, and since then, we've all felt complete." I stroked Patrick's ears, tracing the shape of them. "He's a kind man. He sees the good in everyone, even wretched souls like us."

"Take...this off," Patrick muttered.

I was surprised to hear him speak. He hadn't for several days.

"Take what off?"

"You know what." He opened his eyes. "The damn cuffs. No more." He paused and swallowed. "I'll do whatever you want. I can't stand the burning. No more." He gritted his teeth and hissed a breath in through them.

"I'll ask George."

"Just do it."

"I have to ask George."

"What does he want?" George was at the door. He'd likely heard Patrick speaking from the opposite side of the cabin.

"He wants his cuffs off."

George rubbed his chin, appeared thoughtful, then, "One, release one cuff. That will half his torment but keep his strength sapped."

"Please," Patrick said. "I'm begging you."

"Yes, okay." Something in my guts twisted uncomfortably at seeing him reduced to a begging man. It didn't suit him. "I'll do it now."

George pulled a key from the pocket he kept his watch in. "Here."

He tossed it into the air.

I caught it.

"You have to promise to maintain control," I said.

"Aye, I promise." Patrick's attention was on the key.

I slid on the rubber gloves then released the cuffs. I kept one fastened around his left wrists. The contact of silver on skin was all we needed to hold him prisoner, not necessarily his hands locked together.

"Key." George held his hand out.

I threw it back, frowning a little. Didn't he trust me with it?

"I'll stay with him," I said to George. "Answer his questions."

"Yes, he'll be more alert now." George nodded then turned. He left the room, shutting the door behind him.

Patrick moved his legs, then his body, turning from his curled-up position onto his back. He let the arm with the cuff hang over the side of the bed, the metalwork swinging downward.

"Better?" I asked.

"Yeah." He stared up at the ceiling and blew out a breath. "Why does this thing hurt so much? It's like fire, being burned alive."

"It's silver." I got onto the bed and stretched out next to him. I bent my elbow and propped my head on my hand so I could look at his face. "Silver is like Kryptonite to vampires."

"Huh, I knew you guys read too much Marvel."

I chuckled. "I'll read anything when I'm bored enough."

He studied me, his eyes clearing as if the reduced discomfort was allowing his thoughts to gel cohesively. "You've been sitting at my side for weeks, Rhys. Do you never sleep?"

"No." I paused. "Do you?"

"No." He shook his head. "That's because of the pain, though."

"But you're not tired?"

"No."

"Have you ever stayed awake for weeks or months before? Even when you've been on missions?"

He was quiet for a moment, and I studied the shape of his brow, his straight nose, and the dip beneath his lower lip. A part of me loved him, I knew that, and accepted it now.

He shook his head. "No, there's no training that will teach a man how to go without sleep. Like air, we need it."

"You say *we* like you're still human." I touched the neckline of his t-shirt. "You're not."

He stared up at me. "I'm a vampire."

"Yes."

"You gave me more blood, yesterday."

"Yes. I wasn't sure if you'd even noticed you were drinking; you barely roused."

"The blood is all I can think of. The taste of it, the smell, getting it into my belly."

"It satisfies you?"

"More or less... I get the feeling deer blood is a bit like having prosecco when I could be having champagne, though."

I smiled and ran my finger up his neck to his jaw line. I liked touching him; his skin was cool and tight over his bones. "You'll get the chance to taste the champagne if you're good."

"Good?"

"Yes, if you can control your urges for human blood."

He groaned. "Aye, human blood, that is what I need."

"So you're on board with being a vampire?"

"I... Rhys... Can you tell me something."

"Of course."

"And answer me honestly."

"Anything."

"Why are you doing this?"

"Doing what?"

"This? Me? Why are you sitting here in the middle of Siberia with me?"

"Because I, we, turned you. We have responsibility to you."

"You seem to take it more seriously than the others, George and Lloyd."

"No, they take it very seriously, trust me."

He narrowed his eyes. "It goes against everything I've been taught, but I kind of do trust you."

"You do." I grinned. His words thrilled me. "Good, because we only want the best for you. We want you to feel like you belong, that we're your new brothers."

He ran the tip of his tongue over his top, then his bottom lip. "Brothers?"

"Yeah, you know, close."

"The thing is, brothers don't usually lie on a bed like this. One touching the other's face, neck…"

"I'm sorry." I snapped my hand away from where I was stroking the patch of skin beneath his ear. "You don't like it?"

He didn't reply.

I squeezed my fingers into a fist. "Can I ask you something?"

"You can now you've allowed me a reprieve from the pain, enough so I can talk."

I hesitated, then, "Are you gay, Patrick?"

His nostrils flared, and he turned.

"You can tell me." I kept my voice soft. "It's okay, everything else is in the past now, your old way of life, old prejudices, anything you worried about."

"You have no idea what it's like in the British Army."

"So tell me." I had to stop myself from touching him again. His t-shirt had wrinkled up, exposing a strip of flesh above his belt. His belly was flat and smooth with a thin strip of hair disappearing beneath his waistband. Below that was an interesting bulge—a cock-shaped bulge—pushing at the material of his combats.

"It's not exactly accepted," he said, "in the military. Oh, they say it is, and maybe in some divisions it's tolerated, but Special Forces…oh no. Being gay there makes you a fucking leper. Chances are some friendly fire would head in your direction when out on exercise."

"So you kept it quiet."

He turned back to me, his eyes searching mine. "I've never spoken to anyone about this before."

I paused. "You've always kept your true self hidden?"

"My true self has fucked a lot of women."

"I bet they threw themselves at you." I smiled, honored that I was finally getting to know him a little better.

"Not quite, but I'm no saint. If it was offered, I took it."

"Are any of us saints?" I risked touching him again and rested my hand on his chest, over where his heart used to beat. "We all do things we regret and we learn from them, and are forgiven for them."

"What have you done that you need forgiving for?"

I was quiet, then, "Turning you into a vampire?"

"No." He sighed then winced as though the cuff still in place had pained him. "You don't need forgiving for that."

"I don't?"

"No, I've thought it through. I understand what you've told me, and despite my old self saying it's a big pile of shit, my new self believes it. I mean, how else would I be able to do this?" He opened his mouth and slid his fangs down.

"Ah, you're getting good at that."

He slipped them away, and his top lip sat neat again. "And the craving for blood, it's real—it's more than real, it feels like it could become an addiction."

"Which is why we're keeping you here, like this, so you don't go and drain the entire population of the local town."

He swallowed, seeming to imagine draining an entire town.

"Which would be a very bad thing," I said. "We have rules to abide by, and not killing humans is one of them. Which brings me to the question of family, Patrick."

"Family?"

"Yes, who will be looking for you?"

He frowned, and again turned away. He moved his hips and bent one leg, so his foot was flat on the sheet. "No family."

"None?"

"Nope. I was brought up in care, signed up to the military as soon as I was old enough." He paused. "I guess they're my family, my squadron."

"So they'll look for you?"

"Of course." He huffed. "Hardly going to find me here, though, in Siberia."

"No, they won't find you here. No one will." I slid my hand to the base of his t-shirt and straightened it.

He sucked in a breath and tensed.

"What?" I asked.

"Nothing." He closed his eyes tight, sending small lines streaking toward his temples.

"Tell me."

He tutted. "I've got a fucking hard-on, okay."

"You have?" I stared at his groin. Sure enough, the cock-shaped bulge had become more pronounced. There was a seriously hard, long wedge of flesh in his pants.

"Yeah, and I don't fucking know why. Same as I don't know why I crave blood, why I have this urge to run, like the wind, over the snow, to hell with the cold or the distances."

"I know why."

"Why?" He frowned.

"Because." I dipped my head to his, so our lips were nearly touching. "You're a vampire."

"I am." He was breathing fast, almost panting. "I *am* a vampire. Fuck."

"I don't think we should fuck," I said. "I have a mate, Darius, but I can help you out with the problem in your pants."

"What...what are you suggesting?" His eyes widened.

"Shall I show you instead?" My excitement levels were romping up. My cock was stiffening, pushing against my jeans.

"But I can't... I haven't..."

"You haven't been touched by a man?"

"No." He bent his other knee and moved his hips again. "I'd sort myself out, but..."

"But you haven't the energy, not with the silver on. And you really don't want those cuffs to accidently touch your cock, that wouldn't be fun." I reached for his belt. "So let me. I'm here for you, I told you that."

"Rhys." He said my name on a puff of air that washed over my lips. "Please."

"I'll give you anything you need, Patrick." I released his belt then popped open the top button on his pants.

He didn't say anything, just stared up at me and straightened his legs out.

I allowed myself to fall into the depths of his eyes. I pushed at his clothing, and his cock sprang free.

He groaned, and his eyelids fluttered as I took his cold, hard erection in my hand.

"I should warn you," I said. "Coming as a vampire is quite different to coming as a human."

"How...how do you mean?"

"It's more intense, super intense, in fact."

"This feels pretty intense already."

I squeezed his shaft and slid to the base, then up to the top. He had a great cock, thick enough to hurt a bit when lodging deep, sweet pain, that sensual nip, and a good length to hit all the right spots and then some.

"Jesus, I never thought I'd..." He gasped.

"Have a man do this to you?"

"No."

"Enjoy it." I circled his glans and stroked his slit. "No shame, no lying about who you are anymore and what you want."

He canted his hips, pushing into my touch.

I smiled down at him. "Our connection is special, Patrick. It will be forever, for all of time."

"Aye. Oh...more like that."

I set about giving him a hand job. It would be the best one he'd ever had, bar none. I was gentle but firm, not too fast, not too slow. His moans told me I was getting it just right.

"Rhys," he murmured, swelling further. "Oh God..."

I picked up the pace, massaging him with firm, swift strokes. A drip of pre-cum leaked from his tip.

"Come," I said. "Come when you want to."

"I do...I do...oh...." He closed his eyes, pressed his head into the pillow.

I kept on going, slipping my curled fingers up and down his shaft so fast the movement was a blur. Excitement swirled inside me. I wanted him to have this, a moment when he forgot about the pain.

"Ah, fucking hell..." He moaned. "It's here..." Thick, cool cum spurted from his cock. It covered my hand and coated his belly.

I stayed with him, working him harder, my own cock swelling.

His fangs came down. I guessed he hadn't planned that, and he stared, almost manically at me.

"It's good, yes?" I grinned.

He didn't answer. He was overwhelmed by the power of his orgasm. A whole new level of pleasure had besieged him.

After a fourth release of cum, I slowed the pace to little more than a caress.

He was breathing hard. His fangs retracted.

I set my mouth over his and kissed him, softly, gently, and relishing the moment.

When I pulled back, he lifted his hand, the one that didn't have the cuffs on, and touched my face. "Show me your fangs."

I smiled, pulled back my top lip, and slid them down.

"Fuck," he said. "A vampire just gave me my first gay hand job."

Chapter Ten

Darius

"It's two weeks today, Oscar."

He was staring out of the window, hands on his hips and with his back to me. "Yeah, I know."

"So, we can go to Siberia?"

"We can't really, I just said I'd take you."

"Are you going back on your word?" I frowned. I'd been counting the hours until this moment. My need to go to Siberia was very real. I had to see my other vampires, and something deep down was drawing me to Patrick. He was mine, too, I couldn't explain it, but in my dreams he was there, needing me. I had to go and see if it was true.

"No, of course I'm not going back on my word." Oscar turned to face me, his expression dark. "But George is going to be seriously pissed off with me. Lloyd and Rhys, too."

"If they really are, if it's a huge problem, we'll stay a day then come back here."

He made a grunting sound, as though I'd made a stupid suggestion.

I reached for a rucksack I'd already packed. "How will we get there?"

"We could fly, or take a train, but…"

"But what?"

"But it would be easier if I just ran with you on my back."

"What?" I laughed. "Are you serious?"

"As serious as I am when I tell you I'm madly and deeply in love with you."

He looked so worried standing there with his shoulders tense and jaw tight that I went to him.

"Oscar." I slipped my arms around his waist. "I'm madly and deeply in love with you, too, and we've spent weeks showing each other that, but it's time now, to be a team again."

He sighed and slipped his hands to my butt. He drew me close with a squeeze. "I know. I just don't want you at risk, Darius. You're too precious. And your mother, if anything happened to you she'd—"

"So protect me."

"I intend to." He kissed me, his tongue stroking against mine and his sharply stubbled chin scratching my flesh.

When he pulled back, he nodded at my rucksack. "You'll need some warmer clothes."

"I will."

"So we'll go shopping, now. Then when you've eaten, we'll hit the road."

I smiled. So we *were* going today. In just a few hours, I'd see my other vampire lovers again, and Patrick. I'd get to experience Siberia with them, rather than sitting here in a castle—beautiful as it was—wondering what they were doing and how they were faring in the chilly landscape.

Four hours later we were walking out of Krakow, following the river. Oscar said it was best to wait until no one was around before he picked up speed.

I enjoyed my last views of the city, but my thoughts were crammed with what the next few weeks and months would hold.

How was Patrick taking the news that he was a vampire?

Was Rhys okay, having been the one to turn him?

Had Lloyd and George driven each other crazy by being cooped up together with no other entertainment and no Wi-Fi for George's laptop?

Eventually, Oscar stopped by a copse of silver birches. A children's playground stood empty to the right, and on the opposite side of the river, church bells rang out. "Put on your winter gear."

"I've got my thermals on, under my jeans and sweater."

"Good, but you'll need more the moment we stop."

I did as he'd asked, huddling myself up into a new jacket made for extreme conditions. I already wore new boots.

"So I just climb on?" I asked when I'd done up the zip of my mountaineering over-pants. This was all a bit strange, but since there was no body of water between here and Siberia, running over land was our plan.

"Yeah, and hold on tight." He turned and bent his knees.

"A piggyback?" I asked.

"That's the one."

I giggled, sprang onto him, and wound my arms around his neck.

He grabbed my legs. "Hold really tight," he said. "And you might want to close your eyes, too, so they don't water."

"How long will it take?"

"A couple of hours, maybe less."

"Fuck, that's fast."

"Hell yeah."

He gripped me, then lowered his head. It was as if an explosion of energy had burst inside him. He shot forward, me with him, the world around becoming a blur.

I did as he'd suggested and closed my eyes, the wind speed stinging them instantly.

The air shot past my ears and whipped over my hair. Scents came and went, and the temperature changed, from cool, to warm, cold, hot, then really cold. Bitter.

My fingers ached from gripping on, and I huddled my head at the nape of his neck. On and on he raced, until I felt I could go no farther. Holding on was exhausting.

Finally, he slowed.

An icy chill wrapped around me, and frost filled my lungs.

I opened my eyes to the whiteness.

And then he stopped.

"Wow." I stared around. Deep snow stretched into the distance in every direction. There were a few trees, their branches drooping and heavy under the weight of the snow. The sky was crystal clear, not one cloud, not one plane trail.

To the left, a cabin rose from the whiteness, its skinned log walls age-darkened. It had a pointed roof, a small fenced porch, and a few outbuildings. There was smoke coming from the chimney.

"Is that it?" I asked.

"Yeah."

"Why have they got a fire going?" I asked. "I thought vampires didn't feel the cold?"

"We don't." He shrugged. "At a best guess, I'd say the place was damp and they're drying it out ready for you."

I smiled. "See, they are expecting me."

"Not this soon." He frowned. "Come on, we might as well get this over with."

I grinned. Despite Oscar's obvious misery at having to bring me here, I was excited.

We stomped through the snow. It squeaked beneath my heavy boots. My nose was cold, and the air nipped my cheeks. I shoved my hands into my pockets, wishing I'd bothered to get my gloves out of my rucksack before we'd left Krakow.

When we were ten feet away from the cabin, the door opened.

George stood there, as gorgeous as always but with a frown in place.

"Predictable expression," Oscar muttered.

"What the hell…" George said, holding out his palms, "are you doing here?"

"Sorry, boss, he insisted." Oscar nodded my way. "And I couldn't stand to see him so miserable without you all."

George appeared lost for words as he stared at me. His mouth hung open, and he was unblinking. "Get in here, Darius, before you freeze to death."

"I've got the right gear." I stomped up the steps which had been cleared.

"It's minus twenty degrees centigrade today. Humans die in that." George set his hand in the small of my back and ushered me inside. "Not that it's much safer in the cabin."

"Darius!" Lloyd jumped up from a seat, a book slipping to the floor with a clunk. "You're here."

"Yes." My heart skipped a beat at seeing him.

In an instant, he was in front of me, cupping my face and kissing me.

I melted against him. It had been so long. I soaked up his taste, his scent, his touch.

When he pulled away, he glanced at George, then at me. "You shouldn't have come, Darius, it's too soon."

"I couldn't stay away. It hurt a part of me, really hurt." I banged my chest.

"I kept him in Krakow as long as I could." Oscar shifted from one foot to the other, snow sprinkling from his biker boots onto a large red rug.

George threw a log onto the fire then adjusted it with a long iron poker.

"George," I said, hating the tension radiating from him.

Still he said nothing.

"It'll be okay," Lloyd said.

"How will it?" George spun around. "Patrick is a loose cannon, you know that. He's still wearing silver, for goodness sake." He produced a key from the inside pocket of his waistcoat. "In fact, I'll go and put the cuffs completely back on. We might need the collar again, too, Lloyd."

"No." Lloyd shook his head. "He's been calm, shown no signs of trying to escape, losing his control, or screaming for blood. Better than I'd dare hope, if I'm honest, going by how he was at Stonehenge."

"The guy is a highly trained soldier," George said. "He'll show you what you want to see."

"A highly trained soldier?" I raised my eyebrows. "I thought he was a young squaddie."

"No, don't let his youthful appearance fool you. He's Special Forces through and through." George slipped the key away and scowled. "We'll leave the cuffs the way they are…for now."

Lloyd nodded.

"Where's Rhys?" I asked, looking around. The main living area was cozy with big soft sofas, bookcases, and several baskets of logs by the fire. The pictures on the walls were bright and modern; I guessed they were new. To the right was a kitchen area. I was surprised to see shelves full of tins and packets. Seemed they really were prepared for my visit. Just as well I was here.

"Rhys is in with Patrick," Lloyd said, squeezing my shoulder. "He doesn't leave his side; he's feeling very responsible for the situation Patrick has found himself in. It's almost like he's sharing his pain, his burden."

"It's not just Rhys's fault, it's all of ours. Well, it's my demon father's really, but you know what I mean." I paused. "I take it you've explained to Patrick what he is now."

"Yes, and he's understanding of that."

"He is?"

"Why are you surprised, babe?" Oscar said, sitting in one of the big leather armchairs. "You accepted what we told you, even though it was way out of your comfort zone."

I thought back to them telling me they were vampires and I was a cambion. Yes, it had been strange, crazy, but I had believed them. They'd had the evidence to support what they were saying.

"So he knows he's immortal, that he'll only ever drink blood, never sleep, can run and fight and be super-human when he needs to be," I asked.

"Well, no, we haven't told him everything. Best he doesn't know how strong and fast he is for now." Lloyd shrugged. "But he'll find out, once he's out of silver."

"Which will be when?" I stepped to the right and glanced up the corridor. Several doors led off it. I guessed they bedrooms.

"Longer now you're here, Darius," George said. "We'd only given him a thin slice of trust as it was. Now we can give him even less."

"Oh…" My heart sagged. Had I made it worse for Patrick by coming here? I was hoping to make it better.

"He'll get there," Lloyd said. "We all did."

George faced the fire with his hands on his hips

I removed my jacket and outer weatherproof trousers. The coil of doubt was winding tighter. Perhaps I should have listened to Oscar and stayed in Krakow. I supposed we could always go back.

"Darius!" Rhys strode down the corridor. He was grinning with his arms outstretched.

"Rhys." I went to him, falling into his embrace.

He held me tight and I tucked my face against his neck, breathing in the cool scent of his skin.

"I missed you," I murmured.

"And I missed you, too, we all did."

I trembled. Had I messed up all their hard work?

"Hey, what is it?" Rhys held me at arm's length.

I glanced at George who still had his back to me. "Perhaps I shouldn't have come."

"Nonsense."

"It's too soon," George said sharply.

"Too soon for what? For us to be with Darius." Rhys laughed. "I don't care if we have a thousand lifetimes together, I was missing him, and you both were, too, there's no denying it." He gestured to George and Lloyd.

"Not denying it." Lloyd held up his hands and smiled. "Not for one moment. I missed you, Darius, more than words can say."

"So did I." George turned and jabbed his finger against his chest. "But am I the only one around here thinking of Darius's safety?"

"Patrick is under control." Rhys gestured to the bedroom. "He's becoming more mentally stable each day. I'm proud of him."

"You've become close?" I asked.

"Yes, very." Rhys paused. "And that's another thing I'm glad you are here for." He glanced around the room, at the others. "But we'll talk in private."

"Yes, of course. Are you okay?"

"I am, yes." He tipped his chin. "I'll take you to see Patrick now."

Oscar jumped up. "Not on your own you won't, kid."

"No, Oscar, not on my own." Rhys tutted.

He linked his hand with mine and led me down the corridor. When we reached the end room, he opened the door. The light was dim, and the air was cool compared to the living area.

I stepped in. A large double bed dominated the room, and on it was Patrick. Still in his camo pants and t-shirt, he had one arm hanging off the side of the bed, one loop of a pair of silver handcuffs attached to his wrist.

When he saw me, he pushed, a little awkwardly, to sitting. His eyes widened. He opened his mouth, and his fangs slid down. He let out a strange growling noise.

"Fucking hell," Lloyd muttered. "So much for progress."

"It's okay." Rhys moved quickly to the bed. He squeezed Patrick's shoulder. "Put your fangs away. This is Darius, you can't hurt him...you *won't* hurt him."

"Blood."

"Yes, he has blood." Rhys nodded. "But it's not for you; not now anyway."

Patrick was staring at me. "I need blood."

"This is ridiculous," George muttered, placing himself between me and Patrick.

"Get me blood," Patrick said, closing his eyes suddenly. "Get me the deer blood, Rhys, so I can quench my thirst."

Rhys grinned at George, a proud, self-satisfied smile. "See, he's got it under control."

"Now!" Patrick snarled through gritted teeth, his fangs still on show.

"I'll go." Lloyd disappeared, but was back within seconds holding a pewter tankard. "Freshly drained this morning," he said to me.

"Nice." I couldn't quite keep the sarcasm from my tone.

"It's not bad actually." Lloyd shrugged. "For deer, that is."

Patrick held out his unshackled hand.

Lloyd handed him the tankard.

He drew it to his mouth then drank in big, loud gulps. A trickle of scarlet blood dripped from the corner of his mouth to his chin then landed on his t-shirt.

We all watched in silence.

When he'd drained it dry, his fangs retracted, and he wiped the back of his hand over his lips, smearing blood over his cheek. "Right," he said, his attention set steadily on me. "We can talk now, Darius."

Chapter Eleven

Darius

I took a step closer Patrick.

My way was blocked by George's arm. "That's near enough," he said.

I frowned as Oscar and Lloyd flanked me. It was clear they had no intention of letting me touch Patrick, not even to stand by the side of his bed.

"I won't bite," Patrick said, his mouth tilting into a twisted smile.

"He's still got his sense of humor." Rhys laughed.

George huffed.

"Patrick," I said, studying his face. He was handsome, youthful but with a been-there-seen-that edge to him. He had wise eyes, wild, too, but they held depth. "I want to apologize for what's happened to you."

"Why? It wasn't you, was it?" He rested his head back on the pillow.

"It was, kind of… I burned you alive."

"You did what?" He lifted his head and glared at me.

"Phew, I'm glad you can't remember." I shoved my hands into my jeans pockets.

"Why the fuck did you burn me alive?" He stared at his free hand, seeming to check for blisters and scars.

"You, or rather my demon father, was aiming a staked crossbow our way. He was trying to shoot us, and I… I…set fire to it, and in turn, you."

"Darius can create fire from his fingertips," Rhys said. "That's what did it."

"Rhys," I said. Rhys knew I wasn't in the habit of telling people that.

"What?" he said. "He'll find out eventually."

"That is true," Oscar said.

"You create fire from your fingers?" Patrick repeated. "What, like some kind of party trick?"

"No." I glanced at the window. The curtains were half drawn. Outside, the expanse of white stretched into the distance, and swirls of small, dusty ice flakes danced over the glistening surface. "I guess it's because of what I am. If I get emotional, worked up, then I can make fire."

"I can see how that would come in handy," Patrick said. "But tell me this." He glanced at Rhys then back to me. "How come I'm not a pile of ash then?"

"Draining you dry returned you to your former state," George said. "Actually, make that a better state. You have no weakness for illness now; you won't succumb to the ageing process. So long as you have enough blood—"

"Which isn't nearly as much as you think you need," Lloyd said.

"Exactly," George went on. "You will live in your new, healthy vampire body for centuries and beyond."

Patrick rubbed his forehead. His t-shirt was tight on his inked biceps which bulged against the material. "I won't age?"

"No. You won't." Rhys ran his hand over Patrick's short hair.

It was a loving, familiar gesture that surprised me. But perhaps it shouldn't. I'd known Rhys and Patrick would build a bond, *had* built a bond. And that was something I was pleased about. It was just a little strange to see one of my men so easy with another.

"I guess being made immortal is something I should thank you for, Darius." Patrick set his gaze on me again. "I've spent years in war zones wishing for that very thing. Would come in quite handy out on the field now."

"You want to go back to the army?" Rhys said, surprise widening his eyes.

"I...I haven't thought about it. I mean, could I?"

"Not really," Lloyd said. "You'd freak them out on your first medical."

"But an immortal soldier would be damn useful, right? Think of all the shit I could get done. Places I could go where no one else can." He lifted his arm a few inches, the one with the cuffs, then dropped it to the bed again. "If I didn't have this painful fucking thing on, I could do a lot of good."

"We're sorry about that," I said. "Really we are."

"So take it off." His nostrils flared. "I can't stand it."

"We don't trust you not to attack, Darius," Oscar said.

Patrick studied him, as if seeing him for the first time. "You're a big bloke."

"Really? I hadn't noticed." Oscar huffed.

"Gay? Like the others?" Patrick asked, raising his eyebrows.

"What's it to you?"

"Just asking. Rhys said I could ask as many questions as I like."

Oscar was silent for a moment. "Yeah, I am. And this here is my guy." He slid his arm around my waist and tugged me close.

"Sounds to me like your *guy* shares himself around." Patrick licked his lips, his unblinking gaze on me again.

"We have an arrangement," I said, forcing myself not to squirm under his scrutiny. Patrick had something about him. Even in this subdued state he was clearly a man used to winning, getting what he wanted, and was capable of completing his mission.

Is he gay, too?

That thought raced through my mind. I recalled Rhys saying he wanted to talk to me in private. Was it about Patrick's sexuality? Or perhaps Patrick had a wife at home, kids.

I swallowed, a sudden nasty taste. "We need to know..." I looked from Lloyd to George.

"What?" Lloyd asked.

"If he has family." I'd save the gay question for now.

George turned to Patrick. "Tell him."

He rolled his eyes then dipped into the neckline of his t-shirt and withdrew two steel discs. "Military was my family." He let them sway from his fingers. "Grew up in care, joined at sixteen. It's all I've ever known."

"So you're not married? No kids?" I asked, checking out the bare ring finger on his left hand.

"Had my fair share of women," he said. "They've come and gone over the years. But no...never got tied down."

"You should tell them the rest," Rhys said, nodding at us but looking at Patrick.

"Tell them what?" Patrick slipped the ID tag away.

"You know." Rhys swept his gaze down Patrick's body. "About being gay."

"What?" Patrick snatched hold of Rhys's wrist. A surprisingly fast movement considering how lethargic he'd appeared.

"It's okay." Rhys set about peeling Patrick's fingers off his arm. "Everyone in this room is gay, likes to either fuck or be fucked by men." He shrugged. "Your truth is hardly going to change how we feel about you."

"Get out," Patrick said, his teeth gritted. "Get out, Rhys."

"But I..."

Patrick closed his eyes. "I want to be alone."

"Rhys." I held out my hand to him. "Come with me." I hated to see Rhys's face full of confusion and remorse.

"Yeah, go with Darius," Lloyd said. "Patrick has lots of new information to digest. He can lie there for a week or so and think about it."

Patrick shifted so his back was to us and he faced the window. His fingers, on the cuffed hand, were trembling.

"Rhys." I slipped my arm around his waist when he drew level with me. "Let's go and talk."

He nodded.

"Do you want some tea?" Lloyd asked me.

"Yes, please."

"Food?"

"If there's something going."

"Of course, and it will give me a chance to use the kitchen. It's all ready for you."

George was frowning at Patrick as if trying to work out a puzzle. I decided to leave him to it.

"This way." I tugged Rhys from the room.

He followed me, and I tried the handle on the door to the next room along. It opened and revealed another bedroom. The bedcovers were creased and several books at on a dresser at its side. The curtains were drawn.

Rhys stepped in, and I shut the door.

"What's going on?" I asked.

Rhys sat on the bed, his legs apart and his forearms resting on his thighs. He stared at the wooden floorboards beneath his sneakers. "It's complicated."

"I can tell." I took a seat next to him and rested my hand between his shoulders. "Want to talk about it?"

"More than want, I have to, to you."

"I'm all ears."

"Patrick is gay."

"I guessed by his reaction to what you just said, despite the macho soldier image and the comment about lots of women." I paused. "But why did you just out him in front of us? He clearly wasn't ready."

"I know that now." He twisted to face me. "And I feel awful."

I sighed and kissed the ball of his shoulder. "It's done now."

"But it's the truth. I wouldn't have said it otherwise."

"He told you, that he's gay?"

"Yes. We've gotten close. Impossible not to, considering he's my responsibility."

"He's *all* of our responsibility."

"I know that, and I'm glad of the support, but I feel...I don't know, like I want to ease his burden, take some of his pain. This initial phase is hard, and he's suffering."

"And George won't take the silver off?"

"No, not yet, and I agree with that. He needs more control."

I ran my palm down Rhys's arm to his hand.

He linked his fingers with mine and squeezed. "I have to confess something."

I remained quiet.

"One of the reasons I know he's gay is..."

My heart rate picked up. What was Rhys going to say that had made him so nervous? Had he fallen in love with Patrick? Fallen out of love with me?

"You're worrying me," I said, swallowing, my throat suddenly tight.

"I know he's gay because he got a hard-on."

"And..."

"And he let me sort it out for him; he didn't have the strength, you see, so I...well, you can imagine the rest."

I raised my eyebrows. "You gave him a hand job?"

"Yes. And I'm sorry, Darius. It felt like the right thing to do at the time, and it doesn't mean I love you any less, it's just—"

I set my lips over his. Relief washed through me. A hand job I could cope with. In fact, having seen the connection between Patrick and Rhys, I wasn't that surprised.

"You made him feel better when he was feeling like hell."

"Yes. It was something I could do for him."

I stroked Rhys's hair. "You're a good man, Rhys. I'm lucky to have you, and so is Patrick."

"He hates me now."

"No, no he doesn't. He'll come round. Let's face it, if he wasn't gay, he'd be the odd one out in this cabin."

"True." Rhys managed a weak smile. "I did miss you."

"I missed you, too."

"You always make me feel like everything is going to be okay."

"It is, when we're together." I studied his features, taking in his eyes, his straight nose, the shape of his lips. "I don't want us to be apart again like that. I enjoyed my time with Oscar, but it hurt not being with you all."

"You enjoyed your time with Oscar?"

"Yeah…a lot."

"He didn't hurt you?"

"No, of course not."

"Good." He kissed me and stroked my chest, over my sweater. "Though it's probably time for him to share again."

"I agree." I smiled against his mouth. "What did you have in mind?"

He grinned and slipped to the floor with his knees folded beneath him. "Remember in your apartment that time?"

"When?"

He released the top button on my jeans. "When we were watching porn."

"Ah, yes, that." I knew exactly what he was talking about and what he had in mind. My cock tingled, and heat traveled to my groin. "I remember."

"You let me give you your first blow job," he said, tugging at my clothing.

I lifted, and as he dragged down my trousers, boxers going with them, my cock sprang free.

He took the hard shaft in his hand and squeezed.

I groaned and locked my arms straight behind myself. His touch was electric, and it had my balls aching and my belly tensing.

"You are my first love," he said, poking out his tongue and swiping it over the tip of my erection. "I need you to know that."

"Yes, yes I do." I blew out a breath, harnessing self-control as he laved at my slit, then circled my glans in slow, sweeping movements. It was so damn erotic to see him doing that. His hair fell over his brow, and his eyes were closed as though he was savoring my flavor.

He took his time, tasting me, teasing me, then stretched his mouth wide and sank deep, taking me to the back of his throat.

"Oh fuck, Rhys…" I curled my toes in my boots, and my knees shook. The cool wetness of his mouth was bliss.

He cupped my balls, rolled them gently, and sucked back up my length.

I closed my eyes, let my head fall back, and released a low groan.

He was following the circle of his mouth with his fingers, the firm stroke urging me closer to release.

"Rhys." I canted my hips, wanting to go deep again.

He obliged, slipping back down, faster this time.

My asshole trembled; my balls contracted. My arms were tingling, heat shooting through the muscles and tendons to my fingers. I fisted the bedsheet, hoping I wouldn't burn them.

He set up a fast but steady rhythm, working my cock in and out of his mouth.

My breaths were coming in short pants. Sweat tingled in my armpits, on my brow. "I'm going to…oh fuck…"

The breathless words seemed to spur him on. His lips tightened, and he stroked the strip of skin between my sac and asshole.

That was it, my undoing. The pressure was too much. I couldn't hold back. I came, long pulses of bliss dragging up my shaft.

He removed his mouth and used his hand, extending my orgasm.

And then I felt it, the hot, sharp piercing of my skin, over my femoral artery.

"Oh, yes, Rhys."

He sucked my blood, and my climax went off the scale. Another hot jet of cum left me, its release exquisite. My hands were on fire; I was aware of the crackle of sparks and the smell of scorched material.

But still I bucked for more. Rhys feeding off me just increased the pleasure.

And then he lifted his face, his blood-coated fangs still visible. "Fuck." He released me, grabbed a pillow, and smothered the flames at my side. "Get up."

I staggered to standing, clutching my cock.

He set about beating the bed and putting out the small fire I'd left behind. When he'd done it, he turned to me, licking his lips. "Sex with you is always explosive."

Chapter Twelve

George

I was struggling to contain the fear that had created a knot in my belly and sent my thoughts skittering. It wasn't like me to let emotions rule this way, but having Darius here at the cabin, with Patrick not yet under control, sent terror into my dark heart.

Forcing myself to think straight, I stared once more into the flames of the hearth fire.

I couldn't deny that I was pleased with how Patrick was progressing. He'd accepted what he was now, even if he was still thinking of his old life. Plus, he had a special connection with Rhys, and I knew from having a close relationship with Master Concorde that was going to give him strength going forward.

But Darius was here. Right here. Damn Oscar for not keeping him in Krakow longer. I was sure he could have found ways for them to pass the time, even if they'd just stayed in bed.

I frowned and glanced up the corridor.

Darius and Rhys were having some alone time. That would do Rhys good. He, like all of us, needed Darius. And he'd given so much of himself to Patrick lately that some quiet time alone with the man he loved was essential.

A burning scent lined my nostrils, and the faint sounds of Darius orgasming rang in my ears. I tried not to hear them. I wanted to give them privacy, but that was impossible. I couldn't just turn my acute hearing on and off.

Not such a quiet time together then.

I tossed another log onto the fire, happy to listen to the clunk and rattle as it settled. We had to keep this place warm now our cambion was here. The last thing we needed was him getting cold—cold was a killer in Siberia, and it could kill in minutes.

A rush of arousal went to my cock as another groan filtered my way.

I poked at the fire.

"You've got to chill out," Lloyd said. He was pacing in front of the window.

"You don't exactly look chilled."

"Okay, I'll rephrase that. *We* need to chill out and think of a plan."

"So you *do* think it's a problem that Darius is here?"

"Of course I do, but not having him here isn't the solution. We were all miserable without him, and more to the point, *he* was miserable. We haven't committed ourselves to him to allow that. Our job is to keep him happy, safe, and satisfied."

"We haven't committed to him, not formally."

"No, but we will, George. When all of this is over and we can get to The London Order. It's just a matter of time."

"But when will all this be over? And how will it end? Because if Patrick gets hold of Darius now, he won't be able to stop the way we can. He'll drain him dry."

"And he'll become like us. Darius will be a vampire."

"You know as well as I do, we have no idea if cambions can turn."

Lloyd sighed. "Okay, so let's try and think straight."

"Yes, lets." I glanced at Oscar.

He was sitting with his legs and arms crossed and his thick dark eyebrows pulled low. "I'll do what I can to help," he said.

"It would have been a help to keep him away for another few months."

"We've gone over that, George," Lloyd said. "So let's go from here."

I sighed and tugged my pocket watch out. I looked at the face, put it away. I didn't register what the time was.

"Patrick is on minimal silver," Lloyd said. "Hardly any really. The collar was his main bind, and without that, we've managed to build a relationship with him, get him thinking straight and aware of time and place."

"But you saw how he was when Darius walked into the room. His bloodlust is still rampant." I flapped my arms in the air, an unusual gesture, but I didn't know what to do with them.

"But he *did* control it," Lloyd said, shoving his hands into his pockets as though to stop himself copying my exasperated gesture. "He was rational enough to ask for deer blood, and after he'd sated his thirst, he was a cool cucumber, all things considering."

"Cool cucumber?" Oscar huffed.

"You never heard that expression?" Lloyd said.

"No, but whatever." Oscar uncrossed and recrossed his arms.

I tutted. The tension was rising. I hoped Rhys would keep Darius out of the way while we made a plan—if we *could* make a plan, that was.

I rubbed my chin and stared at the flames. I'd seen plenty of other vampires at this stage of their development, but Patrick was different. He'd been an elite soldier. The qualities he'd possessed to perform his human duties would have in turn made him an elite vampire. I didn't want to underestimate him, but neither did I want to break his spirit or tear away the things that could be really special about the new member of our team.

"I vote we take that last bit of silver off his wrist and get him out hunting," Oscar said.

"What?"

"What?"

Lloyd and I had spoken at once.

Lloyd stopped pacing. "Hunting?"

"Deer, bear, the odd husky, whatever he can find. It will use up his energy and give him an understanding of his power. Until he's got an appreciation of his speed and strength, he can't be blamed for overusing it."

"It's too risky." I shook my head.

Lloyd pushed his hood down and scrubbed his hand over his shorn hair. "It is, but…"

"Don't tell me you think it's a good idea, Lloyd."

"It's not great, but it might be the best option we've got."

"How?"

Oscar stood. He went to the kettle which was coming to boil. "If he sates his thirst on animal blood, he'll know he can. Sometimes not knowing if you can get what you need is worse than not having it."

I let his words roll around my mind and tried to picture taking Patrick into the tree line.

Will we be able to control him?

What if a human from the town wanders this way?

Oscar poured hot water into a cup. "Two stay here with Darius, two go with Patrick."

"It could be a turning point for him," Lloyd said. "Once he's out of silver and feeding the way a new vampire would."

"A new vampire in training."

"Well, yes, obviously not like a feral vampire." Lloyd shook his head. "Then we can decide how much we trust him not to hurt Darius."

"Or anyone else. If anyone from the village gets attacked by him, we'll have to move on. Patrick will be too fast for us to run with. We'd have to all walk out of here so he's under control."

"I agree," Lloyd said. "But one step at a time. Let's get him out into the forest, take the silver off, and let him hunt under our supervision."

I didn't like the plan, but I couldn't think of anything else. And we couldn't go on like this. Darius didn't want to sit for years in this cabin.

"Okay, we'll do it." I set down my shoulders.

"When?" Oscar asked.

"Now. Lloyd and I will take him. You and Rhys are responsible, entirely, for Darius."

"I'm quite used to that." Oscar nodded.

I glanced up the corridor again. "It sounds like they've finished their fun in there."

Lloyd's mouth dropped open. "You were listening to them?"

"Hard not to. Our sweet Darius groans and moans when he's coming."

Lloyd looked in the direction of the bedroom. "Lucky Rhys."

"Yes, I agree." I beat down the desire to go in there, strip Darius naked, then bend him over, take his ass. I wanted him to do the same to me. I just damn well wanted him.

But first things first. "Oscar, can you let Rhys know where we've gone and what the plan is?"

"I can do that."

Lloyd followed me into Patrick's room. He hadn't changed position and was still facing the window, a slight tremble shivering constantly over his body.

I rested my hand on his arm. "You're going out."

"What?" he murmured, his eyes staying closed.

"You're going out with us," I repeated. "Into the forest. When we're there, we'll take that cuff off and see how you feel."

He opened his eyes and stared into mine. "I think that will feel fucking awesome."

I couldn't help a smile. "Come on then, Officer."

Lloyd and I helped him to standing. He was as tall as each of us, broad, too. We were careful not to get too near the cuff.

He steps were shuffling, and his head hung low. We made our way out of the cabin and onto the porch.

Once there, he held his face up and breathed deep. His nostrils flared, and he sniffed.

"You can smell more than usual, right?" Lloyd said.

"Yeah." He frowned. "What's that all about?"

"All your senses are heightened. Taste, smell, eyesight, hearing."

"And," I added, "so is your sense of touch, and when it comes to sex, you'll notice that especially."

He turned to me, his eyes narrowed.

"When you have sex now, Patrick, whether it's with a woman or a man, it'll be off-the-scale hot, super intense."

His jaw tightened, and a small tendon flexed in his cheek.

I held his gaze. It reminded me of someone being interrogated. Then it came to me, that wasn't news to him. He and Rhys...

While they've been together and alone.

And Rhys had said he wanted to talk to Darius about something in private. Was it that he and Patrick...?

No, Patrick is in no fit state to fuck, and I'd have heard it.

But they had done something. I'd bet my damn pocket watch on it.

"Come on," Lloyd said, nodding west. "Let's hit the forest. About five miles in should do."

"Do we need kit?" Patrick asked, his useless cuffed hand hanging at his side.

"Are you cold?" I asked.

He shook his head. "No."

"It's twenty below," Lloyd said. "And all you have on are combats and a t-shirt. Can you explain that, Patrick?"

I could almost see the cogs of Patrick's mind working. Perhaps this hadn't been such a bad idea. It was all well and good telling him what he was now, but experiencing it would cement our words and hopefully make him trust us as we needed him to.

"We'll run," I said to Lloyd. "And carry him between us." I curled an arm around Patrick's cool, hard body.

Lloyd did the same.

And then we were moving fast, holding him. We entered the tree line, a swirl of snow in our wake, then dodged between the trunks. We kept on going until the distance between Patrick and Darius felt as safe as it was going to.

"What the fuck"—Patrick slumped against the skinny tree we'd stood him next to. A shower of snow fluttered over us—"was that?"

"An efficient method of getting around. No always suitable, but handy when it is," I said.

He grimaced and held his cuffed arm forward. "You said…you'd…"

"Yeah, and we will." Lloyd pulled a rubber glove from his pocket and put it on.

"But you must promise us a couple of things first." I cupped his chin and forced him to look at me with his red eyes. I needed to know I had his cooperation.

"Whatever you want, George. I understand what you need from me."

Is he just saying that? Is that how he's been trained to respond in a hostage situation?

"First," I said, "you stay within our sight."

"I can do that."

"And second, if we come across a human being…"

"Here?" He glanced around. "Not likely."

"But if we do, then you can't hurt them, can't bite."

"So what can I do?" He paused. "What *can* I bite?"

"Deer most likely. Perhaps an elk, or maybe a bear if one has woken early, but I doubt it."

He licked his lips. "Any of the above will do."

"And it will be hard to stop drinking the blood," Lloyd said. "But that is something you must master. Start working on it now, for until you do, you'll never be able to integrate with your new species."

"I'll do whatever you want." He gripped his elbow. "But take this off, please. I can't stand the burn, the pain, anymore."

Lloyd nodded and took the key from me.

He unlocked the cuff.

It fell to the ground.

Before it had hit the snow, Patrick was behind me with his feet wide, arms out and fingers spread as though feeling the air. He reminded me of a newborn who'd been suddenly unswaddled, yet he was no cute baby—he was one seriously dangerous creature, and we'd created him.

Give me strength, Master Benedict, and give Patrick wisdom.

He looked around, wild and savage. I could believe everything we'd told him had slipped from his mind.

Lloyd pulled out his packet of cigarettes and sparked one up. He blew a stream of smoke from the side of his mouth. It mingled with the small particles of freezing air that danced in the weak light.

"Really?" I said to him. "Now?"

"He's cool." Lloyd shrugged. "See."

Patrick was still surveying the area manically and was now rubbing his wrist, the one that had held the cuff. He didn't seem cool. He looked ready to go on a one-vampire rampage around Russia, feeding on everyone and everything he could catch. And with the strength of his vampire youth and his specialist skills, we would have our work cut out catching him even if there were four of us.

"How are you feeling, Patrick?" I asked, trying to keep my tone calm and neutral, even though that wasn't how I was feeling inside.

"Glad to have the pain gone." He glared at me. "If I do as you've asked, will you promise me one thing?"

"I will." Right now, I'd promise him the damn moon to behave. Master Concorde would have me staked if Patrick went on a killing spree. The thought of having to admit that we took the silver off so early sent dread scouring through me.

"If you promise," Patrick said, "never to put that stuff on me again, that silver, I'll do what you ask." He sniffed, filling his nose with the scents of the forest.

And there was plenty to smell. An elk had passed by recently, and a bear was hibernating nearby, too. Luckily there was no dog. The smell of wolf would likely tip me over the edge right now.

"We can promise that," I said. "We're reasonable men, Patrick, as long as you are, too."

"Good." He licked his lips. "I want human."

"But you can't have human."

"I understand that." His fangs slid down, which didn't instill a whole load of confidence in me. "I'm just telling you what I want and what I would have had I not just made that promise."

"A promise is a promise," Lloyd said. He nodded over Patrick's right shoulder. "There's something back there, go see."

Patrick spun and stepped away, flicking up snow with his boots. "Where?"

"Follow the scent," Lloyd said.

Patrick dragged in a huge lungful of air, his shoulders rising and his t-shirt stretching over his wide torso. He blew it out; there was no evidence of mist hanging before him—his breath wasn't warm. "Yeah, I can smell it."

"It's an elk," I said.

"And I can have it?"

I smiled, pleased that he'd bothered to ask. "Yes. Go hunt."

He was gone.

Chapter Thirteen

George

"Fuck." Lloyd dropped his cigarette and raced after Patrick.

I followed.

We sprinted through the trees, following the blur of camo gear that was Patrick. After dodging trunks, frozen streams, and a clearing studded with clumps of dead grass, we caught up with him.

He'd caught the elk. It was lying on the ground, eyes wide, and frightened as Patrick kept it pinned down.

His face was buried in the animal's fur, at the point of its jugular, and he was feeding noisily.

"He's quick." Lloyd pulled his hoody back into place, shielding his face from what little sun there was. "I'll give him that."

I gulped. Had we made a huge mistake? "Yes, he really is."

"But he's only got elk." Lloyd squatted on his haunches at Patrick's side. He rested his hand on his back. "Is it good?"

Patrick didn't answer. He was feeding as though his immortal life depended upon it.

"He'll need to stop soon," I said.

"Yeah." Lloyd rested his hand on the elk's chest. "I'd say now. This things heart is—"

"Going way too fast, yes, I can hear it." I took a step closer.

Lloyd held his hand out. "Let me handle this."

I stopped and nodded.

Lloyd ran his palm up to Patrick's nape and bent his head close. "Patrick, it's time to stop feeding. If you don't, you'll kill this animal."

Patrick continued to drink.

"And if you kill it, you'll never feed off it again. You need to learn that animals and humans make more blood, but not if you kill them." He curled his fingers around the neckline of Patrick's t-shirt. "You cannot drain it dry."

"Shit, he's not listening." I gritted my teeth.

"He will." Lloyd threw me a frown from the shadows of his hood. He turned back to Patrick. His voice was low, but I could hear him easily. "Do not be a monster, Patrick. Do not be that kind of vampire. There is no reason why you can't still be a good man despite your urges and needs."

I held my breath, hoping Lloyd's words would have an effect.

"Monsters can't live happy lives with good people," Lloyd went on, "and we want that for you, we all do, including Rhys and Darius."

Those two names had the desired effect. Patrick lifted up, breathing hard, blood dripping from his fangs, lips, and chin. He stared at the puncture marks on the elk's neck.

Lloyd pressed his fingers over them to stop the flow. "You did it; it's not easy, but you did."

"I want to keep going." Patrick was breathless, and excitement laced his voice. "Until there's no more, until the veins and arteries are dry."

"But you mustn't," I said.

"I know, I'm just telling you what I want." He threw a steely glare my way. "You might as well know."

"I understand it's hard, it's a battle, and you have to gather all of your self-control and willpower to stop," Lloyd said.

"I have plenty of self-control."

"We've noticed," I said. "You were clearly one hell of a soldier, Patrick."

He sat back, forcing Lloyd to release him. His ass landed on the snow, and he bent his knees, letting his forearms drape over them. He stared at the snow that was being peppered with the blood dripping from his face.

Lloyd released the elk. It scrabbled to standing, it's long legs wobbly and uncoordinated, then burst forward into a leaping run. Within seconds it had melted into the forest.

"You did well, Officer." I gestured in the direction the beast had run, wondering if I should have taken my fill, too.

No, that would have been too much for the creature.

"Thanks." Patrick didn't look at me. "I want to do the right thing, even though this whole situation is freaking me out."

"It would be weird if it didn't freak you out." Lloyd sat on a log at Patrick's side. "When I turned, the thirst was horrendous. My throat felt permanently parched." He shook his head as though casting his memory back. "I was like an addict. Blood was all I could think of, human or animal, whatever, I just wanted blood."

Patrick twisted to face Lloyd. "But you got it under control?"

"Eventually. I was in a silver collar for six months, and every second of wearing it was agony."

"I can attest to that." Patrick glowered.

"Every time it was removed for a trial run," Lloyd went on, "I went out on the rampage. A few of my victims didn't survive. I'm ashamed to say, news of their deaths hit the *London Standard*."

"Along with the birth of who was later to become Queen Victoria and the Shelley scandal," I said, casting my mind back. "Terrible business, that."

Lloyd frowned at me as if wondering why I filled my head with these facts. I didn't particularly, the information just lingered.

"So how did you stop?" Patrick asked, poking at the blood droplets on the snow before pressing them deep. He'd retracted his fangs now.

"Willpower was one thing, but mainly I didn't want to be a killer. I wanted to make the best of the situation, and I dare say it, now that I've met Darius, fall in love and be happy."

Patrick was quiet. He seemed to be absorbing every word Lloyd was saying.

After a few minutes, I stepped close and ran my hand over his short hair. I felt for him, I really did. His emotions were a confusing soup of feelings and instinct. "Is it making sense?"

"Yeah." He set his attention on me. "And I killed enough men when I was a human, saved lives, too, but taken my fair share. Now maybe I can atone for some of that by controlling my urges."

"That's my man." Lloyd grinned.

"And...is it weird if I say I want to make Rhys proud of me?"

"Not at all." I smiled. "I was privileged enough to be turned by Master Concorde, who I hope you will meet one day. I've spent centuries ensuring I do make him proud."

Patrick stood, unrolling his shoulders then rubbing the tattoos on his forearms. "I want to make you all proud. I'm not the kind of guy to let people down, especially not the men standing at my side."

"I understand that, Officer, and appreciate it." I clasped his shoulder. "Now let's get back to the cabin. We'll run, together, but keep it steady."

"Sure." He nodded east. "That way, right?"

"Yes."

Like before, he was gone in a flash.

"Holy Benedict." Lloyd jumped up. "He's seriously fucking fast."

We shot off after him. For a moment I'd forgotten that new vampires had heightened speed, and in all honesty, that just made Patrick even more of a liability.

When we arrived at the cabin, he was nowhere to be seen.

"Shit." Lloyd paced left and right, peering into the distance. "Where the hell...?"

"Hey."

I looked up. Standing on top of the cabin was Patrick. He was grinning, breathing fast, and held a freshly killed arctic fox in his right hand. If his speed and reckless arrival hadn't concerned me so much, I'd have paused to admire what a fine specimen of a vampire he was.

"Get off the damn roof," I snapped.

"Keep your hair on." He jumped down, sailing through the air, then landed softly at my side. He held up the fox. "I thought Rhys might like a snack."

"How the heck did you have time to grab that?" Lloyd said.

Patrick shrugged. "Guess I'm faster than you two."

"Get in." I nodded at the door. "And chill out, Patrick."

Inside the cabin, Oscar was sitting beside a roaring fire reading a thick, dusty book, and Rhys was in the kitchen wearing an apron with an image of a Cossack dancer on it. He had ingredients spread out and was scratching his head as he studied a recipe card.

"Where's Darius?" I asked.

"Lying down." Oscar nodded at the corridor. "He's physically and emotionally exhausted."

Somehow, I felt that was a bit of a dig at me. Darius and I had hardly spoken since he'd arrived, and when we had, I'd been sharp with him.

A knot of regret tightened in my stomach. I had been harsh with him about coming here early and unannounced. But it was fear that had made me behave that way.

I should go to him.

I slipped off my boots. "Watch Patrick." I nodded at Oscar.

"I will, boss."

Patrick was next to Rhys, presenting him with the fox as though he'd been out to buy a goddamn bunch of flowers for him.

Those two!

I wandered down the corridor and stopped at the bedroom with the door closed. I knocked softly.

There was no answer, but I could hear the gentle sounds of Darius's breathing.

I went in, clicking it shut behind myself.

He lay on the bed, beneath the covers, his head on a faded blue pillow and light from the window creating a rectangle on the floor at his side. His eyes were closed, and he was so angelic in that moment it was hard to believe he was half demon.

I sat on the edge of the bed.

He stirred, then arched his back and stretched. His arms came out of the covers, reaching behind himself, and when he brought them down, he dropped them at his sides.

I took his warm hand in mine. "I'm sorry."

"For what." He opened his eyes, and his gaze settled on mine.

"For being less than a gentleman when you arrived."

"I surprised you." He smiled, though there was sadness in the tilt of his lips.

"Yes, you did, but despite appearances, I am glad to see you, more than glad. My soul ached without you." I brought his hand to my mouth and kissed his knuckles. The heat of his skin stirred my groin.

"I know you are, George. I love you and I understand you."

"I'm just concerned about Patrick and his urges. I've seen new vampires before; it can get ugly."

"Patrick is different, though, don't you think?"

I hesitated. "Yes, he's unique, but I still wouldn't trust him farther than I could throw him."

"Which is probably quite a long way."

I chuckled. "You got room for one more in there?"

"In bed? Always." He flicked back the covers, revealing a naked torso.

I smiled and stripped off my waistcoat, then set to work on the buttons of my shirt. Once I'd folded them over the back of a chair, I slipped off my pants.

He watched me without speaking, but his eyes sparkled.

"I hope I don't make you cold," I said, climbing into the bed next to him.

"I'm sure you'll soon warm me up." He snuggled close and kissed me. His cock was already hard and wedged up against my thigh.

I roamed his body, reminding myself of his shape, his long limbs, hard abdomen, and defined pecs. Darius was all I'd ever need. I loved him so much.

His tongue swept over mine, spreading the taste of heat and vitality and man. I moaned softly and gripped his ass, pulling him close so our hard cocks came into alignment.

"Room for one more?"

We broke the kiss.

Lloyd stood on the opposite side of the bed, minus his hoody and t-shirt.

Darius spun to face him. "Yes." He looked at me again. "If that's...?"

"Okay with me?" I smiled. "Sure, a little ménage à trois never did anyone any harm." The idea of seeing Darius pleasured by both of us was a turn-on.

Lloyd shoved at his black denims, removed his boxers, then climbed under the covers.

Instantly, the urgency to fuck ramped up a notch.

Lloyd nibbled Darius's ear and drifted his hands down his body.

I kissed Darius again and delved into his boxers.

A groan tore from my throat as I gripped his hot, solid shaft.

Damn, I've missed his cock.

"George," Darius murmured. "I want you... I want both of you."

"And you'll get us," I said. "I promise."

I stroked his cock, and his eyes fluttered closed. Lloyd's hand was there, too, cupping and massaging his balls.

"There's no rush," Lloyd whispered to him. "Relax, let us adore you."

"Mmm."

I smiled, enjoying his pleasure.

He curled his hand around my shaft and squeezed.

Longing unfurled in my belly, and I pushed into his touch.

He worked me, the way I was working him. The sense of connection and understanding between us was back. It had never really gone anywhere.

Lloyd reached away for a moment, then returned. "Loop your leg over George's."

Darius did as instructed, and I scooped my hand beneath his thigh.

His eyes pinged open. "Fuck. Lloyd."

Lloyd chucked and set his chin on Darius's shoulder so he could see his face. "Your little asshole is going to take us in a minute; you need some lube."

"Oh God…" He moaned. "I've missed you both so much."

Lloyd was finger-fucking him, I could tell by the small movements of his shoulder.

Darius was clearly enjoying it; his cock was rock-hard, his breaths coming in short, sharp pants.

A drip of pre-cum leaked from my cock, and he caught it, using it as lube on me.

I explored the tip of his glans, found the same slickness and copied his actions.

"I'm going to fuck you now," Lloyd said. "And remind you how much I love you, Darius."

"Yes. Yes. Fuck me."

I clasped his leg harder and massaged his cock with a firmer grip.

Lloyd repositioned, then gritted his teeth as he pushed in.

Darius held his breath, his eyes wide and focused on me. Within the depths of his pupils was love and lust, understanding and compassion.

"He's filling you?" I asked.

"Yes…oh…yes." His brow furrowed in concentration. "Lloyd…oh…"

"Fuck!" Lloyd hissed in a breath. "You're so damn tight."

"And you're…big…"

I kept working Darius, stimulating his cock as Lloyd massaged him from the inside.

Darius's hand was motionless on me. All he could concentrate on was what we were doing to him.

Lloyd slipped his arm around Darius's waist, pinning him close, then began to fuck him.

It was a steady rhythm that made the bed frame squeak and tap against the wall.

We ignored it.

Darius was our world.

"Lloyd…George…" Darius gasped.

I cupped his face with my free hand. "We've got you."

"I know…I…" His features scrunched. "I need to come, it's quick but…"

"Come when you want," I said against his lips. "Come. Come now."

"I am…oh…"

His shaft swelled. I kept my grip firm and my movements steady. It pulsed against my palm; warm cum leaked from him, covering my hand and daubing onto his belly.

"In the name of…" Lloyd said. "Fuck, it's here."

Lloyd was coming, too. Not surprising, being that Darius was convulsing against him and likely squeezing his cock like a noose with every release of his pleasure.

His fangs slid down, and he sank them into Darius's shoulder.

Darius cried out, then their groans mingled.

My needs erupted. My gum was tingling, my cock painful it was so hard.

"My turn."

Lloyd grunted, stopped feeding, and pulled out.

I lifted Darius's leg from over mine.

He flopped onto his belly, groaning and with trembles gliding up his spine. His skin gleamed.

I spread his legs, got between them, and arrowed my cock at his asshole.

Take it easy. Be gentle. He's human.

I didn't take any notice of myself. The urgency was overwhelming.

I set my chest over his back and mouth at his ear. "You ready for me?"

"Always, always, George." He parted his legs and arched the base of his spine, offering himself to me.

I took it.

I shoved into his lubed hole. Going to full depth on the first plunge. He could take it—Lloyd's cock had prepared him.

I shunted us both up the bed then paused, reveling in the sensation of his hot ass wrapping around my cock.

"Oh yes, fuck me... I love you... George... Lloyd...oh..."

"That's it," Lloyd said, at my side. "Making him come again."

"I can't. Oh..." Darius groaned and twisted his head from side to side. "It's so much."

"Sure you can." I lifted up, dragging him with me so he was on all fours and I had hold of his hips. "Work him, Lloyd."

Lloyd grinned, his teeth bloodstained, and reached beneath Darius.

Darius jerked when Lloyd took his cock.

"You can come again," Lloyd said in a low, husky voice. "And we'll show you how."

I didn't think it would be difficult. With Lloyd's potent saliva already swirling in his bloodstream, and mine about to join it, Darius would soon have an off-the-scale multiple orgasm.

I ramped up the tempo, my balls hitting hard onto him each time I bottomed out.

When I could hold off no longer, I tipped forward, fangs exposed, and pierced the skin at the nape of his neck.

He cried out, a bliss-soaked noise that echoed around the room.

I began to drink, taking in his magical blood. Every drop was a taste of ecstasy. As I drank, I curled my hips under over and over, pushing us both on.

And then I was coming, releasing all the delicious pressure and finding that moment when nothing else existed except being inside Darius.

"That's it, you're coming again," Lloyd said excitedly.

"Oh...fuck...yes..." Darius was coming again, his asshole clamping and releasing around my cock.

I forced myself to stop drinking, lifted my face, and yelled my satisfaction. I plunged deeper, more of my cool cum filling him.

He was shaking, sweating, his breaths erratic. His heart was thudding as loud as a drum.

"There's no cum," Lloyd said, "but he's definitely..."

"Coming...yes I am..." Darius wailed. "Heaven help me."

"We've got you." Lloyd clasped his shoulder and kissed the top of his head. "We've got you."

Darius suddenly collapsed down. I went with him.

Air huffed from our lungs.

"You okay?" I asked. I glanced at Lloyd; his eyes were flashing with excitement.

"Yeah..." Darius murmured. "Just a bit fucked."

Chapter Fourteen

Darius

I fell asleep again, my asshole tender, my cock spent, and my skin tingling as I cooled.

Lloyd was behind me, George in front watching me—I knew he was. That sensation of being watched when sleeping was something I'd had to get used to.

After a while my stomach rumbled, and the scent of herbs, onions, and garlic floated toward me.

"You hungry?" George whispered, stroking my cheek.

"Yes. A bit."

"So let's feed you; we've had ours." Lloyd kissed my shoulder, over the spot he'd fed from earlier.

"Mmm, that's a good idea. I might take a shower first."

"Sure thing. I'll go check the fire is stoked."

George slipped from the bed, and I admired his ass when he bent to reach his clothes. Next time we had sex, I'd be the one inside him. I'd feel his hole around my cock, let his cool tightness wrap around my shaft.

"You're thinking dirty thoughts," Lloyd said, chuckling behind me.

"Can you blame me?" I twisted to kiss him. "When I have two of the sexiest men alive in bed with me."

"Not quite alive, but we know what you mean." George grinned and dragged on his shirt.

I'd have kept him naked if I'd had my way. He, like the others, didn't exactly need their clothes. But then maybe we wouldn't get anything done. We'd spend our whole time fucking, a bit like Oscar and I had at Foxhill and in Krakow.

"How long are we going to stay here?" I asked.

"At least for the summer." George slipped on his waistcoat, checking the time on his pocket watch before he buttoned it up. "To give Patrick plenty of time to adjust."

"He's doing well, though?"

"Yeah," Lloyd said, sliding his hand over my chest and tweaking my nipple. "Much better than expected for a first run out."

"And for the love of Benedict, the man can run." George blew out a breath and frowned. "One of the fastest I've ever seen."

"And that's a problem?"

"It is while he's still volatile." Lloyd swept over to my other nipple.

"And a liability." George walked to the door. "So the longer we're here the better. We have nowhere else to be."

"The agency will be wondering about me." I sat, locking my elbows behind me. "It's unusual for me not to take modelling jobs most days."

George grinned. "I emailed them, said you were taking a sabbatical."

"You did?"

"Yes. They were fine about it."

"And who did you say you were?"

"I didn't. I emailed from your account."

"You hacked it?" I didn't know how I felt about that. I didn't have secrets from George, or any of my vampires, but still…

"I'm sorry." He shrugged. "We had other things to worry about at the time, like destroying your father so he didn't deliver a whole pile of evil onto the world."

"I guess." I glanced at Lloyd who'd also sat.

"Yeah, sorry about that." Lloyd shook his head. "But at least it's done now. Not like we have Internet connection here, is it."

"True."

"And you can go back to your career anytime you want. In a hundred years, you'll still look the same."

"I'm still getting used to that concept." I shook my head. "But I do need to touch base with my mother. I told her I'd be off line for a while, traveling, but as soon as we've got some signal or Internet connection I want to speak to her."

"Of course." George nodded. "I'll make sure you can, soon."

"Thanks. Right, I'm going to shower, and then food."

"Rhys is rustling you up some culinary delight," Lloyd said, flinging back the covers and exposing our nakedness. "I'll go tell him you're nearly ready for it."

Three hours later, I was lounging on the sofa with Rhys. He'd made elk steak with garlic butter, white berries, and cabbage dumplings. It was a bit of a mixed plate, but I was hungry, and each individual mouthful was delicious.

The fire glowed, keeping the room warm.

Lloyd and George had taken to one of the bedrooms to study some old maps of the area they'd found.

Oscar was sitting in what appeared to be his favorite chair—maybe because it was big and he fitted well in it—reading.

Patrick was at the table in the kitchen area. He had a pencil and was sketching.

Oscar kept glancing at him—more than glancing, watching him. As though he didn't trust him not to leap up and bite me or run out of the cabin at any moment.

I wasn't getting that vibe from him, though. Patrick seemed calm and in control. Getting rid of the silver had been the right thing to do—having someone in the cabin in agony had made for a tense, uncomfortable atmosphere.

"Did you enjoy your dinner?" Rhys asked, lacing his fingers with mine.

"Yes, you're a great cook?"

"You think so?" He seemed surprised at the compliment.

"Yeah, I hope you'll cook for me some more."

He grinned. "You know I will. You need to eat every day, right?"

"Three times a day would be ideal." I chuckled.

"Yes. Of course." He leaned over and kissed my cheek.

I caught Patrick watching us.

Suddenly, Oscar stood. "I need to go out."

"You do?" I asked.

"He needs to feed, deer or elk," Rhys said. "Been a while since you had a good fill, hasn't it, Oscar."

"It has, and it's easier to have control if I'm not over thirsty." He glanced at me.

A small tremble wound up my spine. I knew Oscar would never hurt me intentionally, but even so, it would be good to ensure he felt under complete control of his bloodlust.

"I'll be back soon." He strode to the door. Holding the handle, he paused and set his attention on Rhys. "You got this in here?"

Rhys glanced at Patrick. "Yep."

Oscar went, leaving a chill from where the door had opened and closed.

I shivered.

Rhys reached for a blanket and set it over my knees, pulled me close against his hard body.

"I love that you cooked for me." I stroked his cheek then kissed it.

"I love taking care of you." He smiled.

"Maybe you'll let me take care of you later." I slid my hand down his chest and beneath the blanket. "Repay the favor from earlier."

"I'd like that."

The heat of Patrick's gaze lay heavy on me.

As I turned to him, he stood, his wide shoulders tense and his hands in fists.

"What?" I asked, sitting forward.

Rhys tugged me back. "It's okay." He paused. "Patrick, come and sit with us."

He moved to the fire and stood with his back to it. "You two really are in love, aren't you?"

"Yes." I studied him. "Did you doubt what Rhys had told you about my relationship with everyone here?"

"No." He paused. "Perhaps, I mean, one guy, four vampires, all fucking." He gestured to the bedroom. "Screwing each other senseless, it's...unusual."

"It's how it is for us," I said.

"And Darius is exceptional." Rhys smiled at me.

"Mmm, you make me feel exceptional." I slipped my hand lower and cupped his cock. He was semihard.

"And you're completely unapologetic about it." Patrick nodded at my hand moving beneath the blanket.

"What should I apologize for?" I asked. "Being in love or being gay?"

He was quiet. "Gay."

It was strange to see such a big tough soldier struggling with his sexuality. I hoped we'd be able to help him with that.

"Come and sit here." I stopped touching Rhys and patted the cushion beside me.

"Er, this side." Rhys pointed at the gap on the sofa next to himself. So Patrick wouldn't be directly next to me.

Patrick swallowed, then nodded and sat.

A log shifted in the fireplace, sending a crackle of sparks upward. Outside, an owl hooted; it seemed to be perched on the chimney stack.

Patrick looked upward.

"Owl blood tastes like shit." Rhys reached for Patrick's hand. "Most bird blood does, with the exception of golden eagle, that's okay."

"Noted." Patrick was studying the way his fingers were linked with Rhys's.

"We need to talk about how you're feeling," I said, hoping I wasn't pushing Patrick too fast.

"About what?"

"Being a vampire, being here with us…" I nodded at their joined hands. "How you feel about Rhys."

"Rhys," he repeated, a line forming between his eyebrows. "Is…"

"What?" Rhys asked. "What am I?"

"Special to me." Patrick shrugged as though the words didn't mean much.

They mean a lot.

"I can see that he's special to you," I said. "And that's good. We're a team; you're part of it now. We all have unique and extraordinary relationships with one another."

He nodded.

"And you're just starting to get to know us," I went on. "And I'm so glad you've bonded with Rhys."

"Bonded." He blew out a breath. "Fuck, that's one thing to call it."

I smiled. "And if you and Rhys want to be physical, you have my blessing."

"Why would we want to be physical?" Patrick frowned.

His words weren't matching his actions.

"Because we're physically attracted to each other," Rhys said, rubbing his thumb over the back of Patrick's hand. "Aren't we?"

"That..." Patrick swallowed, a loud gulping sound. "Is not easy for me to admit after years of being told gay is a sin and an embarrassment." He stared Rhys in the eyes. "I hope you understand."

"Of course." Rhys grinned. "Take all the time you need. We have plenty."

"The problem is," Patrick said, "I don't want to take my time."

My heart did a little flip on Rhys's behalf.

"You don't?" Rhys said.

"No, and I'm sorry for being mad at you when you spoke the truth."

Rhys and I were silent. Something told me this was super-important to Patrick.

"You told the truth," Patrick went on, "about me, and what I wanted." He paused. "I am gay, you're right. And I've been keeping it hidden, the urge suppressed for years, but now..."

"Now you can be true to yourself." Rhys smiled and stroked his free hand over Patrick's hair.

Holy hotness.

I hadn't realized how sexy it would be to see my handsome young Rhys getting all mushy over a cute soldier, but it was. Far from feeling jealous, I just wanted to watch, see what they would do next.

"So can I...?" Patrick asked, his deep voice low, almost a growl.

"Can you what?" Rhys whispered.

"Give in to my urges?"

Rhys glanced at me.

I nodded, just once, and only a tiny movement of my head.

"Yes," Rhys said, returning his attention to Patrick. "You can."

And then Patrick's mouth was over Rhys's, and they were kissing. A luxurious, stroking tongues kiss that had them sighing and melting together.

My cock tingled, despite having been thoroughly satisfied earlier. They were incredible together.

"Rhys." Patrick pulled back and stared into Rhys's eyes. The red depths flashed and burned. "I want to..."

"What..."

"Repay you." He nodded at me. "Seems keeping tally is something you guys do."

I recalled my earlier comment to Rhys. Patrick had clearly been listening to every word as he'd sat there sketching.

"Now?" Rhys asked.

"I'd bet good money, or rather blood if that's the currency, that you've got an impressive hard-on." Patrick grinned, the sternness in his features suddenly evaporating.

Rhys shifted. "I fucking have now."

I smiled and slipped my hand beneath the blanket again. "Yes, he's hard," I said to Patrick.

Rhys groaned when I caressed his length over the material of his jeans.

"So shall we do something about it?" I said against Rhys's cheek.

He grunted a response, and I popped open the buttons on his trousers. A few more seconds, and I was holding his erection.

"Darius," he muttered.

"Shh..." I caressed his length. "Just relax and enjoy."

"Relax is the last thing I can do when you're holding my cock."

"How about when I'm holding it." Patrick sneaked his hand under the blanket.

I let go of Rhys and allowed Patrick access.

"Ah fuck." Rhys gritted his teeth. "Tell me, is that the first time you've touched another man's cock?"

"Yeah, you're the first." Patrick kissed him again.

The blanket moved, the recognizable up-down motion of a hand job.

I changed position, becoming short of space in my own pants. I was breathing shallow, anticipation raging through my veins.

"Are you gonna make me come?" Rhys asked, gripping Patrick's shoulder.

"If that's what you want."

"Hell yeah."

Patrick grinned. "So come, while I touch you and Darius watches."

"Yes, come," I said, my arms tingling and a familiar heat growing in my hands and fingers. "You two are hot together." And it wasn't just their bodies that looked great together, it was their connection. It simmered in the air. Despite their coldness, it was a burning wave of attraction—one that was too powerful to be ignored.

And we shouldn't ignore it.

"Ah fuck." Rhys drew back his lips, exposing his gums, but his fangs didn't slide into view. "I'm...nearly...there."

"Aye." Patrick stared at the moving blanket. "Come."

"Argh." Rhys canted his hips, his entire body tensed, turning to concrete. Then he came. Curling forward, he gasped and released the pressure and his cum.

Patrick's mouth hung open, and his eyes were wide. He kept working Rhys.

"Fuck, that's it, no more." Rhys clasped his hand over Patrick's. "Damn, you're good at that."

"Had lots of practice on my own dick." Patrick chuckled and set his lips over Rhys's.

I stood, and walked a little stiffly, to a box of tissues. I plucked a few out, then handed them to Rhys. My fingers were hot at the ends; sparks were building. I could feel them simmering and was surprised the tissues hadn't started smoldering.

"Thanks." Rhys shoved the tissues beneath the blanket to clean himself up.

I turned to the fire. It had practically gone out. The room was cooling, which wasn't a good thing for me.

"Damn it," I muttered.

"Darius," Rhys asked. "You okay?"

"I've got..." I spread my fingers then drew them into fists. "You know."

"Sparks?"

I nodded. "Watching you guys was so damn sexy, and now..." A grimace tugged my mouth.

Rhys was up and by my side. "So get rid of them. Don't be in discomfort, you don't need to be, not around us."

I glanced at Patrick.

"He'll be cool," Rhys said. He held his palm out to Patrick. "Stay there, okay. Stay on the sofa."

I was struggling to hold the heat in. My arms were full-on painful now, the sharp heat of it spreading like a whip between my shoulders then contracting my biceps.

"Just do it, Darius." Rhys rested his hand on my lower back. "Get rid of them."

"Ah fuck!" I clenched my jaw, stared at the fire, and shot my hands forward. Bright yellow, orange, and red sparks flew from the tips. They tore the agony with them and bounced and sprang into the dying fire.

Rhys rubbed my back, a soothing gesture, as though he knew the hurt this caused me.

But the moment they were out, I was okay. More than okay. I felt better, lighter, cleansed almost.

The last ones trickled downward. I released a breath and closed my eyes.

I sensed Rhys move away. Another log landed on the fire with a clunk.

I tried to slow my heart rate and pulled in a long, slow breath.

When I opened my eyes, Patrick spoke. "That was...incredible."

"I told you he was unique," Rhys said, encouraging the flames with a poker.

Patrick was suddenly in front of me. Looming over me. His red eyes flashing and his mouth open.

Fear hit me like a punch to the guts. Something had changed. Him seeing me release sparks had excited him.

His nostrils flared, and he gulped in air.

And then Lloyd was there, George, too, and Rhys was dragging Patrick away from me as the poker rattled to the floor.

"What the fuck is going on?" Lloyd demanded.

Chapter Fifteen

Darius

"I'll second that," George said. "What is going on?" He positioned himself in front of me, shoulders tense, hands balled into fists.

Lloyd was pressed up behind me, gripping my upper arms, seemingly ready to race off with me somewhere.

"It's okay. *He's* okay," Rhys said, circling Patrick's torso with his arms and pulling him back toward the sofa.

Patrick went with him, his body stiff and with his attention still on me.

"Doesn't fucking look okay," Lloyd said.

"He's cool," Rhys said.

"Yeah." The word seemed to scrape from Patrick's throat. "I'm cool."

Rhys nodded at me. "You okay, Darius?"

"I'm fine. Nothing happened."

"It nearly did." George huffed.

"I didn't do anything." Patrick still had a manic glint in his eye. "I was just amazed, that's all. Haven't seen a bloke spurt fire from his hands before."

The front door flew open, banging onto the wall. "Sit the fuck down." Oscar marched in, snow fluttering from his leathers and spreading on the floor. "Before I damn well make you, Soldier."

Patrick snarled, his eyes flashing.

For a moment I didn't think he'd do as Oscar had told him. He seemed to be sussing out his opponents, sizing the other four vampires up. I had no doubts that he was a skilled fighter. In his old life he could probably put up a fair fight, but now…?

Luckily, he seemed to think the better of it and sat with a bump. He crossed his arms and glared around the room.

"Lloyd," George said. "Get Darius the hell away from here."

"Doing it."

Lloyd curled his hand over my shoulder. "Go put your warm outer layers on."

Oscar put his hands on his hips and blocked Patrick's way out of the room.

I rushed into the bedroom and pulled open the wardrobe where I'd stored my outdoor clothes. Within minutes I had them and my thermals on. I shoved my feet into the heavy boots I'd bought in Krakow.

"Come on." Lloyd was at the door, his mouth in a tight, flat line.

"I'm ready."

He clasped my hand and led me out. George was speaking, but I didn't catch what he was saying as I was ushered into the sub-zero arctic.

"Did he hurt you?" Lloyd asked, tugging up his hood.

"No, not at all."

He hesitated. "But he scared you?"

I didn't want to drop Patrick in it, when he hadn't actually done anything wrong. "Let's just say I couldn't read what he was thinking."

"He was thinking about your blood, Darius, and you know it."

I glanced at the closed door.

"Come on, we're out of here." He turned. "Hop on, the way you did with Oscar."

"Really?" I stared at his black hoody.

"Yes, now."

His tone had me leapfrogging onto his back. He was cool and solid and gripped my legs as I fastened my arms around his neck.

And then we were moving, fast. The snow whooshed in our wake, stirred up by his speed. The wind howled in my ears, and I closed my eyes. I had to hold on tight and hoped we wouldn't be traveling for long.

Luckily, we weren't, and after a few minutes he slowed.

I opened my eyes to the bright snowfields. Here there were less trees; instead, huge rust-colored boulders dotted the landscape. Before us was a frozen lake glistening in the sunshine, and behind it a mountain range towered upward, froths of white smoking from the highest peaks.

"Wow," I said when Lloyd drew to a halt. I dropped down to my feet and stared in wonder. "This is possibly one of the most beautiful places I have ever seen."

"Yeah, it's neat." He was studying my face. "I'm glad you like it."

"I more than like it." I was kind of speechless. "It's incredible to think there are places on the planet like this that are seen by so few people."

"I know what you mean." He took my gloved hand. "But come on, there's more."

We started trudging east, our boots crunching in the snow. I breathed deep; the chilled air was pure and fresh. Snow hung like fluttering goose down in the air.

"Where are we going?" I asked.

"You'll see."

We trudged past a row of fir trees—how they were still standing with the colossal amount of snow perched on their branches I had no idea.

"Look, tracks," I said, pointing at the ground.

"Deer," he said. "They're close, I can smell them."

"You can?"

He nodded.

"Do you want to feed?"

He laughed. "No, not at all."

Ah yes, I forgot. Lloyd had fierce self-control over his thirst, not only that, he'd had some of my blood not long ago, which he said could last him much longer than mammal blood, even if it were only a few mouthfuls.

"This is what I want to show you," he said. "I found it about sixty years ago. I'd always hoped to bring my special someone here." He released my hand and slipped his arm around my waist. "And now I have."

I stopped and stared, my mouth hanging open. Before us was a huge frozen waterfall. It was as if the clock had stopped on it in the space of a few seconds. The cascade of water now white, deep aqua in places, sparkled. Jagged points hung toward the icy lake like long strands of hair.

"Come on," Lloyd said, urging me forward.

We walked onto the lake, then stood beside the long shards of ice. It was so quiet, so still, the opposite to how it would be standing here in the summer when the water cascaded and gushed.

"It will melt in a few months." Lloyd stroked one of the long ropes of ice. "But only briefly; summer is very short in Siberia."

"At the moment I can't imagine it melted. It seems so huge and permanent."

"I know what you mean." He pulled his packet of cigarettes out and flicked one in into his mouth.

He sparked up, and the smell meandered my way. "Can I bum one?"

"What?" He took a drag.

"A cigarette. I gave up a while ago. Guess I can start again now it's not going to kill me."

He appeared hesitant.

"What?" I asked.

"George won't thank me, but what the heck." He tossed me the packet, then the lighter.

I lit up, enjoying the familiar taste and the warmth of the smoke traveling into my cold lungs.

"Some of it looks like meringue," I said, studying the higher levels of the falls.

"Yeah, it does."

I walked along, letting my gloved hand stroke the icicles. "Hey, look, there's more animal prints." I stopped and studied the pits in the snow before me. Then I realized they were all around me. Unlike the first bit of the lake, here the snow had been disturbed by lots of animals.

"Prints?" Lloyd was at my side.

"What are they, more deer or—?"

"Fuck!" He flicked his cigarette to one side. "Wolf."

"Wolf." I glanced around, my heart rate picking up. "Are these prints from just one or lots of them?"

"I knew George's idea to come to the cabin wasn't the best one he's ever had. This is exactly what I was afraid of." Lloyd's jaw was tense. His sharp blue eyes scanned the area, and his nostrils flared, as though he was hunting for a scent. "For the love of Benedict," he muttered. "Lots, a serious amount of wolves. This is one big pack." He turned. "Get on. Sightseeing trip over; we've got to get out of here."

The urgency in his tone had me discarding my fag and climbing onto his back. The moment I'd latched around his neck, he was running.

I hadn't seen Lloyd spooked before. When my demon father was around, Lloyd was angry and protective. This was nervousness. More than that—this was fear.

I nestled my cheek against the back of his neck and tried to recall what I knew about vampires and wolves. The two species weren't friends, I knew that much. In fact, I'd go as far to say they were sworn enemies. Master Concorde even had a decapitated wolf's head on his cane.

We soon came to a stop at the base of the cabin steps.

"You wait here. Let me check they're under control with Patrick."

"And if they're not?" I asked.

"You and I take a long trip away. Far away."

The idea of a long trip away with Lloyd was appealing, but not under these circumstances.

He stomped up the steps and opened the door.

I wrapped my arms around myself. I was getting cold. Even with the right gear, this was no place to be outside.

After a few seconds, Lloyd poked his head out of the doorway. "Come in, Darius."

I went gratefully into the warm, closing the door behind myself.

Oscar was in his usual chair. Rhys was in the kitchen and appeared to be making me tea. George was feeding logs to the fire.

"Where's Patrick?" I asked.

"In his room," Oscar said.

"He's not...he's not in silver again, is he?" I couldn't bear the thought of that.

"No." George set the poker on its hook. "We promised him we wouldn't do that, and a promise is a promise." He straightened his waistcoat. "We had a talk with him, about controlling himself around you."

"And?" I unzipped my jacket and shrugged out of it.

"He's taken it on board," Rhys said. "You have no need to fear him."

"I don't fear him," I said. "Well...not if you guys are around."

"Exactly." Lloyd took the mug of tea Rhys had made and passed it to me. "Which we have to make sure we always are."

"Thanks." I took a sip. "So why in his room?"

"He said he wanted to mull it all over, what had happened." Rhys shrugged. "He's got a lot going on in that soldier mind of his."

"He's no ordinary soldier, I keep telling you that," George said. "We underestimate him at our peril."

"But he's one of us now," Rhys said. "And he's doing well, you admitted that."

George folded his arms and rocked back on his heels. "Yes, he is, but we've accelerated his training. His transition is going much faster than I'd planned."

"Perhaps we're just a good team," I said, sitting next to Rhys. I knew he felt protective over Patrick, so this must be hard.

"You have to understand," Oscar said, "he's a wild card."

"Enough of Patrick and his bloodlust." Lloyd swiped his hand through the air. "We have another problem."

"We do?" George turned to him.

"Yes. Wolf."

"Wolf!" Oscar leaped up. "Where?"

"About a hundred kilometers west of here."

"In the name of Benedict," Oscar growled. "I'll kill it. I'll tear its goddamn head off and put in on a spike so the eagles can eat its eyeballs."

"Not it, them," Lloyd said. "In the pleural."

The room fell silent.

Eventually, George spoke. "How many are we talking about, Lloyd?"

"More than I could count. The scent was overwhelming when the wind brought it in from the trees."

"And are they *just* wolves?" Rhys asked.

I frowned, and again a snippet of information came back to me. Shifters. Oscar had told me it was wolf shifters who'd killed his first love, Jack.

"Just wolves," I repeated.

"We have no way of knowing whether or not it's the Carlton Pack," George said, "going on tracks and scent."

Lloyd paced to the window and stared out. "I thought they were miles from here. When we were last at The London Order they'd been reported as having a permanent base in Canada."

Oscar made a weird snarling noise and slammed one fist into the other.

George glanced at him. "Yeah, I know. But they could have moved, especially over the winter months when the sea is solid between the two continents."

"Why would they move?" Oscar said.

"Perhaps they'd become too large to sustain in one area or they wanted to spread their territory, who knows." Rhys sat on the sofa and crossed his legs.

"If it is the Carlton Pack, I'll—"

"Oscar, take it easy." Lloyd rested his hand on Oscar's shoulder. "We've spotted them before they've seen us, or at least I hope that's the case."

"If they're nearby, it's put a time limit on us being in the cabin, though." George pulled out his watch and checked the face. "And I didn't think time was going to be an issue."

"Where will we go?" I asked.

"Not sure, and Patrick, to be honest, is a liability running; he's so damn fast. We'd have to figure some other transport out."

"I'll go and see if he's okay." Rhys stood. "It's not good for him to have too much time in isolation." He wandered across the room and down the corridor.

"Good idea,' Lloyd said.

Within a second, Rhys was a back, eyes wide, hand on the timber wall. "He's gone."

"What?" I jumped up.

"Tell me you're fucking kidding," Oscar said.

"No." Rhys pointed in the direction of the bedroom. "The window is wide open. Patrick has gone."

Chapter Sixteen

Patrick

Seeing Darius shoot sparks from his fingertips had created a new kind of hunger in me. It was a hunger for him, what he was, how he was...the taste of his blood.

And damn, I wanted to screw the guy, too. Screw him all day and night until we were both exhausted and sated.

I'd nodded and apologized while George had given me a lecture about self-control. As if I didn't know about bloody self-control. It's what I'd been trained in, that and combat and survival, and munitions and...the list went on, but he didn't seem aware of that, and I couldn't be fucked to tell him.

'No matter how much you want to bite Darius, you must summon your willpower. We all have to. When the time comes, if the moment is right and you two have a connection, then you will be able to feed from him, the way we do. But until then, Officer, you must wait and learn and prove you can control your thirst.'

The trouble was, I couldn't control it. Right now, I could hear Darius's voice coming from the living area in the cabin. It made my dick hard and my upper gums tingle.

"It's not fucking fair," I muttered. "If they all feed from him, why can't I?"

I stood from the bed and paced. It didn't help, so I dropped and pumped out five hundred press-ups—my arms didn't even ache.

I stood before the window, staring out at the vast white wilderness. It had been so erotic giving Rhys a hand job. Feeling and hearing his pleasure and the spurt of his cool and slick cum was an experience that would always stay with me.

"What if Rhys, Darius, and me...?" I'd said the words quietly, but even so, speaking them seemed to make it true.

What if we all get naked together?

I ran my hands over my hair. Holy fuck. I'd only just admitted I was gay, and here I was fantasizing about a threesome—a threesome with a vampire and a guy with a demon father.

I closed my eyes tight, screwing them up until there was nothing but blackness. Perhaps this was all a dream and I'd wake up and find myself back at base, kit bag at my side, some march in the Beacons planned for the day.

Opening my eyes, I sighed. This was no dream. This was real. And I couldn't even remember when it had all started. George had said that I was possessed; that was how I'd ended up at Stonehenge. I couldn't remember that happening. Last I knew I was walking back to camp after a few pints with the lads.

They'd be wondering where I was. As would my senior officers. Likely my name would be mud for going AWOL.

I should get in touch?

No, Rhys had told me that was a terrible idea. I had to fall off the face of the planet and into this new world. It was the only way. Trying to combine real life, my old life, with what I was now would never work.

My gum still tingled. My skin itched. I had a weird longing, an ache. Was it for blood, sex, or simply to run?

Run.

I shoved at the window, and it opened easily despite being frozen.

I had to run. I had to do something. This bedroom was a prison to me, the same way the silver had been.

I sprang onto the ledge, looked over my shoulder at the closed door, then shot into the open air.

On and on I ran. I knew they'd be furious but I couldn't help it. It was that or go crazy and start messing things up, breaking stuff...biting stuff.

The whiteness was startling, and the scents were a barrage of new information—pine, deer, fungi, owl, elk, bear, wolf, husky, human.

Human.

I stopped, barely out of breath and not at all cold despite the snow falling around me.

Going after a human feed was forbidden. I'd had that drummed into me like a damn mantra. But even so, my gums itched, and my fangs slid down. The longing inside increased.

"No." I snarled, forcing my fangs away and turned from the direction the scent was blowing in from.

I picked up the pace, removing myself from temptation. The imagery of myself sinking fangs into a warm human's neck, piercing the skin then supping on thick, warm blood hung before me.

I tried to push it away.

Ran faster.

I went through a forest, past a frozen lake, over a small mountain dotted with caves.

And then I saw it.

A train of twelve fluffy white dogs. They were barking and working hard, leaving a long, snake-like trail in their wake.

Behind them was a man. He was huddled against the weather, hood up, shoulders hunched.

All I could think of was the blood inside him, coursing around his veins, hot and vital.

My fangs slid down again, and I sucked in cold air, dragging with it a wisp of his scent mingled with the stench of dog.

I set off after him.

It was fate, wasn't it? This man out here alone, in the direction I'd run to escape another human scent. He was meant for me. God, or whoever, whatever, had sent me this gift.

I can almost taste him.

Stopping feet apart in front of the huskies, I held my hands wide and stared at my meal.

The dogs ground to a halt, their reins slackening. Their barks increased in frequency and pitch; a few of the front ones whimpered and slunk back, bumping into the ones behind.

"*Kto ty!*" The man pulled a scarf from his face.

He was asking who I was. Did he really want to know? Would he have such a scowl on his half-frozen features if he did? Or would he be screaming in terror?

I licked my lips, stepped past the dogs, then opened my mouth and revealed my fangs.

"*Chto ty takoye?*" His eyes widened. His lashes were kissed with frost, and frozen droplets of breath hung in his moustache and around his mouth.

"You want to know what I am?" I asked, grinning.

He flicked the reins attached to the dogs. "*Idi begi idi seychas.*"

They all leaped up and yanked at the sledge. Within seconds it was pulling away from me.

I hissed in frustration. Did he really think he could outrun me?

"Stop!" Tight arms wrapped around my waist, the strength of them knocking me off balance. "You've done enough damage already."

"Oscar!" I grunted and tried to shake him, but the guy was big and strong.

I swept my foot against his, got lucky and sent him to the ground. I went with him, hitting the snow in a plume of white.

"Patrick," Rhys's voice. "What the hell are you doing?"

I didn't answer; I was desperately trying to get Oscar into a headlock.

"Put your damn fangs away and stop this." Lloyd glowered down from within his hood.

I got my elbow around Oscar's neck, dragged it into a classic lock, and rendered him disabled.

"Get the...fuck...off...me," Oscar managed. "Before I stake your damn heart."

"Patrick, let him go. What's this going to achieve?" Rhys again.

I looked at him. There was pain and disappointment in his eyes. I hated that. I released Oscar, shoved at him, then jumped to my feet. "Don't touch me again, Oscar, I don't like it."

"Patrick." Rhys clasped my shoulder. "It was for your own good. You can't go hunting the citizens of Oymyakon."

"The man saw him," Lloyd said, nodding in the direction of the huskies and sled which were now disappearing into the tree line. "Fangs exposed, red eyes...shit!"

"This is a problem." Oscar rubbed his neck and glared at Patrick. "*You're* a problem."

"So I'll just fuck off and leave you all to it. If that's how you feel."

"Of course that's how we feel," Lloyd said. "Which is a damn shame when you were doing so well."

"Yeah, what changed?" Rhys asked.

I sighed, hoping it would expel some of the frustration swirling inside. "I guess I just...I want it all now."

"Want what? Blood?" Rhys asked.

"Yeah, that, and you and Darius and...I haven't been true to myself for years and now I can be, and I'm telling the truth when I say I've had pain in my life, mental and physical, but now I feel great, on top of the world." I paused. "The last thing I want to do is be cooped up in a damn cabin with a bunch of control freaks."

"It's for your own—"

"Don't say it's for my own good, Rhys." I turned from him, pinched the bridge of my nose, and closed my eyes.

Was I really going to kill that innocent man?

Would I have been able to stop drinking from him, the way I had the elk?

I didn't know the answers to those questions.

Opening my eyes, I studied Oscar, Lloyd, and Rhys. Clearly, they did know the answers. I would have drank and drank until he'd lain dead and drained on the snow.

And perhaps I'd have enjoyed it so much I wouldn't have cared, a bit like when I used to enjoy a good medium rare steak with a peppercorn sauce and a glass of merlot.

"We need to get back to the cabin," Lloyd said. "He might return with more townspeople."

"Yeah, come on." Oscar nodded east.

I hung my head. "Am I coming with you?"

"Of course you are." Lloyd frowned at me. "Everyone makes mistakes."

"And you've done yours now." Oscar shook his head. "No more chances. And if you ever try and put me in a headlock again—"

"I'm sorry." I'd done more than try. I *had* put him in a headlock. But he knew that, it didn't need spelling out.

"I mean it." Oscar frowned, his gaze unwavering.

I glanced away. I wanted to promise him I wouldn't mess up again, but at this moment in time I really didn't know if I could keep my word.

"Don't be so sad." Rhys ducked to look into my face. "I still love you."

"You...you love me?"

"Sure, can't you tell?"

My heart lifted at that, and I smiled. "I'll try really hard not to let you down again, Rhys."

"I know." He paused and held out his hand. "Come on, let's get back. You first."

I nodded, then used that explosion of energy within my core to break into a super-fast run. Again, everything blurred, but at the same time I could see it clearly. There was no way I'd run into anything, it was there, before me to dodge, if only for an instant.

I went back over the mountain and past the lake. In the forest, I spotted a young deer, grabbed it around the neck, and kept running. It struggled, but that didn't break my hold on it; in fact, I barely felt it.

When I reached the cabin, I was the first one to arrive. I guessed Darius and George were inside, warm and safe.

With excitement churning through me, I jumped up onto the log shed, still holding the deer. It would be an apology gift for my fellow vampires. They could drink from it, and if they decided to kill it, Darius might have veal for his dinner.

A swirl of snow told me of their arrival.

Three figures ground to a halt at the base of the cabin steps.

"Now where the fuck is he?" Oscar snapped.

"Damn it." Lloyd spun around. "This is getting ridiculous. He's as slippery as an damn eel."

Rhys saw me.

I grinned and held up the deer. "Hi."

"He's there." Rhys pointed.

"What the...?" Lloyd's mouth hung open.

"I got you a wee bit of dinner." I jumped down, deer aloft, and grinned. "Want some?"

Chapter Seventeen

Darius

I heard voices outside and ran to the door. The blast of icy air as I opened it took my breath away—the temperature was falling now night was approaching.

"You found him," I said, taking in the scene before me.

Patrick was holding a deer which appeared to be barely alive. Oscar was scowling at him, Lloyd's face was hidden by his hood, and Rhys was beaming ear to ear.

"What the hell happened?" George slipped his arm around my waist.

"We'll come in and tell you." Lloyd stomped up the steps.

"Get in there." Oscar shoved at Patrick's shoulder.

"All right, keep your hair on," Patrick said, tensing.

"Shall I?" Rhys said, taking the deer from Patrick.

"It's for you. A gift."

"Thanks, but... I don't need to feed, and this is a very young one."

"Oh, okay."

Rhys set the creature on the frozen ground. It stood on wobbly legs, huffed out a breath, and then leaped into the snow, making in the direction of the forest.

The four vampires came into the cabin and sat.

George and I stood by the fire. I waited for the air to warm again now the door was closed.

"Well?" George said.

Patrick's eyebrows were pulled together, his mouth a tight, flat line. Something had happened, other than the deer, I was pretty sure of that.

"We found him a long way east of here," Lloyd said, "in a valley."

"A valley that had a husky sled going through it," Oscar added.

"And?" George asked. "I'm guessing by your faces there's more."

"And within a second of seeing it, he was down there, fangs out, ready to attack the driver." Oscar folded his arms, his glare boring into Patrick.

"But he didn't hurt him, didn't do any harm," Rhys added quickly.

"No harm?" Oscar grunted. "The man saw him, saw what he is, *exactly* what he is."

"And that news will be all around the town by now," Lloyd added. "I'd put money on it."

"I agree." George rubbed his temples. "Damn it!"

"I'm sorry," Patrick said to me. "Really I am."

I managed a weak smile. He looked so fed up and ashamed of himself. He'd been doing so well; it was tragic that he'd gone and spoiled it by giving in to his urges.

"We have to get out of here," Lloyd said. "And stay away for a long time."

"How long?" I asked.

"Until this entire generation has gone." Oscar tutted.

"What, really?" That seemed a little extreme.

"Yes." Rhys rested his hand on Patrick's forearm and squeezed. "It has to be until it's gone from living memory. Somewhere as isolated as this, it's the only option."

"Fuck." Patrick muttered. "I'm sorry. I know this place is important to you all."

George sighed. "Yes, but there's other places we can go."

"And let's be honest, this isn't exactly ideal for Darius." Rhys gestured to me.

I was rubbing my hands together; just a short time outside without gloves had numbed my fingers.

"Mmm, somewhere warmer would be good." Lloyd wore a worried expression. "We hadn't expected Darius to be with us this soon, spring perhaps, when the temperature isn't so lethally cold."

"But…" I shoved my hands into my jeans pockets. "Would it really be lethal to me? I thought you said I was immortal."

"Only," George said, "when it comes to ageing and disease. You could still freeze to death, get hit by a bus, shot, or a stake through the heart."

"Great, thanks for those cheery images." I huffed.

"Sorry." He rubbed his temples. "We'll get packed up and go."

"What do we have to pack?" Rhys asked.

"Food, water, supplies for the half human in our group." Oscar shook his head. "Get a grip, kid."

Rhys scowled at him and went into the kitchen area. He began banging around and opening and shutting cupboard doors.

"Where will we go?" Lloyd paced to the window and looked out.

It was getting dark. Long finger-like shadows stretched from the woods, spreading an eerie purple hue over the snow.

"I'm not happy about running, not with the Usain Bolt of the vampire world with us." Lloyd nodded at Patrick.

"I agree," George said.

"Me three," Oscar added.

"I'll go slow, really I will." He licked over his top gum, as though checking his fangs.

"Not a risk we can take. We need to stick together." George gestured to the maps he'd been studying with Lloyd. They were neatly folded beside a book titled *The Demise of the Romanovs*. "Fifty kilometers south of here is a train line. If we follow that another fifty kilometers, we'll get to a small village."

"How often do the trains run?" Rhys asked.

"Passenger trains are rare, but a colossal freight goes through once a day, if memory serves me correct, and slows at the village to a near walking pace to unload mail and drop off supplies."

"And if we jump aboard it will take us out of Russia." Rhys grinned.

"Yes, and into Mongolia. We'll be safe there. It's as deserted as here, almost, and warmer."

"You spent quite a bit of time there, didn't you?" Lloyd said to George.

"Yes, up in the roof of the world." George paused and smiled. "Bayan-Ulgidd."

"And you liked it?" I asked. Mongolia wasn't a place I knew much about.

"I did."

"Why?"

George paused, pulled in a breath. "I needed to be alone, and the mountains, the lakes, the glaciers helped me come to terms with who and what I was. I enjoyed the isolation; it gave me headspace."

"When was this?"

"A few centuries ago." He shrugged. "The only person who knew where I'd gone was Master Concorde. He checked in on me a couple of times, but other than that I was alone for thirty years."

"Thirty years," Patrick said. "That's some finding yourself expedition."

"I have eternity, so time is irrelevant. It is for you, too."

Patrick was quiet at that. I could almost see the information sinking in afresh, despite that fact it was something he knew already. Being told you would live forever—providing there were no stake-heart incidents—wasn't a concept that could be comprehended overnight. I was still getting used to it myself.

"You said you had a place there..." Rhys tapped his head and screwed up his eyes. "Was it a cave?"

"Yes." George smiled again. "It was. Up in the cliffs near the border. I saw only a handful of Kazakh people during my time there. Mostly they were shepherds with goats and yaks, or horseback hunters with their eagles."

"Do you think the cave is still there?" I asked.

"It won't have gone anywhere." He took my hand, checking I was warming up. "And I left a few things in it, in case I ever needed it again. Chances are it's as it was when I left it all those years ago."

"And you think we should go there?" A hundred kilometer walk across a dark frozen tundra didn't particularly appeal. I needed to know the trek would be worth it.

"Yes." Oscar stood. "We should. Damn shame we can't run, but it's obviously not an option with a new vampire." He squeezed Patrick's shoulder.

It was almost as if he was reassuring him, forgiving him, and that pleased me.

George lifted my hand to his mouth and brushed his lips over my knuckles. "Yes. I do. You'll be warmer there, and safer. If the Siberian villagers descend with spears and stakes, it could get nasty." He shook his head. "And I don't fancy explaining a bloodbath to Master Concorde right now. There's enough going on."

"And there's those wolf tracks." Lloyd turned from the window. "They've unsettled me. I won't be sorry to go."

"There's no evidence that it's the Carlton Pack," Rhys said from the kitchen.

"No evidence that it isn't either." Lloyd snapped the zip of his hoody up to his chin. "We'll go as soon as we have enough supplies for Darius." He looked at George, not for confirmation, but more of a challenge to him. Would he disagree?

"Absolutely, Lloyd." George nodded. "The sooner the better."

Within the hour, I was muffled up against the cold in my thermals and thick jacket, trousers, and boots. Only my eyes had to cope with the extreme conditions. I had a soft woolen snood pulled over my nose and mouth.

I was sorry to leave the cozy cabin but knew my vampires would care for me in the desperately low temperatures.

It will all be okay. Be positive.

Yes. In fact, I was looking forward to seeing Mongolia. I'd traveled the world with my modeling career, but that had been to high-fashion destinations—New York, Paris, Milan, Sydney, Singapore, Rio de Janeiro. Now I was exploring remote, nature-rich destinations. I should feel privileged.

We trudged on. My breath fluttered around my face, the warm air crystalizing. For a long time, we walked in silence with only the sound of our boots crunching through the snow.

George heard an eagle owl and pointed it out as it flew silently—to my ears at least—alongside us for a few seconds. It's grace and beauty took my breath away, as did its size.

We walked through the trees, huge blocks of snow crashing down from the boughs whenever the wind blew. They landed with dull thuds, seeming to send a tremble through the earth.

Despite my face, hands, and toes being cool, my core was warm, and I was happy to keep on going. Which was just as well, because the vampires were stomping along at a good pace. Getting to the railway track quickly was clearly their priority.

Patrick's energy was still revved up, and he shot between the trees from time to time before coming back.

"Would you stop that," Oscar said. "It's making me nervous."

"We're going so slow." Patrick moaned.

"Rhys?" George raised his eyebrows at Rhys. "Do something."

"Yeah, okay." Rhys grabbed Patrick's hand, linking their fingers. "Stick with me, okay."

Patrick hesitated. "Sure, whatever."

They fell into step just in front of me. I enjoyed seeing their connection. Rhys had had to come to terms with no longer being the youngest in the group, but also with responsibility. He'd done it, though, admirably.

And damn, they were hot together. I wondered what fun we could all have in the cave, when it was warm enough to be naked for a length of time. Complete privacy, hot guys I loved. It could be the recipe for the best vacation yet—when we got there.

"Are you sure we're going the right way?" Patrick asked.

"Why would you think we're not?" George stopped and faced him.

"Because you said we had to go south, and we're going west, have been for about ten minutes."

George frowned and pulled out his pocket watch.

"How they heck do you know?" Oscar said. "It's dark."

"The moss on these birches." Patrick released Rhys and smoothed his hand over a dull patch of moss running down the length of a tree. "It grows on the north side of trunks, where the sun doesn't shine." He nodded in the direction they were walking. "Which means we're going west."

"He's right. We are." George slipped his watch away. "Come on, we'll adjust our direction."

Patrick grinned at Rhys and took his hand again.

"Clever dick." Rhys chuckled.

"Shit, look." Lloyd stopped and pointed at the ground.

"What?" My question had been unnecessary. The moment I saw wolf tracks in the small clearing, I recognized them.

"For the love of Benedict, there's so many." George spun around. "Everywhere."

"This is one seriously big pack." Oscar kicked at the prints, as though that might destroy the creatures who'd created them. "I've never..."

"Seen so many." Lloyd peered into the darkness.

Squat firs surrounded us, snow stuck to their branches in big frozen clouds. The light of the waxing moon highlighted their tips, but beneath them the shadows were black and ominous.

I shuddered, not from cold but from the thought of flashing canine eyes watching us.

"I can smell them." Lloyd stepped closer to me, his hoody brushing my shoulder.

"You can?" I gulped.

Rhys nodded. "Yeah, me, too."

"Fuck." Oscar paced to the right and studied the tracks heading beneath a particularly large tree. "They went in every direction from here and—"

"Sh!" George held up his hand.

"What?" Patrick said, his red eyes wide.

Oscar silenced him with a look.

George spun around, then back again. "They're..."

I tried to see into the blackness. My heart was thudding. I was sure I could smell wolf now—a thick, meaty, wet-dog scent.

"They're all around us..." George finished, backing up so he was standing directly in front of me.

Lloyd slid his arm around my waist.

Oscar, Patrick, and Rhys moved in until I was shielded from the forest and whatever lurked there.

To my left a tree shivered, snow skittering from it like icing sugar.

"We'll have to kill them," Lloyd said. "All of them."

"It depends how many they are." Oscar's voice was tense.

"And whether or not they're Carlton Pack," George said.

"Yeah." Rhys set his hand on my shoulder. "If they're Carlton Pack, we're up shit creek without a paddle."

"Would ordinary wolves close in on us like this?" I asked, biting back the fear on my tongue. It tasted acidic and bitter.

A shadow spread ahead of me, slow and stealthy, stalking over the snow.

"No, Darius," George said gruffly. "Ordinary wolves would steer well clear of vampire scent."

"Then we know what we're dealing with." As I'd spoken, big, thickly set wolves, more than I could count, emerged from the shadows. Their coats were black, their skulls huge and their jaws powerful. But it was their growling mouths, bared teeth, and flashing yellow eyes that chilled me the most.

There was no doubt they were on the hunt, the low growling that hummed through the air evidence of that.

"Let us pass," George said. "We don't want trouble."

A massive wolf, its shoulders at least as tall as my hips, broke away from the pack. He glared unblinking at George and came closer still. Saliva dripped from his mouth, and his growl vibrated into my chest.

"We're here on official business of The Ancient Order." George tilted his chin. "We are of no concern to you."

The wolf moved its weight onto its back legs then rose so it was standing on two legs. Its fur shimmered, as if sprinkled with diamonds then began to fade away. In its place was pale skin. The face changed, the muzzle, teeth, and pink gums retracting into a square-jawed human face.

"Jesus, what the...?" I gaped at the sight before me. Yes, Oscar had told me about shape-shifting creatures, but hearing about them and seeing them were two different things.

What had been a wolf was now a man—a tall, naked man with shaggy black hair, a dense beard, and muscles that would put a weightlifter to shame.

"You're trespassing." The shifter's voice was a deep growl.

"Get out of our way before I fucking make you," Lloyd said, baring his gums but not his fangs. He sucked in air, grimacing, as if the taste of dog lacing it made him feel sick.

"Lloyd, don't..." George said with a small shake of his head. He turned back to the shifter. "Not trespassing, just passing." He nodded ahead. "Let us be on our way. As I said, we don't want trouble."

"Who have you got there?" The shifter took a step closer and pointed at me.

I glared at him. If he was the enemy of my lovers, he was also *my* enemy.

"Someone we're protecting on instruction from The London Order. Master Concorde himself, to be precise."

"I have no care for your order or for Concorde. You dirty vampires are the scourge of the earth." He clicked his fingers at several wolves standing behind him. "Shift. Let's rid Siberia of this plague."

Chapter Eighteen

Darius

"No!" I gasped, gripping George's jacket through my gloves. "Let us carry on with our journey."

My words didn't resonate.

To my left and right, more wolves changed into big, strong, naked men. Each sported a bedraggled beard and long hair. They were all roped with muscle.

"We should run," Patrick said. "Get the heck out of here."

"We won't get past them," Rhys said. "There's too many, and if they get us to the ground, they'll rip our limbs off and our heads."

"Fuck." I thought of Patrick, a new shot of fear piercing my heart. He hadn't drunk from me at midnight equinox. If he were killed now, he'd be destined for an eternity of damnation burning in Hell. "We should do what they say."

Lloyd looked between me and Patrick. "Yeah, we'll make our move when the risk isn't so great."

"That plan...doesn't suit me." Oscar stepped to one side, swinging his right fist and baring his fangs. His knuckles connected with a shifter, sending him reeling.

But before Oscar could get another hit in, five shifter men were on him and they were all tumbling to the ground. Snow puffed up around them, arms and legs tangled. The loud grunts shook the air and in turn the trees, toppling more snow downward.

"Oscar!" I shouted, lunging forward.

George and Lloyd grabbed me, pulling me from the rolling tumble of bodies. But then they were dragged off me, more shifters, a blur of them, an army it seemed, surrounding us all, tearing us apart.

Patrick's face melted into a sea of them, then was gone, the same happened to Rhys.

Lloyd was fighting, but only for a moment, then he threw his head back and a long, gurgling yell tore from his throat.

To my left, George slumped to the ground, as if the energy had been sucked from him.

"No, please, we mean you no harm." I lunged forward, was jostled to the left.

A huge guy with dark eyes and frost hanging in his beard grabbed my wrists and snapped handcuffs on me.

"What?" I yanked my arms apart, or tried to. The cuffs were old-fashioned style, two chain links. The flat part on the left side had a keyhole. They were silver.

Silver.

No wonder my vampires had succumbed. They'd been shackled with the one thing that caused them pain.

"Don't do this." I tried to push through the bare bodies to where Lloyd was hunched over. "Lloyd. Lloyd."

My heart was breaking. Terror heated my veins. My shoulders, arms, and hands tingled. Fire was building.

"You." The lead shifter clasped my shoulder and held me firm. "You are not a vampire." He scowled at my hands.

"Get off me. You have no right." I shook him off.

"I have every right. This is my land...our land. You were not invited."

"We're leaving. Let these men go, let us be on our way."

"Men. Ha! These aren't men, they're bloodsuckers, they have no morals, no heart. Our mission is to rid the world of them."

"You can't say that or do that." I felt for the cross that hung around my neck. It was beneath many layers of warm clothes, but still, it was there. "I'm sure there are some vampires around who are not altogether...wholesome, but these are good vampires who try their best to do no harm. If anything, they—"

"I have no interest in their non-lives." He leaned closer, his lips peeling back into a snarl. "Or your opinion." He kind of growled, then stepped back and jerked his head to the left. "Get them. We'll go to Sunezh and present to the council."

"Sunezh?" I said. "Where the fuck is that?"

"You'll see soon enough." He turned his back on me, dropped forward, and shifted back into a wolf.

It was the strangest sight, to see flesh turn to fur and a tail to appear.

"Go."

A shove to my back had me stumbling forward. Frantically, I searched out my vampires.

They were being hoisted to their feet, their heads lolling and shoulders hunched. It was clear the pain was all-consuming and took away their strength to even stand unaided.

How did we get in this mess?

Why didn't they fight more?

Oscar was groaning. He also had a silver collar in place. His attempt at fighting and his sheer size had earned him that.

My eyelids stung; tears were threatening. But I forced them not to fall. They'd only freeze.

I had no choice but to trudge after the lead shifter. All around me were wolves—huge, scary wolves with piercing eyes and big teeth.

The cold of Siberia was dangerous, but these creatures were more so.

We went west. I knew that now because of the direction the moss grew on the trees.

There was no rail track, no sign of human habitation. It struck me that nothing around me was human, not the wolves, the vampires. The forest was wild. Nature ruled here.

I became hungry and thirsty as the night drew on. But there was no stopping, no rest break. The lead wolf continued to trudge forward, through valleys, over small mountains, and around a dense forest. A vast lake stretched to our right at one point, and blue-green-yellow northern lights danced on the horizon, silk scarves wafting in a breeze.

My concern was growing for my vampires. I knew silver wouldn't kill them, but knowing how they were suffering was like a knife stabbing at me over and over.

Eventually, we came to the edge of a fir forest and onto a vast plateau. In the far distance, a crook of blue seawater carved into the land, waves crashing against the shore. To the south a bald eagle perched on a tree; its branches had come off worst in a battle with a lightning strike.

The wolves stopped, the air filling with their warm, doggy breath. Silence enveloped us.

Before us was what appeared to be a town of low wooden cabins set amongst the rough, rocky terrain. Most of the buildings had smoke swirling from chimneys, and a few structures appeared to be larger, like barns. Through the white morning haze, people and wolves moved about, charcoal-hued and stooped, figures from a Lowry painting.

I guessed it was Sunezh.

Part of me was relieved the long, cold trek was over, but equally a new terror had set in. What did they have planned for us? One thing I knew for sure, it wouldn't be coffee and cake.

We headed down the slight incline to the bleak town. I surveyed my surroundings, wondering if we'd be able to make a run for it should the opportunity arise.

When we reached the outskirts, the lead shifter, who I'd been behind the whole time, reared up and turned back into his human form.

"Take them to the Rasputin building." He gestured behind himself. "Lock them in, then everyone get some rest. It has been a busy night, and with our new captives, we have decisions to make."

His words sent a shiver up my spine. What the heck did he mean by decisions—decisions on how to kill us?

We were taken to a skinned-log cabin with snowdrifts climbing up its walls and icicles reaching down from its roof. The one window was black. No smoke rose from its chimney, and it seemed to have squatted into its forlornness.

The door was opened, revealing darkness inside.

"Get in," I was told, the instruction accompanied with a shove on my shoulder.

I stepped in, my footsteps echoing. There was no furniture, though through the dim light it was apparent a fire was ready to be lit, and a basket of logs sat next to it. The walls were roughly hewn planks strewn in shadows, and the window had a net curtain made of cobwebs.

The five thuds of my vampires being slung into the cabin sickened me.

I rushed to help Rhys as he was the closest. My emotions caught in my throat as I lifted his head the best I could with my cuffs on.

His features were twisted in pain, his fangs on show. His hair was messy, and his eyes squeezed closed.

"Rhys."

"Get...it...off."

"Yes...yes..." I gently lay his head on the floor again and then tugged at his cuffs. "I will."

He cried out.

"Shit. I'm sorry." I stared at them. Like mine, they were solid, and without a key, there was nothing I could do.

The cabin door slammed shut. A bolt slid into place, the sound disturbingly final.

I shivered. Despite being in the right clothes, I'd been in sub-zero temperatures for a long time with no food and drink.

"Darius," George mumbled. "Eat something." He'd dragged himself to the side of the room and slumped against the wall.

"George." I rushed to him, examined his cuffs, too. "What can I do to help you?"

He opened his eyes; they were full of pain. "Stay alive."

"Yes...but..."

"No buts." He nodded at the fire. "Light that and eat."

"Yes, okay, I'll just..." I crawled over to Oscar. He was flat on his back, clearly unconscious.

"Shit, shit, shit..." I hovered my hands over him. Seeing big, tough Oscar so debilitated was horrendous. I studied the collar. It was like the one Patrick had worn—silver with a small amount of leather.

But then I saw it; there was no lock, just a buckle.

"Wait, hang on..." I reached for the leather strap. "I can get this off."

Oscar didn't move while I undid it.

But the moment it was off, his eyes pinged open. "Darius."

"It's off." I slung the offending item into a dusty, dark corner.

"Thank you." He pulled in a deep breath then winced and slowly raised his arms to look at the cuffs. "Bastards."

"Yes, they are. But that's better without the collar, yes?"

"It is." He closed his eyes and rested his hands on his belly again. "Thanks, babe."

Next I went to Lloyd. He was facedown with his arms beneath him. "Lloyd, are you okay?"

Of course he isn't.

I rolled him onto his back.

He groaned, his face twisting in pain.

"I'm sorry, I'm so sorry," I said, setting a kiss on his lips.

"Not...your...fault," he whispered.

"I'll get the cuffs off, as soon as I figure out how."

"Do what George said: light the fire, eat."

"I will." I sat back onto my heels, hands on my thighs.

Patrick was sitting against the wall, back rod straight, staring ahead unblinking.

"Patrick." I half crawled, half scurried to him.

"I...hate...silver..." He'd spoken through clenched teeth.

"I know." I stroked his hair. "I know you do."

"You've got to get it off...off all of us."

"I will."

"Damn these wolves." He moved his eyes to look at the door; his head stayed still. "Damn them to Hell."

His words sent a shiver up my spine and over my scalp. "I'll figure it out."

I kissed his brow then stood.

"The fire..." George muttered. "You need heat."

Luckily, the desperate situation had turned my insides to fire. And now the long, cold walk through the tundra had come to an end, my adrenaline had nowhere to go. Instead, it turned into a new type of energy, heat. My chest was broiling with it, my shoulders, neck, and arms picking up temperature.

As I walked to the fireplace, staring at the logs and kindling, the blistering pain of flames seared down my arms to my fingertips. There were sparks there, lots of them.

I grimaced, removed my gloves, and angled my splayed fingers at the stack of wood. I needed to get rid of the sparks. They'd reached the point they were too painful to hold in.

The shower of light fizzed onto the logs, flashing and illuminating the room.

Several pieces of kindling caught, and within seconds were producing small orange flames.

I kept on going, letting the pain and heat flow from me. Each passing second was a relief.

By the time I'd finished, the fire had caught, and flames licked upward. The room took on an amber hue, and shadows crept over the floor.

I blew out a breath and dropped my hands. The cuffs were a hindrance, but at least they hadn't prevented me from sparking.

"Eat now..." George muttered.

The backpack was beside Rhys, so I pulled it open. Inside was sustenance for me. I was grateful the wolves hadn't taken it from Rhys. I knew I needed to eat, even if the vampires didn't.

Maybe that's exactly what they need.

"George." I cupped his chin. "Do you want to feed from me?"

"No, not now. You...first...eat."

"Okay, but after I've eaten?"

He nodded. "Maybe...if you're feeling...strong enough."

"I will be."

I unwrapped a sandwich filled with venison and pickles and munched it. I then ate an apple and half a bag of nuts and seeds. There were several cartons of orange juice, so I pierced one with a straw and stood by the fire, drinking it. All I was doing was refueling, filling myself up so I could care for my vampires.

Staring into the flames, I tried to get my thoughts straight. It was clear I was the only one who could think properly. Pain had rendered my usually strong lovers weak.

I have to get their cuffs off.

We have to get out of here before the wolves kill us.

But how in the name of God was I going to do that? And would He help me if there was a way?

Chapter Nineteen

Darius

I didn't feed the vampires after I'd eaten. George had managed, in a quiet, strained voice, to tell me to save my blood for when they'd need it most.

I had no idea when that would be but was happy to take his advice. It was what I was used to. George always had a handle on things. It was the way he operated. Seeing him incapacitated was more disturbing than I wanted to admit.

Weariness had come over me as I'd stared out of the window, then paced between it, the door, and the fire. After a few hours I'd curled up on the floor, in front of the flames and fallen asleep.

When I woke, the stark white light of midday was angling through the glass to land on my eyelids. It blinded me when I opened my eyes, and quickly, I turned away.

"Darius," Lloyd whispered. "They will...come for you...soon."

"What?" I stood. "How do you know?"

"I'm guessing, but it's an educated one."

"Why just me?"

"Because you're different," Oscar said. "They'll want...to know why."

"But see if you can...figure a way out..." Rhys raised his head and looked at me, the action of doing so seeming to take all of his energy.

"Of course I will." I crawled over to him and rested my hands over his face. It would have been nice to have woken up and it had all been a dream, this being taken prisoner business. "I'll figure it out, don't you worry." I brushed my lips over his.

The door burst open, bringing with it an icy blast.

"Get up," a bearded man, not naked this time, barked at me. "You!"

I sat back on my heels and glared up at him. Who the fuck did he think he was?

"Now."

I had no choice but to stand as two of his companions gripped my biceps and dragged me to my feet.

Each of my vampires grunted, as though in complaint, as if trying to come to my rescue. But it was no good. The silver was very efficient.

"It'll be okay," I said. "I'll be back soon."

My captors tugged me to the door. My heavy boots dragged on the floor, and I stumbled. But I didn't fall. Their hold on me was too tight.

It was snowing, but not much. The tiny flakes were dancing in the air and in no hurry to land.

We made our way between cabins, and I had a good look at my surroundings. Now it was proper daylight, it was easier to get my bearings.

The sprawl of cabins seemed to stretch on indefinitely, peppering into the tree line. This was a huge community; no wonder we'd been so outnumbered in the forest.

Wolves strolled around—black, gray, and a few brown. They were all huge. They all eyed me with suspicion.

But there were also humans dressed for the cold weather. I guessed they could shift when they wanted to and wear nothing but fur.

We passed what seemed to be smoking huts that smelled of fish, then a barn full of bleating goats.

Finally, we arrived at an extra-large cabin with a low roof and double doors.

The wooden doors were opened, and I was ushered inside. For a moment, I paused to let my eyes adjust to the dim light.

Fires were lit on huge iron plates that hung on chains from the ceiling. Both wolves and people stood around, their attention on me.

At the far end of the room was a huge chair, the back of which appeared to be made of long white bones. In it sat the shifter we'd met the night before, the one with the massive black beard and mean eyes.

"Bring him here." He banged his hands on the arms of his chair. Or was it a throne?

"Yes, Siros."

Again, I was shoved forward. A few people stepped out of my way as if wary of me.

When I was ten feet from him—Siros, I presumed—I was released from my cuffs.

I tipped my chin and sucked in a breath. The scent of old dog blankets that needed a wash had my stomach roiling.

"What is your name?"

"Why should I tell you?" I replied in my best defiant tone.

"Because I will chop off your head if you do not."

That seemed like a good enough reason. "Darius Linnet."

A wolf approached me, a sleek, pure-white creature with startling blue eyes. He sniffed my leg and then my hand, his nose damp on my skin.

I resisted recoiling. I didn't want to show weakness.

"Do you agree?" Siros raised his eyebrows at the wolf.

It bobbed his head, as if nodding.

Siros stood and glared at me. "Now I know your name, I will ask you *what* you are?"

"What do you mean?" I glanced at the quizzical faces around me. Some had apprehension in their eyes, I didn't know why.

"Exactly what I said." His voice was loud and gruff. He was clearly a man who was used to getting what he wanted and being obeyed. "What are you?"

"I'm from the UK. British."

"That is your nationality, not your species."

"My species?"

He stamped his foot on the floor, shaking a stacked table nearby, the crockery clattering. "You know what I mean. Now speak the truth before we get it out of you by other means. Means you will not enjoy."

"I'm sorry but I don't understand. My species, I'm a man, human."

"You are not entirely human." Siros glared at me. "There is something else in you, we can smell it. Every single one of us."

"You can smell it?" I raised my hand and sniffed my knuckles. I smelled how I always did. Well, a shower wouldn't go amiss, but I wasn't too stinky.

"Yes." He stepped closer, towering over me. "We can smell human and…" He paused. "Something dark, dangerous…evil."

"Ahh." Now I got him. "You can smell…"

Demon. Shit, should I admit that here? That might get my head chopped off pretty swiftly.

"Tell me."

I sensed I had to give him something. "I…I have an unusual heritage, it's true."

"Unusual, as in…" He sneered. "You might as well tell me, because I'll get it out of you, even if it costs you your life."

Clearly, I had no choice. "My father was an incubus. He seduced my mother. He made her believe he was the man of her dreams."

"An incubus." He stroked his beard, tugging it to a point. "You mean a demon."

"I guess." I pulled a face. "You know what they say, you can choose your friends but not your family."

"Which brings me to my next question."

I waited for him to go on.

"Why, Darius Linnet, half human, half demon, are you hanging around with filthy vampires?"

"Firstly, they're not filthy."

"We'll have to agree to disagree."

Fair enough. "And I'm with them because they helped me destroy my father."

"You destroyed your father? A demon." He glanced at the albino wolf then returned his attention to me. "I can understand why you would want to, but I don't believe you. Demons are not easy to kill, not by any stretch of the imagination."

"It's true, I killed him, and it's no odds to me what you believe."

"How did you destroy this demon?" another man, with a thick ginger moustache and a hood drawn up so it shaded his face, asked.

"He was trying to possess me, use my body for his own evil plans while my soul rotted in Hell. It won't surprise you to know I didn't fancy that fate."

"How did you know this?" Siros asked. "That he was trying to possess you?"

"The vampires told me."

He laughed. "And you believed them?"

"What they said made sense. I'd been having strange dreams about my father, not that I knew at the time it was him. And then he was getting closer to me in daylight hours, too, stalking me, his presence beginning to build in menace." I paused and unzipped my jacket. I reached beneath my sweater and tugged out my cross.

Siros folded his arms and stared at it. It was clear I had his—and everyone around me—complete attention.

"My demon father had no respect for my belief in God," I went on, "something my mother instilled in me. She's a good, kind woman and brought me up to do no harm and respect others. Killing my father didn't come easy, but I had no choice."

"I'll ask you again: How did you do it?"

"With the vampires' help." I pulled in a breath and tried to stay calm. Knowing they were suffering hurt the very core of me. "They helped me, protected me, and when the time came, they finished the job off so there was minimal collateral damage. So you see"—I slipped my cross away and held out my hands, palms up—"we're not bad people. We're simply passing through. We did the world a great favor by getting rid of an evil demon who had untold powers and planned to wreak havoc across many continents for many years."

Siros was silent. He folded his arms and rocked back on his heels.

The white wolf reared upward. Its fur slid into nothingness, and in its place, skin appeared, very pale skin, almost translucent, the blue-hued veins beneath the surface visible. The wolf face distorted, retracted, then formed human features. A long, straight nose, wide pink lips, and light-blue eyes with white lashes.

"He's telling the truth." The tall, white man stepped up to me.

We were the same height, just over six feet, and similar build.

"Why would I lie?" I said. "And who the heck could make that kind of shit up?"

His lips curled, almost a smile.

"So what shall we do with him?" someone asked to my right. A female muffled up in furs against the cold.

Siros was quiet.

So was the man standing before me.

"Let us go," I said, filling the void. "We mean you no harm. We are simply getting out of Siberia and off your territory, which we didn't know this was, by the way." I paused, wondering if I was making a good case. I didn't know but kept on trying. "We destroyed a demon, probably saved untold lives and countless suffering by doing so. We want to live a quiet life, together."

"You do know," the albino said, "that vampires are not truly alive, they just exist."

"Isn't that what we all do? Exist?"

"They have dead, black hearts Their only goal is to drink blood and fornicate." He raised his pale eyebrows.

"Their hearts might not be physically like ours, but I can assure you they're not dead." I paused. "And as for drinking blood and fornicating, you like meat, and I'd bet good money everyone here enjoys sex."

There were a few mutterings in the crowd. The woman huddled in furs gasped.

"Live and let live," I said, stepping around the albino so I could see Siros more clearly. "The god I was brought up to follow says do no harm. What good could come from you harming us or keeping us captive like this?"

"What good." Siros laughed, but it was without humor. "I'll tell you what good."

I waited.

"Disposing of you all would rid the world of vampires and a half demon. And not even you, Darius Linnet, with your cross and your god can convince me that would be a bad thing."

"What...what are you saying?" A thread of unease grew in me. It tugged and tugged until it was a tightly knotted rope in my belly.

"I'm saying"—he tilted his chin—"the night after full moon you will all be staked through the heart then decapitated."

"What?" I hadn't heard him right. Surely.

"Heart." He tapped his chest. "Head." He made a slitting motion around his neck. "It is the only way to be sure a vampire is dead."

I was going to be sick. My ears buzzed, and the foul taste of terror filled my mouth, thickening my saliva.

"And then your bodies burned on a pyre of birch." He punched the air with his fist. "And we will have honored our gods by performing this great service."

A cheer went up.

"Take him away. Take this demon from my sight."

The yelling got louder. Whoops and whistles mixed with barks and howls.

"No, no..." I was hauled outside, my eyes watering. This couldn't be happening. This wasn't right, it wasn't just. I needed humans, human law, the police, the British Embassy.

How can they get away with this? With killing us?

I struggled against the huge hands holding me. Twisted and turned. I had no idea what I'd do if I escaped. There was no way I would leave my vampires here to suffer such an awful fate. But I couldn't do nothing, so some kind of survival instinct kicked in.

"Get off me. Let me go."

"Be quiet." I was yanked to the left and dragged back past the barn of goats then the smoking sheds.

Two men and one wolf accompanied me. As we approached the cabin George, Lloyd, Rhys, Oscar, and Patrick where holed up in, I stopped struggling. This wasn't the way to escape my situation. Even if I broke free, where would I go? The harsh landscape was as effective as prison bars.

I was drawn to a halt beneath the small overhang outside the door. A crescent moon had been carved into the wood.

The two burly men holding me released my arms and set their attention on the wolf. He was sleek and dark, his fur shined with health, and his eyes held intelligence.

He bobbed his head as though nodding.

The two men left, their boots thudding on the ground.

And then the wolf shifted. He stretched upward, standing tall, and his gleaming fur changed into dark-olive skin. He was clean-shaven, his cheekbones high, his lips plump, and his face...beautiful.

I stared at him, an avalanche of recognition tumbling through my mind. "Nicoli?"

Chapter Twenty

Darius

"Shh, Darius." Nicoli glanced around. "Do not make it seem as if we know one another."

"What the fuck are you doing here?" I asked. The last time I'd seen this man we'd been on a catwalk in Milan. It had been his first big gig, and he'd been nervous. I'd given him a cigarette and attempted to lighten his mood and boost his confidence as we'd chatted on a fire escape.

"I could ask you the same thing." He jerked his head at the door. "And what the hell are you're doing with them?"

"But I mean...you're a shifter?"

"The secret is out, but so is yours, Darius." He released a misty breath. "Demon father, huh."

"*Dead* demon father."

He looked over his shoulder.

I did the same.

"I shouldn't be talking to you like this," he said.

"So why are you?"

"You were kind to me, in Milan."

I shrugged. "I was only doing what anyone would do. You were nervous."

"I was nervous." He paused. "Because some of the other guys, from Head Talk Agency, had been taking the piss out of me, winding me up. They knew it was my first time for Valentino and were determined to make sure it wasn't a fun experience."

"Damn, I hate those blokes."

"Me, too. Shit, I have to get you in here." He opened the door. "In."

"But…" My elation at seeing a familiar face vanished. "Nicoli, please…I mean…can you help us? We're in quite a fucking predicament, in case you hadn't noticed."

"I can't set your vampires free if that's what you're asking. It goes against everything I believe in. But you, Darius"—he hesitated and swallowed—"are a good man, I know that in my heart, and the last thing I want is to see you hurt."

"So please." I was begging; I didn't care. "Help me to help them. We just want to get out of here and be on our way. We never wanted any trouble." I bit back the emotion. "And I certainly don't want my lovers to be staked and beheaded."

"Your lovers?"

"Is that so hard to believe?"

"I never even knew you were gay." A smile tugged his lips. "I'd have asked you out if I'd known."

Despite my perilous situation, a sharp giggle, a small explosion of emotion, burst from me. "Seriously."

"Yeah, you're hot." He winked, then glanced in the direction we'd come. "Listen, Siros said he'd…you know"—he slashed his finger across his neck—"you all tomorrow night. That's because tonight there's a big ceremony to celebrate the full moon. The town will be practically empty; everyone is heading north to a coastal cove where legend had it the moon rose from at the dawn of time."

"Okay?"

"And I'm supposed to bolt this door." He nodded at the thick bolt. "I offered to take the task on as soon as I saw you last night, in the forest."

"You were there?"

"Yes. I'd been out running with the pack when we picked up vampire scent." He smiled. "I have to say, I thought there was something familiar mixed in with it. Hadn't pinpointed it was you until I saw you, though."

"This is a lot to take in...you're a wolf shifter."

"Yeah, and you fuck vampires."

"I can't deny that."

He shuddered. "Personally, I can't think of anything worse."

"That's okay, I'd imagine they'd feel the same way about going to bed with you."

Again, he checked the surroundings.

We were alone.

He cupped my cheek and lowered his face. "It's not so bad here, Darius. You could stay, with me. I could explain to Siros and—"

"No." The thought horrified me. I was itching to get out of Sunezh—I needed to leave the way I needed to take my next breath.

He sighed. "Ah well. It was worth a mention." He stepped back. "I'm afraid I don't have the key to those cuffs, but I've heard they can be picked if you have enough stamina and a pin."

"I don't have a—"

A steel paperclip spun in the air before me. I caught it.

"Thanks."

"I'm denying everything if you get caught."

"I don't blame you."

He pulled the door closed. This time there was no slide of metal on metal.

"Thank you," I said to the wood. "Nicoli."

"Darius," Patrick's hoarse voice came from the corner.

"It's okay." I looked between them all. Usually so vibrant, strong, and fiercely protective, to see them this way broke me.

But at least I had a plan. If I could unpick their locks after nightfall, we could make a run for it when the wolves were at their lake.

I twirled the paperclip between my thumb and index finger. I'd never even attempted to pick a lock. I'd seen it on the movies, sure, and it seemed simple enough. But nothing was ever really like the movies.

And whose lock to pick first?

My attention landed on Patrick again. He was a loose cannon, but I had a feeling if I freed him, his Special Forces skills would come in handy.

I dropped down beside him. "I'm going to try and get these off."

"Aye, do that." His chest sagged, as though breathing out the last of his breath.

"Fuck," I muttered, unfurling the paperclip then stabbing at the hole.

"No," he said. "Put the tip inside…then bend it so it's a hook."

"Yes, okay." Thank goodness, he was with it enough to help me.

I did as he'd instructed, creating an angle at the end of the clip.

"That's it," he mumbled. "Now it's the shape of the key…almost."

"It is?" I frowned at it.

"Aye… Now put it in again…" He grimaced. "And feel for the wee latch."

"Latch?" I had no idea what I was feeling for but shoved the metal hook into the keyhole.

"It's there, just poke it, then turn the paperclip." He raised his head, dropped his crown to the wall with a thud, and groaned. My fiddling with the cuffs was causing him pain, creating burning in his vampire skin.

"Shit, I can't do it."

"Aye…you can."

I had no idea what I was doing and prodded and poked, frustration building. My hand shook; sweat popped on my brow despite the now cold room. The world spiraled down into a single circle of metal. I tried to stay calm. All I heard was the beating of my own heart and my shallow breaths.

Then, suddenly there was a sweet little click, and the tension went from the cuffs. I pulled them, and they opened, sliding away from Patrick's wrists.

In a flash, he was up on his feet, eyes glinting, fists clenched. His fangs slid down, and he let out a strange snarl.

Fuck. I'd made a mistake releasing him first.

"Patrick." I jumped up. "We need to release the others."

"Help us," Rhys murmured.

George, Lloyd, and Oscar were watching, their gazes misty, but with it enough to know something was happening.

"Patrick!" I said again. I was frozen to the spot. What the hell was he going to do next?

He stepped up to me fast and gripped my upper arms.

I stared at his fangs, at his wild red eyes. Another shot of fear infused my bloodstream.

"Darius," he said, his voice low and rough. "You did it."

"Yes." I nodded. "And now the others. We're a team, Patrick. We have to help them."

He stared at me, my words seeming to need time to sink in. His fangs slid away, and I took that as a good sign.

The next thing I knew, his mouth was over mine and he was kissing me wildly and with heated passion.

A thrill went through me, despite our circumstances.

He circled his arms around my body, dragging me close to his cool, hard, muscled torso.

I groaned, tension leaving me, the tension that had been simmering between us. It was all okay, he wanted me, the way I wanted him.

His tongue swept over mine, and I chased for it.

And then he pulled back, a smile spreading. "We have to unlock the others."

"Yes." I was a little breathless.

He snatched the paperclip from me then darted to Rhys.

Within seconds, his cuffs were off, and he was on his feet. "Fucking hell." He smoothed his hand over his hair. "If I never encounter bloody silver again, it will be too soon."

"Are you okay?" Patrick slid his hand around the back of Rhys's neck and cupped his nape.

"Yes. Help George, Lloyd, and Oscar."

"On it." He stooped beside George, and within seconds, George was also free.

"Thank you, Officer." George stood and dusted himself down, tilted his chin, and drew in a breath. "And well done, Darius. Clearly you missed your vocation as a petty criminal breaking and entering."

I laughed, relieved that my vampires were back.

Oscar stood next, frowning at the door. "I should go and rip the head off every damn wolf here."

"That would take a long time," I said. "There's hundreds, maybe thousands."

He grunted and took my hands. "Did they hurt you?"

"No, not at all." A tremble shook my belly. I'd have to tell them what was in store if we stayed—stakes and decapitation.

Lloyd was the last to have his cuffs removed, and he kicked them into the dying embers of the fire. "Bastards."

"We need to get out of here," I said. "Soon."

"Too damn right we do," Rhys said.

"But how?" Lloyd adjusted his hood and stepped up to the window. He peered through the cobwebs. "I'm guessing we're being guarded."

"Not very well," I said. "And..."

"And what?" George asked, tipping his head.

"And it just so happens I have a friend out there?"

"What?" That seemed to capture Patrick's attention. "An ally?"

"Yes, seems so. A guy I worked with in Milan, a model. Had no idea he was a shifter, and he had no idea about me, but then why would he? Seems I'd been a big help when he was particularly nervous before a catwalk and..." I paused, knowing I was waffling. "And anyway, I reckon he feels he owes me one, hence the paperclip."

"He gave you that?" Patrick said.

"Yes, on the way back to the cabin."

"Good of him." Patrick nodded.

Lloyd turned. "I say we break down the door and get out of here. We'll have to run."

"Wait," I said.

"For what? For them to kill us?" Lloyd frowned.

"My friend, Nicoli, he told me the town will be deserted later. The wolves are going to the coast to worship the moon or something."

"Ah." George nodded. "Of course, it's full moon."

"Never did get the wolf obsession with the moon," Oscar muttered.

"So if we wait just a little while longer, we'll have a really good head start before anyone even knows we're gone."

"They couldn't catch us anyway, not if we're running." Rhys folded his arms.

George was quiet for a moment. "And we'll have to run." He glowered at Patrick. "It's more risky to try and walk out of here than it is to have him as a loose cannon. We'll have to take our chances with Patrick running with us, or *away* from us."

"I am *not* a loose cannon." Patrick set his hands on his hips. He had the whole mean-killing-machine look going on. If anyone had ever given off loose cannon vibes, it was Patrick in this moment.

I suppressed a flutter of interest and beat down the need to get to know more. His kiss had left me curious. Turned out the whole rough-and-ready soldier thing really did it for me.

What would he be like to fuck?

"I beg to differ," George said. "You, Patrick, are one big liability."

Patrick's drooping mouth tugged my heartstrings, as did the flash of pain in his eyes.

Rhys must have seen it, too, because he took Patrick's hand and stepped close, so their shoulders touched.

"We'll head south, to Mongolia, your cave," Oscar said, stooping and redoing the laces on his chunky biker boots. "How long do you think it will take?"

"A few hours running. I vote you carry Darius, Oscar."

"Exactly what I was planning on doing." Oscar stood. "And you, Rhys. Keep hold of his hand. It might be the only way to stop him ending up in Timbuktu."

"I have no desire to go to Timbuktu," Patrick muttered.

I stepped up to him and cupped his cheek, aware of the others watching me. "Can you make me a promise?" I asked quietly.

He nodded then licked his lips, leaving a soft sheen on the bottom one.

"Stick with Rhys, don't go anywhere on your own." I paused. "I want to see you at the cave, Patrick. You're important to me, you're important to all of us."

I wanted more than to see him, I wanted him full stop. And I wanted him to truly become one of mine, part of my harem. I hoped he could see that in my eyes. It was a truth now, the way it was going to be between us.

"Go to the cave with Rhys," I said in the same gentle voice. "The only way you can get through this is by being with people who care about you..." I hesitated. "People who love you."

He swallowed, his throat moving. "Aye." He glanced at Rhys then back to me. "I can promise you that, Darius."

"Good." I tipped forward and swept my lips over his. "I'll see you there."

Chapter Twenty-One

Rhys

We could have smashed down the door to our cabin-prison now our silver shackles had gone, but it was quieter and easier to simply open it.

Lloyd did just that.

Outside, twilight had stolen the day and bruised the sky purple, lilac, and pink. It wasn't snowing, but a carpet of freezing fog glistened around our feet the way fake smoke might at a disco.

"This way," George said, slipping to the right, toward the nearest tree line. His shoes crunched on the packed snow. "You ready, Rhys?"

"Yes." I gripped Patrick's hand tighter. All the demons in Hell couldn't make me let go. Where he went, I went. We would be as one. It was how it had to be.

Darius stepped out. Unlike us, his breath hung in the air, sparkling and catching the weak light. "You okay?" I asked.

"I'll be better when we get out of here." He paused and glanced about, his eyebrows pulled together. "The wolves didn't have a nice day planned for us tomorrow."

"What did they say, when they took you?" Oscar asked, standing directly in front of Darius, arms out at his sides, as if waiting for Darius to leap onto him.

"It doesn't bear repeating." Darius shivered. "Let's just get going while the coast is clear."

"I agree." Lloyd pulled the door of the cabin closed. "This place stinks of wet dog."

Darius jumped onto Oscar's back. Oscar held him, took one last look around, then sped off to the right.

George and Lloyd followed.

"Ready?" I asked Patrick.

He nodded, once, his lips pressed tight.

I held our joined hands up. "No letting go. We do this for Darius, right?"

"Aye, for Darius."

I smiled. It was clear Patrick and Darius had feelings for each other. There was a seed of what could be love germinating. I hoped it would. I more than hoped, it was a very deep longing. Having both Patrick and Darius in my life, as lovers, as companions for all eternity, would be a dream come true.

"Come on." Patrick leaned forward, touched the tip of his nose to mine. "What are we waiting for?"

"Nothing. Absolutely nothing."

I harnessed my speed then let it burst through my body, giving my legs super-human powers. We were running fast, our feet barely seeming to skim the snowy arctic tundra.

The tree line came and went, as did the forest. In the distance, George, Lloyd, Oscar, and Darius kept up the pace.

Patrick was tugging me; his need to go faster had our fingers tensing to stay gripped together. But I wouldn't let go. Nothing on Earth or in Heaven or Hell could ever make me let go of Patrick.

The sky darkened and become black velvet stitched with silver gossamer stars.

Scents came and went. Bear, deer, horse, the occasional human.

Finally, the snow turned patchy, the ground beneath wet.

We didn't slow. There was no tiredness, no fatigue, and no breathlessness. We ran. It was what we were good at...well, that and drinking blood. Oh, and fucking, yeah, that was a speciality.

When the wet earth turned sandy, anticipation built I'd heard George speak of the cave in the past. It was a place he remembered with fondness as he'd found his spirit there, or so he'd told me once. The peace and isolation had been healing for him. It was also what we needed now.

The full moon cast an eerie glow on a range of white-tipped mountains to my left. Their peaks were soft, as though filed by the wind, and they sloped gracefully to the meadows below. We jumped streams and rivers, circled a yurt village, then steered wide of a shepherd and his goats who were napping under a tree.

We caught up with Oscar and Darius and ran side by side.

Darius had his eyes closed, his cheek pressed against Oscar's nape. I hoped the ordeal wasn't too horrendous for him. The sooner we got there the better. He needed food and drink and to rest.

After what felt like forever, George and Lloyd slowed on a dusty track.

We all followed suit.

Before us was what appeared to be a stack of enormous boulders. They were piled high like a cliff, and on the first ridge about ten feet up was a small, perfectly square opening. Beside that appeared to be a carved-out window.

"It's a cave house," Lloyd said.

"I did some modification. I was here for thirty years." George shrugged. "Darius, this is the best way up. Copy my footsteps."

Darius slid from Oscar, his feet landing on the dirt and puffing sand up over his shoes. "I thought it would be warmer," he said.

"It will be when the sun comes up," George said. "Cold nights, hot days here."

"Ah, okay." He rubbed his gloved palms together. "I'll be glad to ditch some of these clothes."

Oscar raised his eyebrows. "None of us are going to complain if you want to get naked, Darius."

Darius laughed, a lovely light sound that settled in my heart. We'd escaped the Carlton Pack and in doing so escaped with our lives. The wolves were not known for their benevolence or mercy when it came to vampires. Not that I cared about what would happen to me, but Darius...and Patrick.

Patrick hasn't drunk from Darius at the sacred place at the sacred time. If he dies now, he'll be locked in eternal damnation.

That thought speared through me. When cuffed in silver, trapped in agony, I'd hardly been able to think straight, which with hindsight had been a blessing.

"Well done," I said, smiling at Patrick and finally releasing his hand. "You stuck with us."

"You shouldn't have ever doubted me." He looked upward, as if assessing his new surroundings—escape routes, possible sniper hide-outs, danger, what he could use. "I was made to be part of a team. No one gets left behind and all that."

"Good man." Lloyd clasped Patrick's shoulder. "I'm proud of you."

Patrick didn't speak. But his eyes narrowed, and he pressed his lips together.

Lloyd's praise had meant something. Which in turn meant Lloyd meant something to him.

I smiled. Patrick was part of us, part of our team. And I'd bet human blood that George and Lloyd felt the same way. Oscar, I wasn't so sure. Not yet.

"We'll get a fire lit for you," George said, navigating the narrow track on the side of the rocks. "Because of the cliff face opposite, the flames are hidden from the plain. No one will come investigating."

"It's certainly secreted away." Darius followed George, having to stoop on one particularly steep section.

"I didn't want to be found back then, and I don't want to be found now."

"It's true we need to lay low for a while," Oscar said. "But Patrick is coping well with his youth."

Oscar's words surprised me.

George paused and nodded at Patrick. "Yes, perhaps we'll be able to present him at The London Order sooner than we first thought."

"What's the—?"

"I'll tell you later, Patrick," I said, not bothering to hold in a smile. Pride was bursting through me. My first turn was coping well. Oscar had said that. George agreed. Something was going right.

Soon we were all in the mountainside cave. It was long and thin, and in sections, partitioned by wonky bits of furniture and curtains.

"Changed much?" Lloyd asked. He picked up what appeared to be the femur bone of a deer.

"Bit dusty, a few rodents have been and gone, but no, not really." George placed his hands on his hips. "I made that table and chair, and the cot at the back."

"Cot?" Darius asked, moving a frayed bit of hanging material to one side.

"Bed," George said. "A straw mattress surrounded by timber planks. A few pillows and blankets."

"But you don't sleep." Darius frowned.

"No, but would you want to sit on that hard chair for thirty years?" George raised his eyebrows.

"No, I guess not." Darius grinned. "I like it, it's cozy. Needs a bit of a sweep, but it's okay."

"Don't forget you're looking at it in moonlight. In the harsh light of day, you might think differently." George laughed.

"Hey, I like it because it's special to you." Darius slipped into George's arms and kissed him full on the lips. "And you're special to me."

George returned the kiss and drew him into a hug. "Thank Benedict we got you out of Sunezh." A shiver wound over his shoulders. "They'd have shown you no mercy, Darius. You were with us, which makes you one of us."

"I know." Darius squeezed his eyes closed. "And thanks to Nicoli for helping us."

"Never thought I'd see the day." Oscar poked a rock with his boot. "That a shifter piece of shit would help us."

Darius pulled away from George. "I guess it goes to show you can't tarnish them all with the same brush. The same way shifters aren't all bad, all vampires aren't good."

"Aren't they?" Patrick asked.

"No." George sat on the chair. It creaked.

"Why, what do they do wrong?" Patrick seemed genuinely curious.

"What do you think?" I said.

"I know killing is frowned upon. I've had that hammered into me often enough by now."

"Yes, but also they feed from humans they shouldn't feed from," George said.

"Like who?" Patrick frowned. "I mean, how come you all feed from Darius?"

"Feeding is permitted if an affirmation ceremony overseen at The Order has been performed," George said.

"And they know how to stop and how to care for their human," Oscar added.

Patrick nodded, the new knowledge seeming to settle into his brain. "And you've all done this ceremony, with Darius?"

I looked at George. He looked at Lloyd who adjusted his hood. Oscar cleared his throat.

"Fuck." Patrick shook his head. "You haven't, have you?"

"It's in the diary," I said. "Our situation is different, and Master Concorde knows we've claimed Darius. That he's ours. It's just the affirmation formalities."

"Formalities. Sounds like you've broken the damn rules you keep harping on about."

"It's not like that," George said to Patrick. "We have to keep Darius safe."

"And it doesn't mean we're not committed to each other," Darius said. "I think you've seen the evidence of that, Patrick."

Patrick was quiet for a moment. "Aye, I have."

I released a breath I hadn't even known I was holding.

"So going back to your question, Patrick," George said. "Some humans, those with rare Bombay blood, must be declared."

"But are not always." Lloyd huffed. "Aimery and Ryle; I swear their wife Bea is Bombay and they're keeping it quiet."

"We have no proof," George said.

"And it's none of our business," Oscar added. "Besides, as you just pointed out, we're hiding a cambion."

"Which isn't against vampire law," Lloyd said, wiping his hand over a dusty shelf and sweeping off several small pebbles which clattered to the floor. "So we're not doing anything wrong."

"Cambion." Patrick frowned. "That's you, Darius, right?"

He nodded.

"And why are you a secret?" Patrick asked.

Silence descended.

I glanced at George.

He nodded at me.

I cleared my throat. "He has to be, otherwise everyone would want his blood."

"What is special about it?" Patrick held up his hands. "I'm not saying you're not a great guy, damn cute, too, Darius, you are, but..."

"Because of my heritage, my blood holds a very specific key," Darius said. "If drunk at a certain time, at a certain place, it can save vampires from an eternity burning in Hell."

"Burning in Hell?" Patrick twisted to face me. "I thought we were immortal."

"You can die if you're staked through the heart," I said quickly and rested my hand on his shoulder. "Which you won't be, so don't worry."

"And we'll use the key to unlock your destiny as soon as we can," George added, "at the next equinox."

"We won't let anything happen to you, Soldier," Oscar said.

Oscar really is warming to Patrick.

"Thanks," Patrick mumbled. "So now what? Here?"

"We'll rest up for a few weeks, give Master Concorde time to finish his business in Krakow and get back to London."

"And then go see him," Lloyd said. "Present Patrick as a new vampire and have a private affirmation ceremony to make Darius belong to all of us."

"Or maybe I should claim you." Darius placed his hands on his hips and surveyed each of us in turn. "You are, after all, mine."

"True." Oscar chuckled. "We are."

"But first we need supplies." George rubbed his palms together. "It's okay for us here, but Darius needs more."

"I'm okay," Darius said. "There's still some food in that bag, and there must be a stream down there I can—"

"There's nowhere near enough food, babe." Oscar took Darius's hand. "We need to make this place more comfortable and get you some decent food and drink. No reason not to."

"Er, apart from the fact we're miles from anywhere."

"That makes no difference when we can run." Lloyd stepped to the door. "I'll come with you, Oscar."

"How far to the nearest town with stores?" Oscar asked George.

"About a hundred and sixty miles east."

"Cool, we'll be back in an hour or so." Oscar kissed Darius's hand. "Be good, okay."

Darius laughed. "I'll try."

Chapter Twenty-Two

Darius

George set about lighting a fire in the small stove. A crooked chimney made of tin cans led to the window.

Rhys went to collect firewood down near the meadow.

Patrick stalked around the cave and the ledge, seeming to familiarize himself with every nook and cranny. He felt the walls, sniffed the scrappy material, and a scooped up a drip of water leaking from a crack in the wall with his fingertip.

Would he have done this before he was a vampire, or is it a new thing?

I wasn't sure. Patrick was someone who was always hyper-alert. I guessed that was the way he was wired and trained. Only now he had highly acute senses, unimaginable speed and strength, and a thirst that would likely need sating at some point.

I paused lighting a huddle of candles on a shelf and rubbed my palm over my neck.

Patrick would want my blood.

And I'll give it.

A shiver of fear wound up from my belly. Patrick's thirst would be like every other part of him. Intense. Wild. Feral.

Could I handle it?

Could my other vampires handle *him*?

"You seem thoughtful," George said, twisting to look at me.

"What? Er yes."

"What's on your mind?"

Patrick slipped out of the doorway and onto the ledge.

"Where are you going?" George called.

"To help Rhys."

"Ah okay." George's attention returned to me. "Well? What's on your mind?"

"Him. Patrick."

George was quiet for a moment, then, "What about him?"

"He's one of us, right?"

"Yes. He is."

"And as such, he's…"

"Yours." He paused. "We understand that."

"You do?"

"Yes. You've let him into your heart, he'll be included in the affirmation ceremony, and now you want to let him into your body." He stood, turning from the stove and the small flames taking hold of the kindling.

A new shiver tapped up my spine. It traveled down again, taking heat and awareness to my asshole and cock.

Take Patrick into my body.

Yes, I will. We'll fuck. Soon.

"It will be his first time with a man." George placed his hand over mine, the one at my neck. "And his first time as a vampire. It will be a dangerous situation. He'll want to feed when he comes, the instinct to heighten the pleasure for both of you and taste your blood will be more than he can be expected to control."

I gulped. "I understand that."

"So it will only be permitted," George said, drawing his face close to mine, "if he's under close supervision."

"You want to watch?"

He smiled. "I'm not opposed to voyeurism, but no, not me…Rhys."

"Rhys?"

"Yes, he'll need to be close. Patrick listens to him. If he loses himself in you, then Rhys will be able to bring him back…hopefully."

"Fuck."

"Yes, fuck." George smiled. "I wouldn't normally have wanted you to be with him so early in his vampire youth, but I see the way you look at each other. Oscar and Lloyd agree. You need to get it out of your systems." He paused. "We think then you and Patrick will be able to hold it together when we go to The Order in London, not give it away that you're with all of us. You have to seem like you're only with Rhys, remember."

"Yes, I remember." I paused. "And you've all spoken about it? You, Oscar, and Lloyd. About me and Patrick...doing it?"

He shrugged and set a soft kiss on my lips. "We talk about you a lot, Darius, in all manner of contexts. Let's just say we're a little bit obsessed."

"With me?" I slipped my arms around his waist, a bubble of emotion expanding in my chest. "Really?"

"Yes, with you, our beautiful cambion, our savior, the only man we'll ever want and who'd we'd all die to protect from any kind of hurt or harm."

He kissed me again, a lovely lazy kiss with stroking tongues and chests pressed together.

George was so special to me. I'd given him my virginity; he was a tower of strength and wisdom. I couldn't imagine my life without him.

"I love you," I whispered.

"And I love you more than you'll ever know."

"Oh, sorry to intrude." Patrick was at the doorway with a bundle of dry, sun-bleached sticks in his arms.

"Not interrupting," George said, keeping me held tight. "I'll kiss our guy whether you're here or not."

I giggled but was silenced by another of George's delicious kisses. My knees weakened, and the heat that had journeyed to my dick earlier intensified.

A good fuck after all that stress will do me good.

George pulled back, his groin in line with mine, and by the expression on his face, he'd felt my growing erection through our clothes.

"And I think now would be as good a time as any." He raised his eyebrows at me.

"What? With…?"

"Yes." He touched his lips to my left ear. "It's best while Lloyd and Oscar aren't here. They'll fret, lurk over you, put you both off your stride, if you know what I mean."

The word stride is suddenly so damn sexy.

"Where's Rhys?" I asked, my throat a little dry, my cock hardening by the second.

"He's only a few steps from the cave entrance. I can hear him." George released me and stepped away. He picked up the chair by the top rung of its ladder-back and walked up to Patrick. He clasped his shoulder. "He's all yours."

"What?" Patrick frowned.

"Darius. He's yours, we're happy to share. But I'll only say this once." George threw a glance at me. "If it's anything other than pleasure, you cause him pain or even a second of fright, then I'll personally drive a stake through your heart."

Patrick clutched the woodpile a little tighter, his attention going from George to me then George again. He shifted from one foot to the other, his square features set deathly serious and the tendons beneath his inked forearms tensing.

He doesn't want me. Fuck. We…I've read this all wrong.

"I don't understand," Patrick said quietly.

"Yes, you do," George said, still gripping his shoulder. "You and Darius are meant to be, you belong together, the way we all do. It's time to seal the deal."

Rhys emerged, also carrying desert-dry logs.

"Ah, Rhys, there you are. Patrick and Darius are going to use the bedroom area. You'll need to supervise...closely."

Rhys dropped the wood into a basket. Dust puffed into the air, and he wafted it away. "What?" He swiped his palms together; the clap echoed around the cave.

"You heard," George said.

"Okay, I'll rephrase that." Rhys blew out a breath. "You mean *now*?"

I set my attention on Patrick. "Yes, now."

All three vampires looked my way.

I held Patrick's gaze. If his kisses and scorching attention had meant nothing, he'd have to admit it.

"Now," Patrick repeated, his jaw tight. "Okay."

A sudden dart of nerves attacked me. He'd agreed. That one word—*okay*—had sealed the deal. I was thrilled, excited, but also...

I hope he can control his thirst.

Patrick dumped the wood into the basket. It didn't land as neatly as Rhys's, and a few sticks scattered onto the floor.

He ignored them. Sucked in a deep breath, his t-shirt stretching over his pecs, then stepped up to me.

He didn't speak, just took my hand and led me behind the flimsy curtain to the mattress. His broad shoulders were stiff, every movement of his body oozing erotic determination.

I walked a little awkwardly. My cock didn't understand the risks involved in fucking Patrick. I was turned on, seriously horny. I wanted Patrick so much I ached.

Rhys appeared at my side, his jaw tight. "You okay with this?" He stroked the back of his finger down my cheek.

I nodded. "I want you and I want Patrick. You're both mine." I squeezed Patrick's hand. "And now it's time to make it real."

Patrick pulled back his top lip. His fangs slid down. "My cock's got fucking zipper marks on it." His eyes flashed as he undid the top button on his trousers.

"Hey, no, put your fangs away," Rhys said, pressing his palm flat on Patrick's chest and giving him a small shove. "I'll tell you when, and I'll tell you when to stop, too. Okay?"

Patrick didn't answer.

"Okay?" Rhys said more firmly.

"Yeah, okay." Patrick shoved at his trousers, and his fangs slipped away. "But let's get this show on the road."

"So much for the shy virgin," I said, also undoing my trousers and eyeing Patrick's long, thick erection.

Patrick grinned. "I've waited my whole life to be with a man. Now I have two of you, I'm not waiting another second."

Suddenly he was kissing me, his big, work-hardened hands roaming underneath my jacket and sweater. His touch was cool but sent flames of desire skittering over my flesh.

I stroked my tongue against his, absorbing his unique flavor and pleased there were no sharp teeth.

They could come back at any moment.

Moving that thought aside, I lifted my feet in turn as Rhys slipped my boots, trousers, and boxers off.

The cool air licked over my skin; I was glad of it. I was hot. My heart was racing. My cock throbbed.

"You're so beautiful, Darius," Patrick murmured then dropped my jacket from my shoulder. He then tugged at the base of my sweater. "So fucking hot."

"So let's fuck," I said, running my fingers over his short hair and squeezing in close.

His nostrils flared, and his eyes flashed. "Who's fucking who?"

"You fuck me," I said. I was happy with being bottom or top, but with Patrick, I had an urge to feel him inside me, and his big soldier cock working my hole.

A low growl came from his throat, and then I was on my hands and knees on the scratchy mattress. I snatched in a breath as Rhys dropped down next to me.

"I won't let him hurt you," Rhys said, setting his hand on my lower back.

"I know…I trust you…oh…fuck."

Patrick wasn't messing around; he'd palmed my buttocks and spread them, the tip of his cock at my entrance.

"Hey, use this. Prepare him," Rhys said.

"Lube, yeah, shit, I nearly forgot."

I was glad Rhys hadn't forgotten.

A shiver went up my spine, and by the time it had reached the top, Patrick had penetrated my asshole with his greased finger and pushed knuckle deep.

"Fuck, he's too small," Patrick said, desperation in his voice.

"No, he's not." Rhys rubbed a circle on my lower back. "Stretch him."

"Does your cock fit in here, Rhys?"

"No…I only bottom."

"Oh…" Patrick stilled for a moment. "That could work out well for us then."

"Why is that?" Rhys asked.

"I only want to top."

"You…" I managed. "Might like me doing this to you…sometime, Patrick." I was breathless. "But right now, just hurry up and fuck me."

Rhys chuckled. "I love it when you get all demanding."

I groaned. I just wanted to come. My cock was tapping up against my belly. My skin had goosebumped, and my pulse thudded in my ears.

Patrick added another finger, filling my ass.

I squeezed my eyes closed and arched my back, raising my butt cheeks.

"Jesus give me strength," Patrick muttered. "I'm going in."

Suddenly his fingers were gone. They were replaced with the smooth round tip of his cock.

"Take it easy, remember he's human," Rhys said.

Patrick eased forward, opening my hole.

I stretched for him, then some more. He kept shoving in, faster now, filling me, creating a dense, thick sensation that was half hurt, half pure pleasure.

And then he rammed to full depth, shoving the air from my lungs. It burst from my throat, and I cried out.

"What the heck...?" George's voice.

"It's okay," Rhys called.

"Ah, fuck..." Patrick said, gripping my shoulders, his big hands like slabs of concrete. "I'm fucking inside you, Darius."

I didn't need telling. My asshole was spread wide around his cool root; it was as if he'd possessed my soul as well as my body.

"I need his blood," Patrick gasped.

"Not yet," Rhys said, his hand lifting from me.

"When?"

"When you both come, and just a few mouthfuls."

Patrick groaned, half withdrew, then slammed back in.

Again, I grunted. I squeezed my eyes closed, and moisture gathered in them.

He'd rubbed over my prostate, the divine pressure going straight to my cock. My balls tightened, and I fisted the blanket covering the old straw.

"Ah God, this is better than any woman." Patrick pulled almost out, steamed back in. "Why did I wait so long?"

He set up a fast, furious pace. There was nothing soft and romantic about it. This was carnal. Taking what was needed. Racing toward satisfaction.

"Ah, yeah..." I managed, "like that...I'm going to...come...soon. Don't stop."

"He won't stop." Rhys set his hand over mine, as if reassuring me that he was there.

"Oh, but I want to come..." I moaned, pressing back for more when Patrick bottomed out again.

"I know you do, and you can—"

"Come." Patrick was fucking me even faster now, steaming in and out of my ass. His body slapping up against mine. If he hadn't been holding me tight, I'd have been through the cave wall.

"Oh yes, I'm coming," I cried, "it's here..." Pre-cum seeped from my slit. My balls had retracted.

"Bite him now," Rhys said, tapping my right shoulder. "Just here, but stop when I tell you to."

As the first spurt of release gushed from me, Patrick sank his fangs into my shoulder.

The effect was instantaneous. The intensity of my climax tripled, quadrupled. His saliva sent me spiraling into new dimensions of bliss. I forgot all time and meaning, person and place. Pleasure soaked in ecstasy was all that existed.

I cried out on each plunge of his cock and burst of release from mine. My head was spinning and my asshole contracting around him. My arms and legs were weak, but he held me firm, his hips continuing to thrust as he drank with his chest molded onto my back.

"That's it, no more," Rhys said sharply.

I opened my eyes, but everything was dark and blurred. My heart beat so fast I was sure it would burst right out of my chest.

"Stop." Rhys's voice was distant, as if he were speaking underwater.

Still Patrick fed, his mouth burning hot over my skin. My cock hurt; the orgasm was extending so long, draining me dry.

I groaned and twisted my neck, trying to get away.

"Stop now!"

Suddenly Patrick was off me and out of me, completely.

I fell to the blanket, sucking in air and shaking.

"Thank fuck," Rhys said, pressing his hand over the puncture wounds on my shoulder.

"I'm sorry," Patrick said. "I couldn't stop, I..."

"No, don't say that, you could stop and you did." Rhys was breathing heavily, too. "You just needed a bit of help, that's all."

"Fucking hell," Patrick said. "Is he okay?"

"Yes, he's fine." Rhys's lips were by my cheek. "Or he will be in a minute." He kissed me. "It's okay, I'm here, you're all good, my love."

I managed a weak smile. My asshole was still being treated to aftershocks and was stinging pleasantly.

"I never want to hurt him." Patrick slid his hand up my right leg, over my right buttock, then set it on the small of my back.

"You haven't. He just needs a minute."

"Good." Patrick panting. "Because I just came so hard. That was the best orgasm of my life."

"I told you," Rhys said. "Darius is special."

Chapter Twenty-Three

Lloyd

Oscar and I returned to the cave as the sun spread golden fingers over the eastern meadow. We'd bought fresh and tinned food, bedding, and toiletries from a small shop in Uligii the moment it had opened.

We'd been treated with suspicion and weren't surprised by that. We didn't look like the usual tourists or backpackers. But our money was good, so we'd gotten what we'd needed before making sure we were out of sight to start running again.

"It's quiet," Oscar said, striding up the steep incline to the cave's entrance.

I didn't answer. If Darius was sleeping, I didn't want to disturb him. The guy must be shattered; we'd walked miles to the wolves' town the night before, and then he'd had to cling on to Oscar for hours to get to the cave. Not to mention the terror of not knowing what was going to happen to us all.

I stopped as a strange smell caught in my nostrils. "What's that?" I sniffed.

"What?" Oscar paused.

"Dog, I can smell dog, or wolf or hyena or something."

"There's no hyenas here."

I shrugged. "I can smell what I can smell." I paused. "It's very faint, though, coming from the north."

Oscar's nostrils flared. "I can't smell anything."

I moved my head, sniffed again. "Neither can I now. Perhaps it's my imagination."

"Yeah, just a new place. I scented a fox earlier, might be that."

"Could be."

I'm not convinced.

"Hey," George called, standing from the seat placed just outside the entrance to the cave. "Get everything our man needs?"

"Yeah." Oscar held up a bulging bag. "He won't be hungry or thirsty."

"Where is he?" I asked.

"Inside."

"Alone?" Oscar nodded at the doorway.

"No, with Patrick."

I raised my eyebrows.

"And Rhys. Rhys is in charge, and it sounds like he's handled the situation well."

"What situation?" I asked, drawing the words out as my mind kicked into gear. Had they been fucking?

We'd all known it was going to happen, sure, but this was much sooner than expected.

"Shit, you let him—" Oscar dropped the bag and rushed to the doorway.

"Hold your horses." George placed his palm on Oscar's wide chest. "It's all over."

Oscar's eyes widened. "And he's—"

"Okay, yes. Darius is fine. You really think me and Rhys would have let anything happen to him?" George grinned. "In fact, by the sounds of it, he had a great time."

"Bloody hell." I rubbed my temples. It was a good job I hadn't known Patrick and Darius were getting their first fuck out of the way. Patrick's primary feed from our beautiful, treasured cambion was a risky business. I'd have struggled to keep my cool. I'd have wanted to be there, ready to tear Patrick away should the need arise and then kick him into next week if he took one more drop than he should have.

"I wish they'd waited for us to get back." Oscar frowned.

"Why? So you could huff and stomp about, stop them even if they didn't need stopping?" George sat back down. "Rhys had it. Have some faith in him, Oscar."

"He's just a kid."

"No, he isn't." George shook his head. "He's made his first turn and he's taking responsibility for it. I've been impressed with the solid relationship he and Patrick have formed."

"They're in lust," I slipped my hood down and glancing at the sun that was rising higher, a golden aurora spreading from it. "Which isn't a problem. In fact, it benefits us."

"It does?" Oscar said.

George sighed as if weary with the trail of the conversation. I hated it when he did that. It was like saying he was the sharpest out of us all, the most intelligent.

"Yes," I said to Oscar. "It makes Patrick more controllable if he's got strong feelings for Rhys."

"Exactly," George said, crossing one leg over the other and bobbing his foot.

"I'm going to check on them," Oscar said. He gave George a look that dared him to argue.

"Sure." George wafted his hand in the air. "Go ahead."

I was about to follow when the same smell as before caught in my nose. It was the vaguest hint, barely there, but I knew what it was—damp, musty cloth was unmistakable. "Have you seen anything about overnight?" I grimaced as I studied the landscape.

"Antelope in the distance, and there's a family of gerbils living on the cliff wall opposite. They make a lot of noise talking to each other."

"No foxes?"

"No."

"Wolves?"

"No." He frowned. "Why?"

"I thought I could smell canine. It's gone now." And it had; the particles of it in the air were so few and far between it kept coming and going. Whatever it was coming from, or whoever, was nowhere close.

George pulled his pocket watch out. "The Carlton Pack wouldn't have been able to follow us here this quickly. No way."

"I agree." But I couldn't help feeling uneasy. "I might go check out the area."

"There's nothing here but animals."

"You know it well, George, it was your home. This is new territory for me. I want to get my bearings."

He slipped his watch away. "Go ahead then. Not much happening here. Darius will sleep for a few hours. He's exhausted."

"And that will do him good."

I wandered back down the ledge path. A viper, flat-headed and decorated with brown diamonds, slithered out of my way. At one time I'd have frozen in fear, but its venom couldn't hurt me now.

Once at the base of the canyon, I headed toward the meadow. There were a myriad of smells to siphon through. Although this part of Mongolia was barren and all around was still and quiet, it didn't mean there weren't living things scrabbling around and scraping out a life.

Creatures with blood—warm, rich, delectable blood.

I stroked my tongue over my top teeth. A familiar need tugged at my belly. Perhaps if I spotted an antelope I should feed. It had been a while, and after wearing silver, I was in need.

Ideally, I'd feed from Darius. But he had five vampires in his harem now. We'd have to take our turn, plus ensure he had enough healing tea.

I sighed and continued to walk, happy to go at a slower pace. I'd known as soon as Patrick had been turned that he'd become part of our team, our gang. It was the only thing that could happen, given the circumstances.

And I reckoned I liked him well enough. What I knew. And there'd be plenty of time in the infinite future to really get to know him. I figured any guy who'd fought bravely for his queen and country couldn't be all bad. He did seem to have some pretty useful skills from his human life, too.

But most importantly, Darius was happy. That was my main focus now. Ensuring he was happy.

I pulled up my hood and shoved my hands into my pockets. My boots thudded on the hard ground.

Soon the going underfoot softened. Patches of emerald-green grass sprung up, and within half an hour I was walking on lush meadow.

I spotted the antelope in the distance and changed my direction.

I hadn't smelt dog again.

Or was that wolf?

But the moment I turned, there it was. And it was stronger this time; the fuggy scent that rolled my stomach was definitely in the air.

I stopped, raised my face, and closed my eyes.

Inhaling deeply, I suddenly knew I wasn't mistaken.

There was a wolf nearby. Only one, I'd bet blood on that.

"How the heck?" I shook my head, narrowed my eyes, and stared into the distance.

The meadow was fractured by several rivers, meandering through it like the branches of a tree. The water came down from gently sloping hills into the valley, and fir copses peppered the gentle slopes.

It was then I saw it.

Movement.

Not human.

Not antelope.

Wolf!

A swarm of anger surrounded me, fizzing in my ears and pricking my skin. I harnessed my energy and burst into a run.

The creature was galloping my way, but I'd have him pinned to the ground and at my mercy within seconds.

And then he was before me.

I slowed, wanting to see his reaction.

If it were just a regular wolf he'd stop and snarl, bare his teeth, and his eyes would flash. He'd look at me with hunger, as in, 'dinner' hunger.

If it were a shifter from the Carlton Pack there'd be recognition, surprise, perhaps he'd even shift. Any hunger would be an appetite to drive a stake through my heart and have me hung, drawn, and quartered.

The wolf saw me and slowed.

I stood, feet hip width apart, fists clenched. Ready for attack or to be attacked.

Not that a wolf would have much luck on its own against me. That was why the cowards stuck together in packs.

He came to a halt, huge paws lost in the grass, ears pricked forward. The sun glinted off his thick coat, and his eyes narrowed.

Oh yeah, he knows exactly who I am.

I pulled back my upper lip and slid down my fangs. I figured that would let him know the mood I was in.

He was panting, his pink tongue visible.

"Shift," I said, a snarl in my voice. "And face me like a man."

For a moment I didn't think he would. And I wouldn't have blamed him— he had more fighting strength as a wolf. But he reared onto his back legs. His fur shimmered then slid away, revealing tanned flesh, muscular limbs, and a six pack a cover model on *GQ* would be proud of.

His face morphed from wolf to human. Neat features, long, straight nose, wide lips, and perfect skin. If he wasn't a disgusting dog, I'd have said he was attractive.

But he was a disgusting dog.

"Where's Darius?" he said.

My lover's name on his lips generated another snarl from me. My gums tingled, and anger squeezed my heart. "That is of no concern of yours."

"He's my friend." He nodded over my shoulder in the direction he'd been traveling. "I want to know he's okay."

"Darius isn't friends with dirty old dogs."

He frowned. "I'm Nicoli; he must have told you about me."

I was silent, trying to remember the name of the shifter who'd left the door unbolted.

"Or maybe he doesn't tell you everything. Maybe you're not as close to him as you think you are."

"How did you get here so fast?"

"Clever thing with wheels, goes on tracks. Sometimes travels overnight, for miles. You can ride it, called a—"

"Shut the fuck up." I was in no mood for mongrel sarcasm. "And we are close, couldn't be closer."

"I can't believe he's shacked up with vampires." Nicoli stepped to the right, his gaze drifting down then up my body as if seeing me through my clothes. "Darius Linnet could have anyone he wanted."

"Do you think he'd be better off with your sort?" The idea was preposterous.

"Actually, I do." He stopped and grinned, a lopsided smile that I'd bet got him lots of men, or women, into bed. "I offered him that."

"You offered him what?"

"To stay with me. To be mine...my lover."

"And obviously he said no, because he's with us."

"Where?"

"Somewhere safe."

"How do you know, you're here? Anything could be happening to him. If he was mine, I wouldn't let him out of my sight."

"You forget, there's five of us. And he'll never be yours."

"That's for him to decide." He walked past me as if continuing his journey and his search for Darius.

I snapped my hand out and gripped his upper arm.

He spun, teeth on show, a low growl coming from his throat. "Don't touch me, you disgusting creature."

"Say that again, and I'll suck you dry."

Yuck, even the thought of wolf blood makes me want to gag.

He laughed and yanked his arm. "No, you won't."

I released him, a scowl streaking over my brow. "So you followed us, for what? In the hope you could win Darius's heart?"

"I've known him a long time, we have a connection." He paused, glanced at his feet, then up at my face again. "I've known him longer than you have. We're friends."

I pressed my fangs onto my bottom lip. The desire to bite, fight, kill was had my skin itching.

But I wouldn't.

Or at least I'd try not to.

Not if this mutt was a friend of Darius. The last thing I wanted was him upset.

"Though I'd like Darius to be more than friends." Nicoli raised his eyebrows. "He's got the cutest ass I've ever seen. I'd like to—"

"I'm trying really fucking hard not to kill you right now."

Nicoli smirked.

"So shut the hell up," I said.

"You're not brave enough to ask him, are you? Ask him to choose."

"It has nothing to do with bravery, and for the record, I'm confident he'd choose us. He left with us, didn't he."

"He has a strong sense of duty."

"For the love of Benedict." I turned, retracting my fangs and squeezing the bridge of my nose. This guy was insane.

"So take me to him. Let me ask him."

"You really want to walk, as a shifter, our mortal enemy, into a cave full of vampires and try and take our lover?"

"Darius should get to choose."

"He has." I pointed at my chest. "And he chose me, us, so get the fuck back on that train and get out of here."

"I want you to take me to him, now."

I saw red, blood-red. It seeped down from the top of my vision, closing out everything except for Nicoli's face.

And then I was over him. I couldn't remember it happening, but I had him pinned to the floor, neck bared, and his body trapped beneath mine.

He twisted and bucked but to no avail.

I was much stronger than him, and fueled with my fury, he didn't stand a chance.

"I've been...in love with him...since I met him in Milan, four years...ago."

"Do you think I give a damn?" I circled my hand around his neck, felt his carotid beneath my fingertips.

"You going to kill anyone who wants him?" He swallowed.

I wrinkled my nose; his doggy smell was repulsive this close.

"Because he's beautiful," Nicoli went on, his voice strained but his gaze steady and holding mine. "Everyone he meets falls in love with him." He paused, his nostrils flared. "There's a reason he's a world-famous model."

"I love him for who he is not his looks."

"But his looks attracted you to him."

I compressed his neck a little tighter.

He grunted and gripped my wrists, tugged.

"You know nothing about it," I said. "Nothing."

"And...I don't want to know about you and him. I just—"

"Want to speak to him, I know." Suddenly I'd had enough of being so up close and personal with a stinky wolf. I sprang back, swiping my palms together and dragging in fresh air. "Well, that's never going to happen, not on my watch. So get on your way."

Nicoli stood, then made a show of brushing the dirt from his naked body. When he'd done, he straightened. "I will have my time with him."

"You had it, he said no."

"He was under pressure, he was scared."

"And now he's happy with us, we protect him, care for him." I cupped my groin over my jeans. "Keep him more than satisfied. You can't compete with us, five of us, with saliva that makes his orgasm ten times more powerful than they could ever be with you."

"You feed from him." He shook his head. "That's sickening and immoral."

"And so are you." I stepped away and pointed at the mountains. "Back the way you came, now. I won't say it again, I'll just rip your head off and feed it to the eagles."

He studied me, as if assessing whether or not I was serious. Fidgeting from one foot to the other, he glanced at the meadow then at the mountains, squinting in the sunshine.

"I mean it, I'll just kill you."

"Why haven't you?" he asked.

"You gave us a head start in Siberia, I owed you, that debt has been paid. Consider us even."

He took a step backward.

I raised my eyebrows.

"I'm outta here." He held his hands up.

I thought it was a gesture of surrender, but then he tipped forward, shifting into his other form as he fell to the ground.

He landed on paws, his back hunching as it was coated in fur. The stench of wolf increased, and before his face had fully morphed, he sprang into a gallop.

I watched him head for the mountains, relieved that I hadn't killed Darius's friend, but also mad the guy had had the nerve to follow us, to think for one second Darius would leave us for him.

When he became nothing more than a dot in the distance, a pinprick, I turned and went back toward the cave. I hadn't been wrong when I'd picked up the scent of wolf, even though it had been so faint it would have been easy to convince myself it was my imagination.

Chapter Twenty-Four

Darius

I woke in Rhys's arms and with my head on his chest. Patrick was lying behind me, spooning my body, and his cool, hard abdomen and groin molded to mine. I still wore my sweater, but it had rucked up my back.

I stirred and yawned, letting them know I was awake.

"You okay?" Rhys whispered, kissing the top of my head.

"Yeah." I reached for Patrick's hand that was resting on my waist and threaded my fingers with his, hugging him closer. "Never better."

"I'm sure that's not true." Rhys chuckled. "This is a crappy old straw bed in a cave. You've stayed in some of the most expensive hotels in the world."

"Yes, but you guys weren't there." I stretched upward and kissed Rhys, then turned and brushed my lips over Patrick's cheek.

His eyes had changed from vibrant, neon-red to a much darker red, maroon almost. "How do you feel?"

He smiled, just a little. "Like I'm not a virgin anymore."

"Good." I kissed him. "Because you're not." I paused. "And how did my blood taste?"

"Like manna from Heaven."

"That good?"

"Hell yeah." He rested his fingers over the bite marks I knew would be healing. "I'm already looking forward to fucking you and feeding from you again."

"So am I." I grinned.

"You have to share, Patrick, remember." George was standing at the end of the bed with his hands on his hips.

Oscar was at his side.

"Yeah, I remember." Patrick pulled back, as though embarrassed to have been caught talking softly to me as we snuggled close.

Perhaps it doesn't suit his macho image.

I smiled at that. He was coping so well, considering.

"You need tea." Oscar held up a mug. "Drink this, Darius."

"I will." I stretched then yawned again. "But I'll get up. I'm getting stiff lying here; it's hard."

"Stiff, huh?" Rhys said, following the line of my waist and hip with his palm. "And which bit is stiff?" He hesitated. "And what's hard?"

"Hey, kid," Oscar said. "Let him have his tea before any more of that."

"Just because you had Darius to yourself for weeks and weeks." Rhys lifted his touch from me.

"Can't say that was a hardship." Oscar held out his free hand. "Come on, up."

I accepted his help, and he tugged me to standing. My sweater fell into place, skimming the base of my abdomen. "Thanks." I took the tea. My throat was suddenly dry. I took a sip.

"You should put some clothes on your lower half," George said. "Or your dick will be getting sucked before you've finished your tea."

"You think I'd complain about that?" I raised my eyebrows at him.

A swift slap landed on my ass, a fast-hot sting.

"Ouch!" George had spanked me. "What the…?"

He laughed at my surprise. "Drink and we'll see, shall we?"

A shadow loomed at the door.

Lloyd.

The moment I saw the set of his shoulders, I knew something was up. "What is it?"

"Nothing." His voice was gruff.

I hesitated as his one word settled in my brain. "Don't lie to me, Lloyd."

"Shit, sorry..." He sighed. "Nicoli, the wolf shifter from the Carlton Pack, was on his way here."

"What?" I processed the information. "Where?"

"A few hundred kilometers north."

"Nicoli who?" Rhys asked, standing.

"The shifter who left the door unlocked back at Sunezh and told us it would be deserted later that night."

"Fuck really?" Patrick's eyes widened. "How the heck did he make it this far south so fast?"

"Train and wolf-speed." Lloyd jabbed his hands into his jeans pockets, his thumbs hanging on the outside and pointing at the bulge in his jeans. "I'm pretty sure it was a lucky guess that he was going in the right direction, nothing more."

I was aware of Lloyd's attention slipping to my flaccid cock. "What did Nicoli want?"

Lloyd sighed. "What do you think?" He stood beside the wall and bent his right knee so the sole of his boot was on the rock. He re-connected his gaze with mine.

"I don't know." I shrugged and sipped the tea again.

"You, of course." Lloyd's jaw tensed. "He seemed to fancy his chances at stealing you away from us."

"Like that would ever happen." I clicked my tongue on the roof of my mouth.

George slipped his arm around my waist. "We'd never keep you against your will."

"I'm very much here at my own free will." I huffed. "I love you all, I'll never leave you, and I told Nicoli that. I thought I'd made myself clear."

"He seemed to think it was worth a second ask." Lloyd's jaw tensed further.

"And you told him it wasn't worth the ask."

"Yeah, that's exactly what I told him."

"And what did he say?" I asked.

Lloyd was silent. I sensed him and George sharing something unsaid, a quick flick of their eyes.

"Well?" I urged.

"He said he will 'have his time with you.'"

"He'll have his time with me. No, Nicoli is wrong." I tipped my chin. "I've made my decision, chosen my men, and it's you, all of you, Patrick included. Unless you'd consider letting Nicoli join our group, being part of my harem." I mashed my lips together, waiting for the reaction.

"Hell no!" George snapped.

"Never." Lloyd frowned.

"Don't even say it as a joke," Oscar muttered. "The thought of having to be within a hundred kilometers of a Carlton Pack shifter makes me want to drive a stake into my own heart."

"Please don't do that, Oscar. I happen to be very fond of your chest just the way it is."

He smiled.

"And Nicoli has gone," I said, nodding at the door. "So we don't need to discuss him anymore."

"Yeah, thanks for sending him on his way," Rhys said.

Patrick stood at Rhys's side, nodded. "Aye, good riddance."

"Yes, thank you." I stepped up to Lloyd and swept my lips over his. "I really appreciate it."

He sent his hand between our bodies and brushed his knuckles over my exposed cock.

A sexy tingle of interest wound up my spine. I raised my eyebrows at him.

"Drink the damn tea." Oscar stepped past us, his bulk casting a shadow.

"Wow, you're extra bossy today," I said, laughing but staying close to Lloyd.

"We're in a new place," Oscar said, nodding at the doorway. "It's making me on edge, plus the scent of wolves is still in my nose. More so now I know one followed us."

"Come on." George slapped Oscar on the back. "I'll show you around the local area, where the springs are for Darius's water and a good place to see to the east, toward the town. You'll catch all the animal and human scents from up there." George straightened his cap and turned up his collar as though protecting his neck from the sun.

"Yeah, okay, we can do that," Oscar said.

They left the cave, slipping into the bright daylight and pulling on shades.

"You need to drink your tea." Lloyd gestured to the mug but his gaze didn't leave mine.

"I'm drinking it."

"Good."

I smiled as my cock stirred. Being this close to Lloyd was always going to get a reaction. "Wanna sit with me?"

"Yeah." He stroked my cock with his knuckles again. His eyes widened, and he smiled, the delicious, dark sexy grin I adored. "Mind if I adore you having your tea?"

"Adore away."

I glanced at Patrick and Rhys.

"Go ahead," Rhys said, "we're going to make our own fun...if it's all right with you, Darius."

Damn, they were going to fuck. I recognized that glint in Rhys's eyes. He wanted to bend over and take Patrick, the new vampire he'd built such a strong bond with. "Why would it not be all right with me?"

"Because..." Rhys cleared his throat. "I'm loyal to you, Darius, you're my man."

"But you want Patrick, too."

He looked at Patrick whose features were tense, as though he was holding back from saying anything. Sensing this was between Rhys and me.

It is.

"I understand," I said, letting my gaze slip down Patrick's naked, sexy body. "And I'm not going to deny two people who are so precious to me something they want." I nodded at the bed area. "Go and have fun, on one condition."

"What's that?" Rhys swallowed and took Patrick's hand.

"You won't blame me for listening."

Patrick grinned suddenly. "I've been quiet for too long. I don't intend to live that way any longer."

Lloyd chuckled. "We got a right one with you, Patrick."

"I'm glad you think so." He tugged Rhys behind the curtain. "Come on, sexy, this is overdue."

My cock surged, going from a semi to a full hard-on.

Maybe I should watch.

"Come on," Lloyd said. "Sit out here, warm up, it was a long cold night for you."

"But it's hot now, for vampires."

He checked his hood. "I'm covered."

With my erection bobbing, I went outside and sat on the chair George had left beside the door. I took another drink of my tea.

Lloyd dropped to his knees at my side. "Can you see them?"

"Who?"

"Oscar and George."

"No."

"I doubt you'll see anyone while I do this." He took my cock in his hand and tipped forward. He swiped his tongue over my slit.

"Ah fuck," I said, my balls contracting. "Really, out here?"

"Of course out here. Relax, there's no rush. I want to hear your pleasure."

As he'd spoken, a long, low groan came from inside the cave.

I smiled and rested my hand on Lloyd's head, over the material of his hood.

He tightened his grip and kissed the tip of my cock.

It was my turn to groan. "Fuck, I thought George was the one with the blow job idea."

"Let's just say he put the thought in my mind." He looked up at me, his face cast in shadows. "Are you complaining?"

"Hell no." I gripped the handle on my mug. "I'm in bloody heaven."

"Good." Again he licked my cock, right around the rim, his gaze not leaving mine.

I moaned and clenched my buttocks. "So damn good, Lloyd."

"This will be better." He opened his mouth and sank deep.

Another moan, tangled with a cry, came from the cave. Rhys being penetrated. I recognized the sound.

I stared at the arid landscape, the gnarly rocks and the lush meadow in the distance. But I didn't really see it. I was too caught up in the suck of Lloyd's mouth around my cock and the exquisite sounds of Rhys being fucked by Patrick.

Patrick was true to his word; he wasn't being quiet and was grunting and huffing with each slapping thrust.

"Lloyd." I curled my toes on the sandy ground. "That feels so good."

He didn't answer, just kept on working my cock. He used his hands, too, stroking and caressing, working his saliva around my shaft.

I sucked in a breath. I'd come with Patrick's cock inside me not long ago, but now Lloyd was pushing me to the brink of release again. My vampires were all so sexy, my body reacted to them every time.

"I'm going to..." I managed, curling forward, still holding the mug, though it had tilted, a drip of tea landing on the floor. The cross pendent hanging from my necklace swung over Lloyd's head. "Lloyd..."

He slipped his hand between my legs, found my balls, and stroked them.

"Oh God." I squeezed my buttocks together. "It's nearly here."

He upped his enthusiasm, working me harder, faster, his tongue caressing me in a blissful tight way.

And then it was there, a swift, intense release.

He swallowed my pleasure, taking me so deep I could feel the back of his throat on my glans.

The pleasure extended, I cried out, dropping the mug and gripping his head. I bucked off the chair, plunging into his mouth.

He took it all, staying with me. More cum shot from my cock.

Lights flashed in my vision, my pulse raged in my ears, and my skin was both burning and cold. "Lloyd." I pulled at his hood, trying to drag his head from my groin. "Here."

He lifted his face and stared at me, eyes narrowed.

I offered him my wrist; the straight blue veins on the underside were visible. "Drink."

"Darius?"

"You...need it."

His fangs slid down. He stroked my cock, firm and determined, and sank into my flesh, piercing it easily with his sharp vampire teeth.

"Ah, yeah..." I gasped.

A new wave of ecstasy shot through me. It bathed all of my nerves in bliss, and I reveled in it, transported to a new high.

A half groan, half yell tore from my throat. It tangled with one vibrating from the cave. Patrick and Rhys coming together, with me—we were all coming.

Lloyd didn't drink much. After only a few seconds, he lifted. Blood coated his bottom lip, but his fangs were gone. "I don't want to exhaust you," he said, then licked his lips. "You've been through enough this last forty-eight hours."

"I care about your wellbeing, too." I was breathing fast, my chest rising and falling.

"That was enough. Thank you." He grinned. "Delicious, and not just your blood, your cock, too." He kissed the tip of my dick, then plunged deep, taking me into his mouth again. This time there was a lingering warmth on his tongue, from my blood.

I dropped my head back onto the rocky wall and sighed, pleasant aftershocks pulsing through my cock and ass.

With my vampires, life was never dull, it was always a roller coaster—a sexy, dangerous roller coaster that I didn't want to get off.

Chapter Twenty-Five

Darius

Four weeks later

Oscar held me tight while I waited for sleep to wash over me. Not that his body gave me any protection from the chill of the Mongolian night, but it was nice to be cocooned in his big arms.

The fire was well-stoked, candles kept the cave's dense blackness at bay, and new, richly embroidered blankets covered me, so all was good in my little world in what felt like the middle of nowhere.

I'm safe, nothing can hurt me.

My thoughts splintered, my mind succumbing to the darkness of slumber. Soon I was slipping into what I knew was a dream, but still, it felt so real.

I was in a white brick courtyard full of flowerbeds overflowing with citrus-orange marigolds. Over the courtyard wall, tall, snow-capped mountains stabbed at a thick blue sky. It seemed as if the darkness of outer space was only an arm's length away from their tips.

Behind me, a building—the same whitewashed brick as the courtyard wall—stood three stories high. Its sweeping, ornate roof was golden and glinted in the pure white light of the sun. The shuttered windows were small, and running along the bottom level was a porch. Each wooden pillar held a prayer wheel, and vast bowls of water dotted with more marigold heads were set at the entrance to an arched doorway.

"Darius."

I turned at my name, my movements floating. My body not quite mine.

A monk stood before me, his blood-red robe skimming the ground and gathered at the waist by a blue rope. He held one hand aloft with his finger pointed, a dazzling green-spotted butterfly perched on the end.

"Yes?" I asked, studying his clear, open face.

He inclined his head, his gaze dipping.

There was something familiar about him, and a soft calmness radiated toward me. It washed over my skin, settling my heart rate and dragging a sigh from my chest.

"Do I know you?" I asked.

He looked up at me again, a smile tugging his lips.

I struggled to recognize him. He was handsome, very handsome; his head was bald and smooth, and despite the wisdom I saw in his eyes, he didn't have a wrinkle or a blemish on his skin. He was youthful and strong.

"What's your name?" I asked.

He blinked, long and slow, then directed his attention to the butterfly. He lifted it higher then blew softly on it.

The pretty creature took to the air, heading in the direction of the flowerbeds.

The calmness around me, the experience of being in this courtyard, was like nothing I'd ever felt before. It was more than contentment, it was safety, it was knowledge—it was enlightening.

"Are you...?" I paused. Master Concorde had told me the cambion he'd drank from was living in Tibet as a monk to keep him safe for all eternity. Was this that immortal monk? Was this man the same as me? Half demon, half human, and a holder of the key? "You are..." I said. "You're a cambion."

There was no other explanation. Why else would my dreams have brought me here?

The monk held out his hand and rested his palm on my cheek. It was soft and warm. "Come to me, my friend." His voice was low but melodic.

"I am, I'm here." I clasped my hand over his. "Talk to me. I have questions. I need to—"

He shook his head and stepped away, forcing me to drop my touch. "Come to me...soon."

He turned and moved, almost floating, to the far end of the courtyard. As he distanced himself from me, my heart rate increased. I spun around. Who else was here? What else was here?

And then I was running, running up steep dirt tracks, hurtling through valleys, racing to get somewhere...

"Hey, hey, Darius. Wake up."

I was frantic. I had to get there again. To see the monk. The monastery was perched on a rugged hill dotted with scraggy rocks. I scrambled, the sharp grit tearing at my knees and palms. My heart was thudding. Only one thing mattered—getting into that courtyard again. Smelling the marigolds, talking to the only other man I knew of who was the same as me.

"Darius, wake up."

Oscar. Oscar was with me. I turned but saw no one, just the empty plains and the towering mountains. I carried on running, my limbs heavy and leaden, my breaths hard to catch.

"Darius, for crying out loud. Open your eyes. Wake up."

My shoulders were squeezed; the voice came louder.

I did as instructed and opened my eyes.

Oscar's face was hovering over mine, our noses almost touching as he gripped me.

"Thank fuck," he muttered. "You okay?"

I gulped in air. "Yes, yes... I am."

"What were you dreaming about?" He paused. "Was it your father?" A shard of apprehension sliced over his features.

"No, no, not him. Someone else."

"Who?"

I gathered my thoughts then kissed him and forced a smile to reassure him. "Someone good this time, or at least I believe that's the case."

"That's a relief." He flopped back down and gathered me close. "Tell me."

"It's the other cambion, the monk Master Concorde told us about. He was there in my dreams and..."

"Go on."

"He wants me to go to him. He's in a monastery, up on a hill. It's white with a golden roof, and mountains surround it. We need to go there."

Oscar was quiet. "We'll see what George thinks."

I sat. "I agree, but I want to go to him. I *really* want to go to him. He's the only other person on the planet who will understand my situation."

Oscar sat, locking his arms behind himself, his t-shirt stretching over his torso. "He'll understand some of it, but remember, this cambion isn't gay, he isn't in love with vampires the way you are. He was sent to live in secret to protect his identity for all of time. Why would he want that secret exposed?"

"I don't know. But I believe he'll make an exception for me."

"What's going on?"

George and Lloyd appeared, their figures shadowy in the dim light.

"Darius had a dream," Oscar said.

George frowned. "Your father?"

"No, a monk. I believe it's the other cambion."

George was quiet for a moment. "He's in Tibet, so I guess geographically we're pretty close. Maybe there is a connection."

"Like telepathy?" I asked.

"Perhaps." George nodded at Lloyd. "Get Rhys and Patrick, they should hear this."

Lloyd huffed. "What did your last slave die of?" Despite his words, he still slipped out of the cave.

A minute later he was back, Rhys and Patrick with him.

"Okay, tell us what happened?" George said.

"Not much." I shrugged and wrapped a blanket over my shoulders. "I just saw him, he asked me to come to him, to visit."

"And...?" Lloyd prompted.

"And it felt right. He felt right. He's kind, concerned, honorable."

"We don't know any of this," Rhys said. "It could be a trick. Don't forget London, at the Tower."

"When the demon was there?" Patrick added.

"Yes." Rhys shook his head. "I'm worried."

"Hmmm." George took his cap off and ran his hand through his hair. "I'm not. Master Concorde has told me of his cambion. He's a good man, kind and peaceful."

"So how come I think you are worried about something?" I asked.

"I'm worried you might expose him for what he is, and in doing that you'll upset Master Concorde. Really not advisable." He slapped his cap back on and straightened it.

"But why would he ask me to visit him? You know my dreams are significant, the really vivid ones at least, and believe me, this was vivid."

"We should take him," Lloyd said. "If that's what he wants."

George frowned.

I had a glimmer of hope. Lloyd was on my side.

"This Master Concorde," Patrick asked. "What would we be dealing with if he was upset with us?"

Rhys took Patrick's hand. "He's a very powerful vampire within the Worshipful Company. Don't forget, we need him to perform a commitment ceremony between all of us and Darius, in secret, to make him ours. Also, we have to present you in halls as a new vampire. An angry Master Concorde would make all of that very difficult."

"Well said." George nodded.

"I saw Master Concorde not long ago, Oscar did, too," I said. "I think he'd understand, especially if I told him I dreamed of being with his cambion." I paused. "And we're so close to Tibet."

"Close?" Patrick said. "Not really...though at running pace, maybe." He grinned. "Could be fun."

"So we can go?" I said, hoping the answer would be yes because I really didn't want to have to argue until I'd persuaded them.

"No." George shook his head. "It's too risky."

"It isn't. Not when you consider what else I've been through since I met you all. I've fought a demon father, been captured by shifters who wanted to decapitate me, all of us, had sex with a new vampire and let him feed. That's risky. What is not risky is going to talk to a monk who has vowed to live a life of peace and harmony."

George folded his arms and nodded at Oscar. "I know what direction Lloyd's thoughts are going in, but what do you think?"

Oscar frowned. "I agree about not wanting to upset Master Concorde, but I don't want Darius upset either. And if he really wants to go to Tibet and see this cambion, we should."

George tutted, clearly frustrated by Oscar's answer. "Well, I still say no. it's too important that we stay in Master Concorde's good books."

"We know he's special to you, George," Rhys said. "But Darius's happiness is the most important thing, to all of us."

"Of course it is," George said. "But we need Master Concorde to keep Darius happy."

"I'm perfectly happy here," I said, "living in a cave with you all. I have everything I need. Food, shelter, *almost* more sex than I can handle."

"I'm glad you feel like that," George said. "But this is the end of the—"

"Don't you dare say conversation, George." I stood, dropping the blanket. "Because one of the things that makes us so strong together is that we decide things together."

Patrick stepped between me and George. He set his hand on my shoulder. "How about we vote on it? That's what we'd do in this kind of situation in the military, unless, of course, someone out-ranked everyone else." He raised his eyebrows at George.

"We're all equal," Lloyd said. "And it's good to remember that.'

"I think that's a great idea, Patrick." Rhys grinned. "We'll vote. Hands up who wants to take Darius to see his monk?"

I raised my hand. So did everyone else, except George.

He scowled and pulled his watch out. "I know which monastery he's in. We'll go at first light."

Chapter Twenty-Six

Darius

Within hours, I was standing at the large gated entrance to the Tsurphu Monastery.

A sign on the weathered scarlet door read *Closed to Visitors* in several languages.

I frowned. "Now what?"

"We go back to the cave," George said, straightening his clothes after our run.

"We can't give up that easily," Rhys said.

"Of course we can't." Lloyd surveyed the high wall as though contemplating jumping it.

"This should do the trick." Patrick reached for a cord hanging from a large brass bell. He yanked it.

Metallic thunder rang out, rising into the blue sky and down the steep rocky slope to the valley and village below.

"No harm in ringing the bell and asking for this monk." Patrick grinned.

I laughed, despite my nerves. Patrick had a nice simple way of surmising situations.

"We don't even know his name." George shook his head. "Who will we ask for?"

Damn it.

"It'll be okay." Lloyd squeezed my shoulder.

The door opened an inch, creaking as it did so.

A face peered out from the shadowed crack. "No tourists here."

"We're not tourists." I stepped close. "I'm looking for someone, a monk. I believe he's here. I also believe he wants to see me."

"We live a solitary life. Many of our monks have made vows of silence, and they have no need of visitors."

"Oh. I see." Blimey, I prayed my monk hadn't made such promises. It had been a long way to come if he couldn't talk to me.

But I won't give up, not that easily.

"Perhaps I could come in?" I said, grinning and hoping this monk would be won over by my model smile the way so many people were. "And see if I can find him."

"What do you want with him?"

He hadn't slammed the door, so I took that as a good sign. "Just to talk. I believe we have a few things in common...family things."

"I doubt that." He tipped his head, squinting at me. "What's your name?"

"Darius Linnet."

"Where are you from?"

"London originally. I've come a long way to find this man." I clasped my hands beneath my chin. "Please, can we come in?"

For a moment he was still and silent.

A bird of prey cawed overhead.

Then the door opened, not fully, but enough for me to slip through.

"Thank you," I said, not wasting a second in stepping over the threshold.

"Only you." He pointed at George, then swept his gaze over the rest of my vampires. "Not these...men."

"But we're together. They are my friends and—"

"No. Monks vow to have respect and kindness to all living things." He tilted his chin. "The key word is *living* things."

I swallowed and glanced at Lloyd and then George. How could this monk know what they were? It was impossible.

"You are welcome, Darius Linnet," the monk said. "Your friends, I'm afraid, are not."

It was clear he wouldn't be swayed, and I really did want to go in. "I'll be back soon, guys."

"I don't like it." George frowned, stepping up to the doorway.

"It's a monastery." I took his hand and squeezed. "No shifters, no demons," I said quietly. "And if I need you, I'll holler. You'll hear me, no problem."

His jaw tensed, then, "Use your sparks if you need to."

"I won't need to." I skimmed my lips over his. "Hang cool, okay."

He huffed and folded his arms, then stepped into the shade of the high wall.

"I won't be long," I said to the others before the monk closed the door with a solid click.

The inner sanctum was cool and smelled of incense. A large lotus flower fountain stood in the center of the courtyard. Butterflies fluttered near it, as though summoning the courage to take a drink. Several sparrows pecked nearby as a scarlet-robed monk swept with an old twig broom. He didn't glance up at my entry and appeared lost in thought.

"We live a quiet life," the monk at my side said. "We don't encourage visitors, but that doesn't mean we won't help someone in need." He clasped his hands together and bowed at the fountain as we walked past it. "And something about the company you keep, Darius, leads me to think you are in need."

"My life has been…turbulent lately."

"I can tell."

"How can you tell?"

He paused at an archway that was decorated with ropes of marigolds threaded on string.

"Your friends are cold, not like you." His nostrils flared a little. "You are warm and different. Your face reminds me of someone I know, which is why I let you enter our sanctuary."

"My face?"

"Is perfect. I'd go as far as to say beautiful."

I touched my cheek. I was more than used to being complimented on my looks, but this was an observation rather than a flattery. "I've modeled in the past."

"Modeled?" He raised his eyebrows.

"Yes, photographs, for magazines, worked on the catwalk, Milan, New York and..." It was clear by his confused expression that what I was referring to was alien. "You said my face reminded you of someone you know. Is he here?"

He didn't answer; instead, he turned and led the way beneath the archway.

I paused, my heart skipping a beat and a bluster of triumph wending through me.

I knew my dream was important

Here I was, standing in the walled garden I'd seen the night before. Bursting with vibrant golden marigolds, alive with birds, bees, and butterflies, and surrounded by the majestic Himalayas.

"I believe it is Llhamo you have come to see." The monk gestured to the far corner of the garden.

Amongst the stunning yellow flowers was a man in a long, blood-red robe tied at the waist with a blue rope. He held a watering can, and his bald head was bowed over an urn containing yet more flowers.

"Llhamo," I repeated.

"He's been with us a long time and is very wise." The monk tucked the tips of his steepled fingers beneath this chin and bowed at me. "Namaste." He retreated through the archway, leaving me alone in the walled garden.

I stared at the monk in the distance.

Was he like me?

A cambion. Half human. Half demon.

And would he speak to me?

Suddenly he looked up, as though sensing my presence.

I took a deep breath, trying not to feel small when all around me I was in the presence of the majestic mountains. I then walked over the neat, well-tended lawn.

As I approached, Llhamo set down his watering can and brushed his palms together, as though removing dirt or dust.

I stopped several feet from him, studying his face, one which I'd seen the night before in my dream.

"You came," he said, bowing and pressing his palms together. "Much quicker than I thought."

"I wasn't far away." I mimicked his bow.

"It was hard to tell where your cave was, from my dream."

"You dreamt of me?"

"Of course. Why would it be one-way?"

"I... I don't know. I guess I never thought of it."

"You would have eventually."

"What do you mean?"

"When you find your place of peace." He gestured around. "That is when the mind, body, and spirit is truly free. But I sense you are a few centuries from that yet."

"Centuries." I smiled. "How long have you been here?"

"I stopped counting decades ago."

His words and gentle tone were a balm to my nerves. It was clear, despite George's fears, that Llhamo didn't mind me visiting him, or talking about himself.

"We are the same," I said. "Cambions."

"The only two at this present time, I believe."

"On Earth?"

"Yes, though I'm sure there are spirits like us, who are awaiting reincarnation."

I nodded. "Perhaps."

"Can I ask you something...?"

"Darius, that's my name."

"Can I ask you something, Darius?"

"Of course."

"When did you last see Concorde?"

"A few months ago, in Krakow."

"And how was he?" He paused. "Occasionally, I send him something. I never expect a reply, though."

"He was working on a jury. Trying to keep rogue vampires under control."

"That sounds like him." Llhamo smiled. "Has he still got that cane with the wolf's head on it?"

"Yes. He has."

Llhamo chuckled. "He always had that with him."

"You were close?"

"Close, yes, not lovers, not in love, but close." He touched his neck. "I let him drink my blood in Kathmandu. So yes, we had a special connection, always will."

I glanced over my shoulder, surprised he'd spoken of the vampire's thirst for blood so openly.

"Do not fear, we will not be overheard," he said. "And if we are, most of my fellow monks are silent. There are only three of us here who speak."

"Why didn't you take the vow of silence?"

"It was a step too far. I'm safe here. I love practicing Buddhism, but believe it or not, I grew up in Paris. Many years ago now. This wasn't how I envisioned my eternity, and being French, I do like to talk."

Any French accent he'd once had was long gone. I smiled. "But you're happy?"

He cupped the head of a marigold, holding it between his fingers. "I'm enlightened, which by definition means I am happy and content with everything just the way it is. I hope you, too, can find enlightenment, Darius."

"So do I. It sounds blissful."

"But I'm not sure you will, not while you keep your vampires close."

I bit on my bottom lip. Life without them was unimaginable.

"They're a magnet for trouble," he went on. "Always on the run from something or hunting someone. They say they can control their thirst, but can they really? And when a love is so wild, can it ever really be trusted?"

"I love them. It's as simple as that."

"And love is why we're here." He smiled, released the flower, and touched my shoulder. "On this beautiful planet."

Warmth from his palm spread through my sweater onto my skin. "So what do you suggest I do, Llhamo?"

He raised his eyebrows a little.

"The monk who opened the door, he told me your name."

"Ahh, I see." He glanced at the archway. "I suggest you find yourself somewhere to live permanently that won't put temptation in the way of your vampires."

"Where?"

"Somewhere quiet and remote, like your cave. Away from wolves—vampires *really* hate wolves."

"I've discovered that."

"And away from humans."

"Okay, I get that isolation is a priority, but what else can you advise?"

"Keep yourself fit and strong. You won't age, Darius, but you would die if you ran out of blood, and from the dream I see you have five vampires to sustain. I only had two, for a relatively short period of time, and that was enough."

I nodded. "Thank you, I'll bear that in mind."

"And the demon, your father," he said, his eyes narrowing. "Where is he?"

"I killed him."

"Good. That certainly simplifies things."

I paused. "Can I ask? Did you kill your father, too?"

"No, Concorde performed that task." He downturned his mouth. "Nasty business. I don't like to recall it."

I decided not to push him. "Anything to do with a demon is a nasty business."

"That is a very true statement." He stooped and picked up his watering can. "And now I must get back to my task."

I was surprised he was bringing the conversation to a close. Was that all he'd wanted to tell me, to find myself somewhere remote to live and stay fit and strong?

"Concorde told me..." I hesitated.

"What?" His gaze connected with mine. "What did he tell you?"

"Er, what I mean is, I can make sparks." I held up my hands and waggled my fingers. "Concorde told me you could make water. Is that true?"

He studied me, seeming to see into my soul. "Yes," he said eventually. "It's true."

He cupped his right hand, the tendons beneath the skin of his forearm tensed. A small sparkle appeared in the well of his palm, glinting in the sunshine. It grew into a tiny dot of dew, then a drip and finally a palmful of pure, clean water.

"Wow," I said. "Impressive."

He tipped it into watering can. "It saves me countless trips to the spring."

"I'll bet."

"Can you show me your sparks?"

"I'm not as good at summoning them as you are with your water." I flexed and unflexed my fingers.

"That will come, over the millennia."

"Perhaps." I tried to summon the fire, willed the heat to grow in my chest, my shoulders, and spread down my arms. I closed my eyes, thought of my demon father trying to possess my body.

But there was no heat, no sparks. The walled garden was simply too calm and serene to invoke any kind of anger or intense emotion in me.

"Hang on," I said. "I'll...keep...trying..."

He smiled.

I concentrated really hard and remembered the moment my father had cornered me in an alley and swirled like a dirt devil, cornering me.

But there was no fire, nor sparks, to release.

"Nothing." I held in a curse word. "Sorry."

"It's okay," he said. "You can show me when we meet again."

"Do you think we will—meet again, that is?"

"Maybe I'm just talking about our dreams. We are cambion brothers, Darius. Unique from everyone else walking the planet today. I can't believe we won't stay in communication somehow."

"I'd like that." I smiled. An urge to hug him came over me, but I resisted. I had no idea what the rules were when it came to monk hugging.

"Me, too." He added another handful of water to his can. "Though I will give you one more piece of advice."

"What is that?"

"Get yourself formally committed to one of your vampires, two at the most. You will invoke suspicion quickly amongst the fanged community if you are seen to be with five. They will all know there is something special about you." He shuddered. "They'll drain you dry at the next equinox. You wouldn't stand a chance."

"Thank you for the advice." I shuddered at the thought of a feeding frenzy at midnight on equinox. "I intend to heed all of it as soon as possible."

"Good." He ducked his head, his hands coming together, the can tipping a little and leaking onto the lawn. "Namaste, my friend."

I mimicked his action. "Namaste."

Chapter Twenty-Seven

Oscar

I paced beside the monastery wall. Hating the sun's rays heating my head and neck. But what I hated more was that Darius was inside the huge building, and without an invite over the threshold, we couldn't follow him.

Him being out of sight didn't sit well with me. When one of his other vampires were with him, that was acceptable—they loved him the way I did. But when he was alone, without any of us, that just made my skin crawl and my dead heart squeeze.

"He's been twenty minutes." George studied his pocket watch for what seemed like the hundredth time.

"And he's got a whole hour." Patrick threw a stone across a ravine. He'd been doing that for a while, seeming to have some kind of target a couple of hundred meters or so away. He was a good shot.

"So why the stress?" Patrick added, landing a bull's-eye again.

"Why the stress?" Lloyd repeated. "What do you mean *why the stress*?" He had his hood pulled up, his shades on.

He reminded me of a sadistic, cunning serial murderer on a movie I'd watched a while ago. Dark, brooding, and damn dangerous.

"Darius can look after himself," Patrick went on. "He's strong, smart, and can make fire if he needs to."

"That's not the point," George said. "We love him, we can't imagine life without him. What if something happens—?"

"Nothing will happen to him." Patrick tutted. "He's in a goddamn monastery, for fuck's sake. I hid out in one a few years ago, had insurgents on my tail and—"

"Patrick." Rhys stepped from the shade. "They're worried, okay."

"I can see that, but I don't know why." He threw another stone. The echo of it hitting the target rattled around the valley.

"Will you stop that, it's hurting my ears," George snapped.

"I'm bored." Patrick clenched his fists and paced in a full circle.

"So find something else to do," Lloyd said.

"Like what?" Patrick paused. "Go down to that village and scare some kids with my fangs?"

I pushed away from the wall, my attention firmly fixed on Patrick. My muscles tensed, ready for action. If Patrick needed pinning down, I wasn't opposed to being the first one to jump on him.

"Of course you shouldn't do that." George glanced my way.

I gave him a tiny nod.

"Don't even say that as a joke," Rhys said, gripping Patrick's arm and pulling him to a halt.

"For crying out loud, would you guys take a chill pill." Patrick shook Rhys off. "I'm not going to, am I?"

"We don't know for sure," I said, eyeing his stance. Was he ready to run, burst into action?

"I'm not, I was joking." Patrick sighed then stepped into the shade of the wall. He slipped off his sunglasses and pinched the bridge of his nose. "You have to lighten up, all of you. I can't stand this intensity. There has to be some fun in life, otherwise, what is the point in existing?"

"We will lighten up," Rhys said. "Soon, I promise, when this is over."

"When what's over? This is it now." Patrick put his shades back on and gestured forward. "This. Is. It." He shrugged. "How we exist. How I exist."

"We have things to do, Patrick," George said. "Important things."

"Like what?" Patrick asked.

"Apart from keeping Darius's true identity a secret and keeping him safe, we need to go to London."

"Why?"

"We need to present you as a new vampire, remember, trained and with thirst under control." Lloyd pointed at Patrick.

"If it is." I glowered at our newest member.

"Yes, Oscar, it is. I've proven that."

"He did," Rhys said. "He fed from Darius, during sex, a high-intensity feed, and he stopped."

"Just," George muttered.

"And your running?" I added. "Can you be trusted to go where you're supposed to?"

"I made it to the cave, didn't I, Oscar, and here, without taking a detour."

Rhys smiled at Patrick. "Perfectly. Well done, Patrick."

Rhys's constant fawning over Patrick was beginning to grate on me. Yes, they were special to each other, they had chemistry, were falling in love even, but Rhys was overdoing the support and kid-glove handling. Patrick was one dangerous vampire with a skill set none of us truly understood yet, and if we didn't keep him under control, no one else would be able to. He was a wild card, a card that had never been played before in the history of time.

"You haven't proven to me your trustworthiness, Patrick," I said. "I'll admit you're doing well, but you've got more challenges ahead."

"Like what?" The jaunty tilt of his chin told me he was happy to take me on in any kind of challenge.

"A plane," Lloyd muttered.

I turned to him.

Lloyd shrugged. "We'll have to fly to London, won't we."

"I guess." It was too uncomfortable for Darius to be carried so far, plus there was a body of water to navigate. But damn, the thought of Patrick on a plane didn't appeal to me.

"I can fly." Patrick folded his arms. "Why wouldn't I be able to?"

"It's good that you're confident," Rhys said.

"I'll tell you why," I said. "Because you'll be in close proximity of a lot of humans. A plane is like a can of tuna to a cat, a bottle of vodka to an alcoholic. There's a lot of warm, fresh blood in one place, and it can't run away. The smell can be overwhelming, the desire to feed almost too much to bear."

"*Almost* too much to bear. So I'll bear it," Patrick said.

Everyone was silent, but their doubts were palpable.

"Listen, I don't know what other young vampires have been like," Patrick said, "how could I know? But I've had to march for days on end in bitter cold and heat, with hardly any rations, sometimes carrying injuries, or an injured colleague, and often with guys closing in who want to shoot me, torture me, or hack my head off on bloody YouTube. I'm used to challenge, summoning my willpower, keeping going when I have to."

Rhys tipped his head and studied Patrick. "You've done all of that?"

"What do you think my role in the British forces involved? I wasn't a fucking cook sitting safely on base or, heaven forbid, a pen-pusher."

George stepped forward. He took off his cap and held it at his chest. "Patrick, we've still got a lot to learn from you, about you, and we will, when this is over and we've got Darius somewhere safe. But until then, know that we're glad to have you with us. More than glad—you're a great guy and an asset to the group. Darius clearly has feelings for you, so does Rhys."

Rhys smiled.

"And if you think you'll be okay on a plane..." George paused. "Then we'll have to take that risk."

"You think?" I said. If Patrick got the scent of blood at thirty thousand feet and couldn't help himself, the shit would really hit the fan.

"What choice do we have, Oscar?" Lloyd said. "We stick together. We've seen what happens when we don't: it makes Darius unhappy."

"Blood brothers," Patrick said. "As we all feed from the same human."

"He's no ordinary human," I said.

"You don't have to tell me that." Patrick nodded at the monastery door. "He's got something no other man has, and I love him." He switched his attention to Rhys. "*Human* man, that is."

Rhys smiled. "I'm glad you love him."

"We all love him," George said. "Darius is our reason for existing. His happiness and safety is our mission on Earth."

A creak came from the door, then it opened a few inches.

I pushed from the wall, peering into the shadows within.

And then it opened farther, and Darius stepped out. It shut again quickly, as if to ensure we didn't slip through. Which, of course, we couldn't, not without an invite.

"Darius," George said, grabbing him in a hug. "We were worried."

"There was no reason to be." He set a quick kiss on George's lips then swung his attention over us all. "Within those walls, all is calm and peaceful; it's a beautiful place."

"Did you meet the other cambion?" I asked.

"Yes, I did."

"What's his name?" Lloyd asked.

Darius hesitated.

I frowned at him.

"Do you mind if I keep that to myself?" Darius said, looking at the ground and poking a stone with his boot.

"Er, no, not at all." Lloyd appeared a bit put out.

I didn't blame him. We didn't have secrets.

"Why, though?" George asked.

Darius sighed. "He's living anonymously, with people who are protecting him by not asking questions, by never revealing his identity or his whereabouts. I'd hate my visit to reveal his concealment to the outside world, be it purposefully or by accident."

George nodded. "If that makes you more comfortable, Darius, then yes, we understand."

"Thank you." Darius nodded. "He didn't say much, other than we are the only two cambions at present and it would be wise to perform the affirmation ceremony to one, or two of you as soon as possible so as not to arouse suspicion among the vampire community about who I really am."

"Why would anyone be suspicious?" Patrick asked. "You look normal—well, fucking gorgeous, but normal." He grinned.

"It's the fact so many of us are in love with him," Rhys said. "Most humans and vampires are couples. There's an occasional threesome, but four, now five of us? They'd either think Darius is a Bombay or a holder of the key."

"Aye, of course." Patrick nodded. "So we go to London, right, for this ceremony."

"Yes."

George, Lloyd, Darius, and I had spoken at once.

Rhys laughed.

I pointed at the valley. "Might as well get going then."

Thank goodness for first-class seats. Without my limbs squished and folded, I could relax on the journey to London.

Relax. Who am I kidding?

Apart from the fact the air was laced with all different blood types and the unmistakable scent of adrenaline—nervous flyers—Patrick was sitting next to me practically salivating.

"Am I going to have to tie you to that fucking seat?" I muttered.

"I'm fine, chillax." He waved away a glass of champagne that was offered to him by a cute air steward with a tight ass and fancy designer stubble. "I'd rather have a flute of the good stuff." He smacked his lips together. "His would be a start."

I gripped his forearm, hard. "Shut the hell up."

"You don't seem to understand the concept of a joke, Oscar." He frowned.

"I understand just fine, I'm just not in the mood for yours."

"What's going on?" Darius poked his head up from the seat in front.

"Nothing," I muttered, keeping a grip on Patrick.

"Want me to trade seats?" Rhys asked from across the aisle.

"Yeah, I'll swap," Lloyd said, his voice coming from behind me.

We had Patrick well enclosed. There was no way he was giving us the slip to lock himself in the loo with some poor unsuspecting traveler and take a long, mile-high drink.

I shook my head. "Nope. I don't need to swap seats with anyone."

Patrick sighed and tugged his arm from my grip. "My ass is on the seat, I'm strapped in, what more can I do?"

"Watch a movie," George said, his face appearing next to Darius's. They were seated next to each other. "Watch four, and then we'll be there and we can all relax...a bit."

"Fuck. If you weren't immortal, you'd have all died of blood pressure problems by now."

"Patrick." Darius smiled at him. "There's a war movie about Afghanistan on. I'm going to watch it. You can tell me what they got wrong afterwards if you watch it, too."

"Ahh, good idea." He stabbed at the control panel. "Aye, I see it. I'll start it now."

I released a tense sigh. Perhaps I'd have ninety minutes or so without having to restrain our sniper with fangs.

I put the same movie on but with only one headphone in. I didn't want to remove one of my most acute senses. Getting lost in a war story and having Patrick go on a reconnaissance mission around the fuselage wasn't on my to-do list.

The movie started. Patrick settled back in his seat, feet up, ankles crossed.

I kept one eye on the action, the other on the vampires and humans around me.

About an hour later, when the lights were dimmed, food and drink served and tidied away, Darius giggled softly then gasped.

My curiosity was piqued.

Leaning forward, I peered into his seat area.

It seemed he and George were having fun beneath the blanket. George was giving Darius's cock attention, perhaps to relieve the boredom of the long flight.

I smiled and settled back, remembering my first flight with Darius. It had been from Paris to London, and I'd told him I was gay. He'd told me he was, too. It was the first time he'd told another person.

I still held that knowledge close. His trusting me had been important for us to keep him safe, but also important because it laid the foundation for what our relationship and love would become.

The air steward appeared from behind a dark-purple curtain separating the staff area from the first-class cabin—the cute one with the stubble and deep-blue eyes. He'd been very attentive to all of us. I couldn't decide if it was because it was his job or if he found us all attractive, each in our own way.

Would he if he knew what we really were?

I smiled at that, but the grin dropped as he made his way toward us. He was walking slowly, as though making himself available should anyone need anything.

A low groan trickled my way. Darius, he was getting close to coming, I would recognize that sound anywhere.

I glanced at Patrick, then past him to Rhys. Both were absorbed in the movie.

The air steward drew closer, his chin tilted, his gaze drifting over his passengers.

I swallowed tightly. There was nothing I could do except see what happened and hope Darius had his fun before they were interrupted.

"Oh, George."

"Shh, Darius..." George said.

A long, quiet groan—muffled by the sound of the engines but audible to my ears.

The steward was alongside George's seat. He paused, looked; his eyes widened.

I bit on my bottom lip. He wouldn't be able to see anything unless George had removed the blanket from Darius's lap, which I doubted. But his expression told me he knew exactly what he'd stumbled upon.

His jaw hung open.

Darius groaned again, a deep, throaty noise.

The steward appeared frozen in time, both shocked and fascinated.

I tipped my head, enjoying his surprise. He should enjoy the sight, too. Darius coming was pretty damn awesome.

And then he took a step forward, his mouth snapping shut. His gaze connected with mine.

I raised my eyebrows, letting him know I, too, was aware of what was going on in the seat in front.

He cleared his throat. "Can I get you anything, sir?"

"Some of what he's having." I nodded forward.

"Oh, er..." A rise of color bloomed on his pale cheeks. "I'm sorry, shall I...I mean."

I chuckled. It was clear big, bad bikers weren't his type. "I'm pulling your leg," I said. "Just jealous, that's all."

"Ah, yes..." He swiped his tongue over his bottom lip, and his gaze took in my folded arms and wide chest. "I have some of that in the..." He glanced at Patrick who was still absorbed in his movie. "In the kitchen area. Perhaps, in a few minutes, you'd like to come and choose, get it." He nodded in the direction of the purple curtain. "And I can make sure you have what you need."

Ahh, so leather-clad bikers do yank his chain. That was a surprise.

"Thank you." I grinned. "Might just do that."

"Yes, do, sir. We aim to be the best of the best here at Dahali Airways. Satisfaction is guaranteed."

I held in a laugh. Talk about laying it on the table. It had been a long time since anyone was brave enough to be so brazen with me. I had to admire him for that.

He glanced at Patrick again, then stood straight and continued down the aisle.

I sat back, still smiling. I wouldn't be taking him up on his offer. I was loyal to Darius; plus, I had no intention of being more than a foot away from Patrick for the entire flight. But it was nice to be offered. Nice to know I still appealed to this generation of cute guys.

Chapter Twenty-Eight

Darius

The Worshipful Company of the Ancient Order had made me nervous before, and it was giving me the heebie-jeebies now. It was a big, imposing building, with tall sash windows, wrought-iron railings, and a huge pillared entrance. But it wasn't that which had my stomach rolling, it was the sheer quantity of vampires within—existing in central London side by side with humans, that would all love to feast on my blood. That was what made me nervous. That was what made my skin itch and my heart pound.

"It'll be okay," Rhys said, taking my hand and giving it a squeeze. "Just like last time, we're a couple. Smile and nod, don't offer any information unless you absolutely have to and then make it vague."

I nodded then followed George, Lloyd, and Patrick up the steps. Oscar walked behind Rhys and me.

We entered the lair. It was so very different to my mother's small house, which I'd just visited. There were no floral curtains, plates of biscuits, Lladro ornaments or bowls of potpourri.

"Well, well, well, here's a sight for sore eyes," Samree, the vampire receptionist said from behind a wide polished desk. "Where have you all been these last few months?"

"Siberia," George said. "To our cabin."

"Ah, the one Master Concorde loves so much." She swept her long-lashed gaze over us all. It settled on Patrick, and she licked her scarlet lips. "And I see you have brought the newest member of your gang."

"We're not a gang," Lloyd muttered.

"Okay, how about brood, coven, pack or...I know, clan?"

"We're friends," George said. "Nothing more."

Samree stood. She snapped her black silk blouse straight then strutted around the desk holding a pen with a long feather wafting from it.

Her skirt was tight and hit just above her knees. Her heels were toweringly high, and her waist so tiny any of the female models I knew would have given secrets of their best fad diet for the same.

She walked up to Patrick and held out the feather. She tipped her head and studied him as she floated it between their faces, just touching his nose. "What's up, Corporal?"

"Officer," he said, holding her eye contact. "Officer Patrick Sinclair."

She smiled. "That wasn't what I asked?" She touched the tip of the feather to his throat, then slid it downward, over his t-shirt, and stopped it where his navel would be beneath the material. "I asked what was *up*?"

Patrick raised his eyebrows, and a smile tugged at the right side of his mouth. It was a damn sexy smile, and my stomach clenched. The guy was hot—hotter than hot, there was no denying it.

"You do know," Samree went on, "that all these boys you're hanging out with are gay, right? They've all resisted me; only true gays can resist me." She giggled, her eyelids fluttering.

Patrick was silent. Chin tilted, gaze unwavering, breaths steady. Though I did see his nostrils flare slightly—was he inhaling her scent or was he firming up his self-control?

"You've hooked up with the more-than-friends crew. The batting-for-the-same team gang," Samree said, her attention unwavering.

George cleared his throat.

I waited for him to speak. He didn't.

"You know that, right." Samree slipped the feather to his groin and stroking it over his camo trousers. "They all like cock."

"There wasn't much choice but to stick with them." Patrick pinched the tip of the feather between his thumb and forefinger and halted her stroking of his pants. "I was turned by Rhys, so we're...an item."

"Ah, I see, an item. So you *are* one of them." She glanced at Rhys and then me. "But Rhys has...Darius, his human. Doesn't he?"

"Why are you always so bloody nosy, Samree?" Oscar muttered. "You don't run this place. It's not necessary for you to know every-fucking-thing."

"Oh, Oscar, of course it isn't. I just like to." She giggled then leaned closer to Patrick, resting her lips by his cheek. "If ever you decide to find out what sex with a female vampire is like, let me know, sexy boy."

"I've been known to show a woman a good time," Patrick said, his voice low. "And I can assure you, I'm no boy."

She giggled again. "Tell me more."

"Let's just say my finely honed skills include female anatomy and—"

Lloyd clapped. "Right, that's enough. Someone sign Patrick and Darius in."

"I'll do it," George said, snatching the feathered pen from Patrick and Samree. "And I'll meet you all in the lobby."

Rhys dragged me from the reception area. He hauled Patrick with him, too. "You were so damn well-behaved on the plane," he muttered. "Why go and say that to Samree?"

"She's hot," Patrick said, "and maybe..."

"Maybe what?" I frowned. My second meeting with Samree hadn't improved my already low opinion of her. She was manipulative, prying, and sex-obsessed."

"Maybe I would like to see what sex with her would be like," Patrick said. "A beautiful woman with fangs and stamina."

"Trust me," Lloyd said, coming up to us. "You wouldn't want to find out, Patrick."

"How would you know?" Patrick came to a halt beside the huge statue of Master Benedict. "I can't imagine you dipping your wick there, Lloyd."

"Too damn right I wouldn't." Lloyd paused. "I've seen her in action, in the dungeon. She has one serious sadistic streak."

"What, with a feather?" Patrick laughed. "I've been on the receiving end of worse torture implements."

"What?" I asked, genuinely horrified that Patrick, *my* Patrick, might have been tortured in the line of duty.

He winked at me. "Another time, Darius."

"No, not the damn feather." Lloyd raised his gaze to the statue. "Give me strength."

"What then?" Patrick frowned up at Benedict.

"Maybe you'll get to see for yourself," Oscar said, clasping Patrick's shoulder. "The dungeon is down that set of stairs."

I stared at the direction Oscar had pointed. When I'd gone down those steps before, into the dungeon, I'd had serious fun with Rhys. I'd fucked him, my first time topping. We'd both come spectacularly—in a private room, though, we hadn't wanted an audience the way many vampires and their humans did down there.

"Master Concorde is in his chambers." George strode past us. His shoulders stiff and his shoes clipping on the hard floor. "This way."

Five minutes later, we were lined up before Master Concorde's desk. He sat with his hands spread before him and his cane propped against the wall at his rear.

"Darius Linnet," he said. "We meet again."

"Master Benedict," I said, inclining my head. "I trust you are well."

"Quite well. How was Siberia?"

"Cold."

He raised his eyebrows. "And...?"

I glanced at George.

"And," George said, "we had a bit of a run-in with the Carlton Pack."

"I'd heard a rumor," Master Concorde said. "Guessed it was you."

"Bloody bad luck," Lloyd mumbled. "They haven't been that far west for years. Seems they've got a whole town running, up by the coast."

"Global warming affects us all." Master Concorde tapped his fingers together. "With a limited time each year to cross the ice between Canada and Russia, they've had to make new plans."

I nodded.

"But you seem to have survived the encounter with them unscathed."

"Yes," George said, "but it would serve us all well to make an announcement about their town of Sunezh in chambers as soon as possible, so word is spread."

"I will do that tomorrow." Master Concorde sat back and stroked his beard. "And I'm guessing the reason you're here is because there is something else you wish me to do tomorrow in chambers."

"Yes." George glanced at Lloyd. "And now, today, here in privacy, if that is still acceptable to you."

Master Concorde was quiet then, "My son, it concerns me that you still wish to all be affirmed with Darius and have your commitment to him in writing when it's clear you are all very committed to him already. Why not have him publicly affirmed as Rhys's human partner and then keep the truth about you all being with him a secret that is never written down or spoken of again?"

"We've thought long and hard," George said. "And it's the best way to ensure Darius's safety in the decades and centuries to come.

If we all have a right to be with him, protect him, feed off him, he stands the most chance of survival."

"Yes," Lloyd said. "If something happens to Rhys, we can all, under vampire law, claim him as ours and take him to safety."

"I love them all equally," I said. "It's what I want, too." I paused. "And to survive, obviously."

"Mmm." Master Concorde stood, scooping up a box of matches. He walked to a thick, cream-colored candle on a tall bronze plinth and lit it. "Do you understand, Darius, how important it is to keep your true identify and your power to unlock the key to eternal damnation a secret?"

"Of course." I nodded. "I'm perfectly aware of that." It was a secret I would keep close forever. I had to.

He held his hands to the flame as if warming his palms, then, "In that case, all face this ancient flame."

Rhys tightened his fingers around mine.

On the opposite side, Oscar took my free hand.

"Darius, do you swear in the name of our revered Master Benedict to be good and true to the city of London?"

"I do."

"Do you promise to uphold the customs of our order and maintain the peace between us and Her Royal Highness Queen Elizabeth the Second?"

"I do."

"Remind me of your situation?"

"I...er..."

"He has a mother, here in London," Lloyd said.

"Ah, okay, we'll miss that out of the public ceremony tomorrow. You know how it upsets the natives." He narrowed his eyes at me. "Tell me about your mother?"

"She is a quiet, religious woman, fit and well. I speak to her often."

"And does she know about your sparks?"

I nodded. "Yes, apart from the people in this room, she is the only other person who does."

Except for Llhamo, he knows.

Master Concorde nodded. "And do you believe that your soul has connected with George's, Lloyd's, Oscar's, Rhys's, and Patrick's?"

"I do. Very much so." I smiled at George, then Lloyd.

Oscar and Rhys squeezed my hand. Patrick tipped his head and studied me; he swiped his tongue over his bottom lip.

I sank a little closer to Rhys, his solid body comforting but offering no protection from the intense scrutiny I was under.

"Now, Mr. Linnet, please hold up your right hand." The Master stared straight at me.

I did as he'd asked, feeling strangely as if I were getting married. Which in a way I was. I was committing myself to these men for all of time.

"Please repeat after me," Master Concorde said. "I solemnly declare that I will be good and true to the Worshipful Company of the Ancient Order."

I cleared my throat. "I solemnly declare that I will be good and true to the Worshipful Company of the Ancient Order."

"And that as a guest in the Sacred Chambers and a house belonging to the company, I will be obedient, respectful, and above all keep information confidential."

"I will."

"And in affirming your commitment to these five vampires, you will forsake others, allow them to feed from you, live as equals, and ensure no harm is done in the pursuit of happiness and satisfaction. Say yes if you agree."

"Yes."

"You are affirmed, Darius." He set his palms on my head. "And I am delighted to have you as part of our family."

"Thank you." A surge of excitement went through me. I'd done it. *We'd* done it. Now we were together forever.

"Congratulations." Master Concorde smiled at me and then at George. "This has been a long time coming."

"I knew if I waited and searched for long enough I would find the man I wanted to spend eternity with," George said. "This is indeed a happy day."

I blinked rapidly, trying not to let pesky drips of moisture build on my lower lids.

"Now if you let me just draw up the contract, you can all sign it, and I'll place it in my private safe."

"Yes, sir," Rhys said. He then turned to me and gave me a kiss. "How do you feel?"

"Married." I laughed, a sudden burst of sound in the quiet room.

"Good." Oscar spun me to face him and pressed his lips to mine. "That's how you should feel."

Next I was passed to Lloyd who didn't speak, but his kiss told me how much the moment meant to him.

"Forever," George said, turning my face to his. "Is not long enough to be with you."

One of those pesky tears did escape; it ran down my cheek, and I let it as George kissed me, too, his tongue stroking mine.

And then Patrick was before me. Big and rough around the edges, the usual glint of unpredictability in his eyes. "Been a whirlwind romance," he said, "but I'm not complaining."

He dragged me close, kissing me with passion and enthusiasm.

I clung to him, adoring being mashed up against his hard body.

Master Concorde cleared his throat. "Er, if you can all please sign."

"Of course," George said.

Patrick pulled back but didn't release me. "I hope we can spend some honeymoon time in the dungeon."

"Yes," I said. "Me, too."

We all signed the contract that bound us together and then watched as Master Concorde used a huge iron key to lock it away in a safe behind a picture of a castle in the middle of a lake.

"You may go," Master Concorde said, seating himself behind his desk again. "And we will repeat this ceremony with Rhys and Darius in chambers tomorrow morning. Ensure you do nothing to suggest there is a relationship between all of you, otherwise tongues will be wagging and suspicion mounting faster than Samree can sniff out a new vampire."

"Yes, Master Concorde."

"And talking of new vampires." Master Concorde turned his attention to Patrick. "I have already been informed about your turning. You seem to be doing very well. I trust Rhys is keeping you in line." He looked from Rhys to George.

"He's doing an excellent job, better than we dared hope." George smiled. "And Patrick is proving to have impressive control over his thirst for such a young vampire."

"Good, good. In that case, you can present him in chambers tomorrow. The sooner he begins to study vampire law and integrate with the community the better."

"Thank you, sir." Patrick clicked his heels together and saluted Master Concorde. "Much appreciated, sir."

Master Concorde gave a rare smile. "At ease, Soldier, and well done."

I went to leave, but when I reached the door, Master Concorde spoke again. "Darius, wait, I wish to speak to you."

I turned to him with my hand on the door. "Of course."

"Alone." His eyebrows dropped low as he studied my vampires.

"Yes, sir," George said. He hesitated for a second and then left.

The others followed.

I shut the door.

"You went to Tibet," Master Concorde said, reaching for his cane and stroking the wolf's head that topped it.

"Yes."

"Why?"

"I think you know why." I smiled.

"You saw my cambion."

I nodded.

He blew out a breath, his eyes closing for a moment. "Why?"

"He is the only other person on Earth like me. We wanted to meet."

"We?"

"It seems we can connect in our dreams."

"Ah, yes, your dreams. Exquisite skill you have there, Darius." He paused. "And how was he?"

"Well, peaceful. He said he was enlightened."

"Then he is a very lucky man."

"I agree." Though in truth, I thought his life was a little dull, if that was it, inside the walled garden of a mountain monastery for all of time. But perhaps my opinion of that would change over the years.

"And what name is he going under now?"

"You don't know?"

"He was given anonymity and protection by the monks. Five centuries ago, I said goodbye to him and the name he used to go under."

"Oh, I see." I paused. "Perhaps I shouldn't break his confidence in allowing you to know his new name."

Master Concorde raised his eyebrows. "He is my cambion."

"He also wishes to live without fear or visitors."

"I can't visit him." Master Concorde frowned. "The monks wouldn't invite me over the threshold even if I said I held the secret to all of Buddha's riddles and prophesies."

"It is true, they don't seem to be very keen on vampires.'

Master Concorde was quiet for a moment. "I admire your loyalty to him, whatever his new name is. I can't fault you for that. But, if you see him again, dreams or otherwise, please tell him I think of him often and my gratefulness for what he did all that time ago is still very much alive within me." He touched the red string on his wrist. "And tell him I wear this."

"Of course, I'll tell him all of that when I see him." I smiled and nodded at the door. "Can I go now?"

"Yes, and congratulations. That's a fine set of men you've got there. The best, in fact."

"I know."

Chapter Twenty-Nine

Darius

"So now what?" I asked after I'd finished eating an egg and bacon roll Rhys had produced.

George checked his pocket watch. "It's too early for a trip to the dungeon."

"But we've got celebrating to do," Lloyd said, winking at me.

"And we need to consummate our affirmation," Oscar whispered by my ear as he handed me a mug of rejuvenating tea.

"Hey." George glanced around the lobby. Several corridors led from it, and a huge sweeping staircase rose upward. "Remember Darius is with Rhys. No one else."

"Yeah, aren't I the lucky one." Rhys ran his hand over my left ass cheek and squeezed.

Instantly thoughts of the dungeon besieged me. It was the only thing that could happen next. "We should do it, show everyone that Rhys and I are still together, stronger than ever, and then…there's still private rooms, right?"

"Yeah, there will be," Oscar said. "And likely free at this time of day."

"I'm liking the sound of this." Patrick rubbed his hands together and glanced at the entrance. "I've fucked in some weird places but never a vampire dungeon."

"Be quiet," George said through gritted teeth. "There are ears everywhere."

"And if there were, you'd hear them, George," Lloyd said. "Come on, there's bound to be something hot going on downstairs, even if it is early in the day. And if not, Rhys and Darius can provide the entertainment." He grinned at me.

My cock stiffened at the thought of the others watching me fucking Rhys and making us both come, no holds barred. Would it turn them all on? I was sure it would but I wanted to find out for sure.

"Yeah, this way." Rhys grasped my hand. "No time like the present."

We navigated down the stone steps to the arched wooden door. Like before, it was shut firm, but the moment it opened, the scent of sweat and sex mixed with incense drifted toward me.

The lighting was dim, candles flickered on wall sconces, and several fires burned in grates.

Stepping farther in, I paused to let my eyes adjust. The bed before me, which previously had been a hive of orgy activity, was empty, but to the left, a male was tied to a cross. A female in a tight black dress and thigh-high scarlet boots held a metallic whip and was speaking into his ear.

"I'm liking this already," Patrick whispered. "And you'd look good on that cross, Darius."

"You've a while to go before you get to tie him up," Oscar muttered.

"I'm just saying." Patrick huffed. "Our guy would look hot on there, his ass striped with a whip and his dick hard."

Oscar didn't answer.

I clenched my ass cheeks, a shimmy of sensation rushing over my skin.

The female brought the whip down on her man.

He jerked, cried out, then groaned, long and low.

She let the whip hang on the floor, reached around him, and appeared to take hold of his cock, her shoulder shifting as she worked it.

"Oh Benedict, yes..." he moaned.

"He's the vampire?" Patrick asked.

"Yeah, seems he's got himself a little Dominatrix human." Lloyd chuckled. "Good luck to them."

We walked past several closed doors and an empty stage.

A booth held three naked figures—a female and two males. She was on her back on a small leather bench, her head tipped as she took a cock in her mouth, her legs up on the shoulders of the guy fucking her.

"Jeez, that's hot," Patrick said, shoving his hand down his pants and adjusting himself. "Spit-roasted well and truly."

For a moment we watched, which is what the threesome would have wanted, and I leaned closer to Rhys. My cock was fully erect now, my skin hot beneath my clothes which were suddenly itchy and heavy.

The grunts and groans of the threesome intensified, and their pace picked up. They were fucking with gusto. Lost in the moment, lost in each other.

"It's Aimery and Ryle," Lloyd said to George.

"Yes, it is, with their mate...what's her name again?"

"Beatrice." Lloyd pushed his hood back so it settled around his neck.

"Yes, that's right." George bit on his bottom lip. "Looks like they're still very much in lust."

"And so am I," I said, tugging Rhys to the right. "And I need satisfying. Come on, new husband of mine."

"Husband." Rhys laughed. "Okay, whatever you want, big boy."

I grinned and tugged him to the next booth along. A fire burned in a grate, casting shadows over the gnarly stone walls. A thick wooden shelf held several candles of differing sizes, and beside it were metal cuffs with a chain between them.

But it was the table in the middle that had caught my attention. It was the perfect height to tip Rhys over, fuck him, and let the others watch.

I didn't pause, didn't hesitate. I needed this. I needed to be inside him, coming…now.

"Darius," he gasped when I pulled him close, squashing my lips to his.

I grabbed his ass and hauled his groin to mine. Both our cocks were hard, our breaths fast, and my heart was pounding.

"You do know I'm going to fuck you, right here, right now," I said against his lips.

"Yes. I want that." He glanced to his left, where the others stood.

"You want Patrick to see?"

"Of course." He grinned. "He'll enjoy it."

"But it's more than that," I said, reaching for the button on his jeans.

"What do you mean?"

"He needs to know that first and foremost you're mine, Rhys. You might have fun with him, a strong bond, but you and me, we fell in love first. I saved you from damnation. It's me who—"

"Who is the love of my non-life, I get it." He ran his hands over my hair, pushing it back from my face. "Never doubt the strength of my feelings for you, Darius. We are meant to be, for all eternity." He kissed me again. "Now deliver on that promise of a good, hard fucking."

I smiled a scorching carnal flush racing over my skin, through my veins, and making my peripheral vision blur. Rhys was all that existed.

"Turn around." As I'd spoken, I'd spun him to face the table.

He landed on it with a thud. He was stronger than I could comprehend, but Rhys tucked that away when he wanted to be dominated. He put it to one side and let me do as I pleased.

Another thing I love about him.

I dragged at his jeans, tugging them down along with his tight black boxers.

His ass cheeks were pert and tanned, and I admired them, releasing my cock and gripping it.

"Fuck me," Rhys said, clasping his right buttock to expose his hole. "Don't mess around, just fuck me."

I knew he'd cope without lube, he wasn't made like me, so I arrowed the tip of my cock at his pucker and applied pressure.

He groaned and wrapped his fingers around the lip of the table.

Impatience gnawed at me. So much had happened in the last twenty-four hours, and I needed relief. I needed to sink deep.

I shoved in, his hole stretching around me. When I gained entry, I didn't pause. I kept on going, pushing into his cold body, taking what I needed.

I seized his hips, drew him onto me as I hit full depth.

He arched his back, an ecstatic wail tearing from his throat.

Gritting my teeth, I pulled almost out, then barged back in. He was so damn tight, hugging me like an elastic band. I groaned, a free, abandoned noise that I hoped would turn my other vampires on. There was no point in holding back.

And then the real fucking began. I thrust in and out, driving us both to orgasm. My balls constricted, and my belly slapped up against his ass.

Suddenly Patrick was there, in front of Rhys, and minus his t-shirt. He shoved at his trousers and released his cock.

I grinned. He had a magnificent cock.

My brain kind of clicked into gear. A wave of panic came over me. It was supposed to be just Rhys and me. We were together, the couple. But Patrick was before us, cock out...

I shot a glance at George.

He nodded, a slight smile tilting his lips.

He thinks it's okay.

Oscar's expression hadn't changed.

Lloyd gave me the thumbs up, clearly understanding my concerns.

And by the looks of it they were unfounded concerns.

Threesomes are popular in the dungeon, common even.

"You need spit-roasting, Rhys," Patrick said, cupping Rhys's chin, the tendons beneath the inked skin on his forearm tensing. "Don't you agree?"

Rhys nodded, but only for a split second because then Patrick was forging his dick in, taking Rhys's mouth at the same time I took his ass.

My pleasure doubled, seeing Patrick's abs tensing, the bliss on his face, and his fingers curling in Rhys's hair was so damn hot.

This is okay. This isn't breaking rules. The others would have stopped it if that was the case.

And boy was it erotic to be having a threesome with these two sexy guys, with an audience too.

I upped the tempo, pounding so fast my hair swung in front of my eyes and my skin became slick with sweat.

I was getting close, the need to release becoming too big to contain. "Ah, fuck yes, fuck...I'm..."

"Rhys is nearly there," Patrick said. "Very nearly."

"I'm am too. Oh God. I'm coming..." I said, my eyes wide. The release had reached bursting point. "Come with me, Rhys."

He couldn't answer, but I knew he'd obeyed my instruction. His entire body shook, his asshole clenched around my cock, and a wild cry escaped his lips seeping out past Patrick's cock.

"Fuck yeah, that's it," Patrick said, his eyes flashing.

Pleasure burst from me, filling Rhys. It dragged up my shaft, sending me spinning into ecstasy. I held my breath, allowed more delicious spurts to burst forward.

"Here." I leaned forward, arm outstretched. "Rhys."

Patrick withdrew and stepped back, holding his still erect cock and panting.

"Drink," I said, putting my wrist at Rhys's lips.

He sank his fangs in, and I slumped onto his back, his skin cool on my hot flesh.

Instantly, new waves of intense bliss shot through my cock, my ass, and my belly. My knees were weak as he fed, my mind full of love and delight. Fucking Rhys was so damn amazing.

But he only fed for a few seconds, and then he released me.

Patrick was there, no longer holding his cock but my forearm.

His eyes were wide and manic, his fangs out, lips peeled back.

"Yes," I said. "You can..."

"Fuck," Rhys gasped. "Patrick."

Patrick had already started feeding, two new puncture wounds in my wrist supplying the blood he craved.

And then Lloyd, George, and Oscar were around us.

"Give him a few seconds." George held up his index finger.

"He needs stopping." Oscar placed his hands on Patrick's shoulders.

My mind was wandering, I was barely hearing their words. My orgasm was extending, the pleasure taking over every sense and thought.

"That'll do," Lloyd said. "He's had as much as Rhys did."

"Stop. Stop." Rhys wriggled beneath me and pushed at Patrick. "For the love of Benedict, Patrick get yourself under control." He was breathless.

Patrick lifted. My blood dripped from his teeth, lips, and chin.

"Oh God," I moaned, the orgasm finally receding. "That was..."

"Fun." Patrick grinned.

"Seriously, Soldier, that wasn't the plan," Oscar said, shaking his head.

"I only took what Rhys took." Patrick slid his fangs away and wiped the back of his hand over his mouth.

I gulped in air and straightened. Lloyd wrapped his arm around me as though concerned I'd fall over.

"We've got an audience." George gestured behind himself.

I turned, refocused, and spotted several vampires in various states of undress, watching us.

"Threesomes are common down here though," I said, to reassure myself that I hadn't misinterpreted their consent for the threesome. I had been in the throes of pleasure after all.

"Absolutely." Oscar nodded. "Sharing a human mate for sex and their blood is acceptable. Even more so with a new vampire who is learning control."

"There won't be a problem," George added.

Thank goodness.

I pressed my palms on Rhys's cute ass cheeks. My cock was still buried deep. "Did you enjoy that, Rhys?"

"Do you even need to ask?" He clenched around me.

I groaned. "Fuck, that feels so good."

"And it's what I want," Lloyd whispered. "To be in your ass."

"So let's go to a private room." I paused. "Or can't we now?"

"Of course we damn well can."

I smiled and withdrew from Rhys. A final tremor of pleasure snaked up my belly, and I tensed. I was hot. Perspiration had formed on my brow and under my arms.

"Walk into that room there with Rhys and Patrick," Lloyd said. "We'll follow in a minute when no one is looking that way."

I didn't answer; instead, I tucked my cock away then helped Rhys to standing. I pressed on my inner wrist, which had four ruby-red drips of blood leaking from it.

"Now," George said. "We don't want to risk anyone else smelling your blood."

Patrick's arm was around me, Rhys at my opposite side.

They were composed and calm as we walked to an open doorway. I was still breathing fast, my cock and balls tingling and my heart racing.

The private room was bigger than the previous one I'd been in. Like the rest of the dungeon, the walls were stone, and there was an abundance of squat church candles on shelves. There was also a cross complete with leather cuffs, a table holding an assortment of whips, paddles, and plugs, and a long mirror.

In the center was a leather bench, the legs wide as if it stood with its feet far apart. At the base of the legs were metal clasps.

I paused. If Lloyd, George, Patrick, and Oscar all wanted to fuck, chances were I'd be going over that.

A new tremble of lust gripped my belly. I'd just come, wonderfully, but the thought of more orgasms was very appealing. Perhaps it would always be this way now. I wouldn't be totally satisfied until I'd had all of my men.

"Here." Rhys handed me a bottle of water. "Tea later, but drink this."

"Thanks." My throat was dry from groaning, gasping, and crying out as I'd climaxed.

"Better?" Rhys asked.

I nodded and put the lid on.

Patrick was watching me intently.

"You okay?" I asked.

"Yes. But I want to finish what I just started...with Rhys." He put his hand down his trousers, which were sitting low and still undone. "My cock aches. I need to come."

"So come," I said. "But over there, so I can see you." I gestured to the head end of the bench.

"Ah, so you've figured out what we intend to do." Lloyd appeared and took my hand.

The door clicked shut. A bolt slid into place.

"Our cambion is smart," George said, slipping off his jacket and hanging it on a wall hook. "He knows what's coming next."

"Yeah, there's only one way to celebrate our affirmation," Oscar said gruffly and undoing his trousers.

Can I handle this?

A thread of doubt tugged at my stomach. All three of my big, thirsty vampires had a look of intent—an air of not-stopping-until-we're-all-screaming.

"This way," Lloyd said.

I followed him. When we reached the bench, he came to a halt and gripped the base of my sweater. "We need you naked."

I nodded and allowed him to pull it off. My nipples tightened when the air washed over them.

"And these." He stooped, tugging my trousers and boxers down. He removed my boots and socks.

"Mmm, much better." Oscar was before me, also naked. He held his big cock, stroking it to a full erection.

"I agree," George added.

I admired George's lean, toned body as he swept his palm over the bench as though removing invisible crumbs.

"Over you go," Lloyd said, standing. "We want to play with your ass and see how many times we can make you come."

I swallowed.

"You'll enjoy it." He kissed me and toyed with first my right then my left nipple. "I promise."

"I know."

"We'll never hurt you," he whispered. "It's all about pleasure, that's the meaning of our existence."

I nodded and smiled. "So you want me over here, right?"

"Yeah, I do."

"We all do." Oscar's eyebrows pulled low. "And the sooner the better."

I tipped over the bench, the surface cool on my belly. My hard cock hung free; there was a groove cut out so it wasn't trapped.

My ankles were, though. Instantly, Oscar, or maybe it was Lloyd, harnessed them to the bench, and I was spread wide for them.

I stared straight ahead, at Patrick and Rhys.

Rhys was on his knees, taking Patrick's cock in his mouth.

Patrick held Rhys's hair, and his hips swung. His head was tipped back, facing the ceiling, clearly lost to pleasure.

It was one seriously hot sight, and my cock surged, my asshole clenching.

"Got lube?" George asked.

"Here."

A lubed finger ran down my cleft to my hole. I wasn't sure whose until I looked past Rhys and Patrick and spotted my reflection in the mirror.

It was George stood between my legs, Oscar and Lloyd at his side, watching him.

He penetrated my hole, pushing in knuckle deep.

It wasn't a big invasion or even unexpected, but being strapped to the bench added a new edginess to it. I liked it, even though it took away my power.

I trusted them all. Implicitly. With my life.

"Relax," George said. "You're going to take all three of us, one after the other, and you're too tight."

"I'm so turned on," I managed, willing my ass to relax. "It's hard."

"*I'm* hard." Lloyd was also minus his clothing and working his cock.

"You can do this." George added another finger.

I moaned and set my attention on Rhys and Patrick again. Patrick was going deep on each thrust, Rhys taking it all.

"He's got such a cute ass," Lloyd said, smoothing over my buttocks.

I groaned, enjoying his touch as George fingered me.

"Cute, tight ass," George said. "Fuck, I'm going in." He withdrew his fingers from me.

I gripped the bench. The desperation in George's tone told me he was on the edge of his patience. He wanted to fuck, now.

His cock was there.

I watched his face, clenched my jaw, and bore down when he entered me.

It was a smooth ride to heaven, and his dense cock pushed straight over my prostate.

I groaned, long and loud, my cock tapping upward and pre-cum seeping from the end.

"I'm going to make you come so fast, Darius," George said, "and you're going to keep on coming while Lloyd and Oscar fuck you."

"Yes. Yes. Do it." I clawed the table, curled my toes, and held my breath.

He pulled out, slammed back in. Gone was gentle, romantic George. Now he was a hard, determined vampire, and I was on the receiving end.

"Oh yeah," Lloyd said, pressing his lips to my temple. "You like that, don't you."

I blew out a breath. "Yes."

"So come when you need to, we'll keep it going. You'll have forgotten your own name by the time we've finished."

"My hands..." I spread my fingers. "It's..."

"There's sparks there, I know. This stone floor can handle it, do your worst."

"Fuck yeah, do your sparks," Patrick said, glancing my way. "You look amazing, by the way...ah..." He drew back his gums, fangs lowered.

Oscar was at his side in an instant. "No more blood for you."

"I know but I...I'm coming." He thrust forward into Rhys's mouth. His six pack tensed, his chest puffed up.

My orgasm was close behind, and I didn't even bother to try to rein it in, delay it. "I'm coming, too..." I cried, heat shooting down my arms to my hands. Sparks flew from my fingertips, cascading onto the floor.

"That's it, yes." George leaned forward.

I watched the reflection of him biting me, sucking the blood from the ball of my shoulder.

On and on my pleasure rolled through me. Cum left my cock, surge after surge. I gasped and writhed, my visual attention locked on Rhys and Patrick.

George suddenly lifted, withdrew, and stepped away.

My asshole clamped shut, quivering; I was still coming. I tried to move but was reminded of the cuffs around my ankles.

I'm at their mercy.

And then Lloyd was there, the wide domed head of his cock parting me again, gaining entry.

"Fuck me!" I cried, blistering heat tearing down my arms to create more sparks.

He did just that, ramming to full depth then hammering in and out of me. My cock ached; it was bliss. I belonged to my vampires.

"Yes. Yes. More," I managed, my words punctuated by his thrusts. "More."

"It's here," he said. "Keep coming."

Sparks bounced onto the floor, reaching Rhys who was on his knees. I stared at them, my climax flashing through my brain, fragmenting my thoughts.

Lloyd's thrusts became more frantic, his body slapping up against mine.

I clenched around his cock and tried to snatch in breaths when I could.

"It's...here..." He tipped forward and hovering his mouth, fangs exposed, over my opposite shoulder.

"Bite me," I cried. "Now."

The sharpness of his teeth set off a new fire of ecstasy raging through me, his saliva taking me to new highs.

I bucked, fought my binds; the bench legs scraped on the hard floor. The room was alight with my sparks. Brilliant flashes of white, red, and orange.

"Jesus, he's wild." Patrick was staring at me, his cock now at a semi.

Rhys got to his feet, touching his lips then slipping his arm around Patrick.

"I can't...it's so much..." I cried. If anything, the orgasm was getting more intense, and it had been mind-blowing to begin with.

Lloyd was in the throes of his climax as he drank from me.

He didn't take much blood, just enough for a taste, and then he was withdrawing.

I took advantage of the moment to suck in air, but my cock was still throbbing, my balls so taut they'd packed up tight to my body.

"My turn." Oscar was behind me.

Our gazes connected in the mirror.

"Yes," I said, seeing the question in his eyes. "I can take you..."

His jaw tensed, so did his wide, square pecs, then he pushed forward. Not as wild and fast as George or Lloyd, but still with determination.

The stretch took me to the point of pain, but he was well-lubed, and I was pliant as my climactic state continued.

He leaned right over me, his chest on my back. "I want to bite you, but..."

"It's okay. *I'm* okay."

"You sure..."

"Yes, do it." I held up the opposite wrist to the one Rhys and Patrick had bitten. "I want all of you, you're all mine."

"Yes, we are," he said. "And right now, you've got me at your mercy."

"I think it's the other way around." I gripped his girth with my asshole.

"Benedict give me strength," he muttered, then slid his fangs down.

They melted into my flesh, a hot knife on butter, and instantly I was coming wildly again. Arching and thrashing, twisting and struggling on the table. Trapped by him in the most heavenly way imaginable. My cock surged, but I was empty of cum. That didn't spoil the pleasure, though. I was coming hard around Oscar's big dick, my body spasming, my heart rate rocketing.

He continued to drink.

My head spun. I closed my eyes, sinking inwards. Lost to the extreme sensations. Nothing else existed. I was in my own orgasmic world.

"That's enough." George's voice.

"Yeah, come on, he's slipping deeper." Lloyd sounded as if he were speaking from a great distance away.

Blue streaks crossed my eyelids followed by stars. I let mind trail them. I had no concerns, nothing to worry about.

Oscar lifted.

I scraped in a breath, my throat dry.

My cock stopped surging and pulsing; my asshole quivered.

"That's it, breathe," Oscar said by my ear and stroking my hair. "Deep breaths, we're done now, you're done now."

"Yes." I tore my eyes open.

Before me stood George, Lloyd, Rhys, and Patrick. All beautifully naked, all semi-hard. They were looking at me with such admiration and love I thought my heart might burst from my chest.

"You're so giving," Oscar murmured. "Have you any idea how much we love you and will protect and pleasure you forever?"

"Yes, I think so."

"Good, because you're ours and we're yours." He nibbled on my earlobe.

A new rush of pleasure slid over my skin.

"Come on, babe.," Oscar withdrew. "Time to get more comfortable."

The next thing I knew, I was wrapped in a blanket and on his lap. He'd settled us into a huge leather chair in the corner.

I snuggled close as Lloyd, George, Rhys, and Patrick sat around. They were all touching some part of me—Lloyd stroking my hair, Rhys rubbing my ankle, George caressing my back, and Patrick holding my hand.

"I love you," I said. "I love you all so much."

"And we love you. We have done since the day we met you," Lloyd said.

"And we'll be together forever?" I asked, knowing it was true but wanting to hear it.

"You can count on that, babe." Oscar kissed the top of my head.

"Good." I closed my eyes, lost to them. Forever was a long time, but even that didn't seem long enough with these beautiful, otherworldly creatures who'd stolen my heart, owned my body, and connected their souls with mine. I wanted forever in this life, and the next, and then whatever else the universe had in store for us.

Epilogue

Five Years Later
Patrick

I studied Darius's handsome profile as he sunned himself under the white-hot Caribbean sun. It didn't take a genius to know why he was a model. The guy was perfect. His features could have been chiseled from Greek marble, his soft pliant lips fascinated me endlessly when he talked, smiled and kissed me. And his body was one that any man, straight or gay, would pause to admire.

And he was mine.

Well...ours.

I tore my attention from Darius and looked down the golden-sanded beach that was lined with swaying palm trees. The waves were rolling in gently, that perfect aqua blue glinting in the sunshine as they crested and tumbled into fizzing white foam. The other man I loved was performing a perfect front crawl parallel with the shoreline.

Rhys adored swimming and was damn quick through the water. He could get around the entire island in a minute or two. It was just as well there was no one to see him speeding through the waves. It was Aimery's and Ryle's private island. They'd kindly loaned it to Darius and Rhys as a honeymoon gift. A decade they'd said, as it could take that long for vampires to take the edge of their lust for a new lover.

Of course we'd *all* come on the 'honeymoon'. What better place than paradise to spend time together, relax, have sex...lots and lots of hot, vampire, blood-drinking, wild, kinky, awesome sex.

Darius sighed and turned to face me. I couldn't see his eyes because he wore shades.

"You awake?" I asked quietly.

"Yeah, how long was I asleep for?" He yawned then stretched, flashing his dark underarm hair. When he dropped his arms he lifted his shades to the top of his head.

"About an hour. Feel better?"

"I didn't feel bad, I guess I'm just lazy. Like *really* lazy these days."

I laughed and reached for his hand. "I'm not surprised you're tired, Rhys, Lloyd and I kept you awake late into the night."

"So you did." He chuckled. "Though I'm not complaining." As if remembering he rubbed over a set of fang marks that were healing on his neck.

George and Oscar were behind us banging around in the villa's plush kitchen. They were bleeding and filleting the fish they'd caught last night when out on the boat.

"They caught marlin," I said, "George and Lloyd."

"Ah, you like that, don't you." Darius smiled.

"The blood, yeah, it's thirst-quenching." I licked my lips. Soon I'd drink some. It took away the urge to feed from Darius every day, which wasn't practical for him. It was one of the tricks I'd learned to help control my thirst. That and diversion therapy which was always good. A run, a swim, a work through some of the martial art moves I'd studied in my previous life. It was how I'd learned to cope with the new me.

"There were bottlenose dolphins out there earlier." Darius reached for a beer he'd stored under his lounger. It had a cooler around it with a picture of a shell on it. "Where'd they go?"

"They scarpered the moment Rhys got in the sea." I shook my head. "Shame really, he likes them."

Darius took a second to locate Rhys who'd almost gone from view. I guessed he was doing a full loop of the island. It didn't hurt to keep an eye on our boundaries; Darius was, after all, one of the most precious commodities in the vampire world.

Darius took a sip of his beer then swiped away a small drip from his top lip. "Can I ask you something, Patrick?"

"You know you can." I sat on the side of me lounger and faced him. "Anything."

"Do you want to stay on the island for the full ten years?"

"Yes." The word had come out quickly because it was the truth. "Why, don't you?"

Was he missing the UK? His modeling career? His friends and colleagues? I hoped not, we all worked hard to ensure he had everything he needed and was happy and content and that included regular FaceTime calls to London to chat to his mother

"Of course I do." He reached across the small gap between our loungers and took my hand. "I'm very content here, who wouldn't be?" He smiled, warmth that had nothing to do with the sun filling his eyes. "It's just…"

"What?" I squeezed his hand.

"I just worry that after your life as a soldier, Patrick, you might get bored here in the Caribbean?"

"Bored." I chuckled. That was not a word in my thoughts or emotions. Despite not sleeping—I had gotten used to that now—I always found something to watch or read, or some kind of physical exercise to enjoy in my new super-human body.

"But your life must have been adventure-filled, and action-packed," Darius said. "You did tours in the Middle East, got involved in rescuing hostages, were dropped into war-ones by parachute in the dead of the night and…"

His words trailed off, all of the stories I'd told him, and the others, over the last few years clearly playing movie-like in his mind.

"It was adventure filled," I said. "But not always in a good way." I tensed my right thigh. I'd been shot there once, the bastard bullet had left a star-shaped scar and a pain that bit like a shark when the muscle was tired. Not anymore though, the scar and the pain were ancient history.

"It's just I remember George and Lloyd talking about how long it takes for a new vampire to settle and they still seem amazed at how quickly you did."

I was quiet for a moment, then, "I had to get myself under control real quick if you remember."

"Yes, I remember." He shuddered. Neither of us wanted to mention the Carlton Pack. Last sighting had been in Yosemite, which was still too close for comfort. "Thank goodness you did."

"And don't forget, all my life I'd been trained and had the mantra beaten into me that I had to be focused to survive, that I had to remain calm with optimal self-surety and discipline." I pulled his hand upward and set a kiss on his knuckles. "And I had great teachers, remember."

"Yeah, George, Lloyd, Rhys and Oscar were amazing."

"Did I hear my name?"

Rhys was walking up the beach. Behind him Lloyd was just taking to the water, naked, his skin pale in the sunshine and his swagger, as ever, mind-blowingly confident. The man was one cool dude and I had the upmost respect for him.

"Hey," Darius said to Rhys. "Good swim?"

"I wish the dolphins would stay for a while. The moment I dip my toe in they disappear."

"I guess they don't like swimming with vampires," Darius said, releasing my hand and throwing a towel at Rhys. "Their loss."

He caught it and scrubbed it over his hair making it stand on end. "It's not like I'd try and feed from them." He pulled a face. "Their fishy blood really doesn't appeal."

"George and Oscar caught marlin," I said, nodding at the villa.

"Now that I don't mind." Rhys grinned and sat next to me, his thigh pressing against mine. "So what were you guys talking about?"

"We were just saying," Darius said. "How perfect it is here, all of us together, fun the only thing in our schedule."

"Fun *and* sex," Rhys bumped his shoulder on mine and winked at Darius. "Sex with orgasms that take even us hours to recover from." He laughed.

I smiled, a lovely feeling of contentment snaking over my cool skin. It was coming more and more these days, the sensation that everything was okay. I wasn't sure if it would stay forever, perhaps I would get bored as Darius worried I might. But for now, no, this was home. These were my men, my new squadron, and the guys I was going to spend eternity with, in this life and the next.

Odd as it might sound, being turned into a vampire had been the best thing that had ever happened to me. I'd found friendship, love and peace when as a human those things had eluded me. So I, for one, had nothing to complain about. Being here, being me, it was good, more than good, it was perfect.

THE END

About Lily Harlem

Based in the UK Lily Harlem is an award-winning, USA Today bestselling author of sexy romance. She's a complete floozy when it comes to genres and pairings writing from heterosexual kink, to gay paranormal and everything in-between. She's also very partial to a happily ever after.

One thing you can be sure of, whatever book you pick up by Ms Harlem, is it will be wildly romantic and deliciously sexy. Enjoy!

Printed in Great Britain
by Amazon